MANASSAS

The Civil War Battles Series
by James Reasoner

Manassas
Shiloh
Antietam
Chancellorsville
Vicksburg

MANASSAS

James Reasoner

CUMBERLAND HOUSE
NASHVILLE, TENNESSEE

Published by
CUMBERLAND HOUSE PUBLISHING, INC.
431 Harding Industrial Drive
Nashville, Tennessee 37211
www.cumberlandhouse.com

Cover design by Bob Bubkis, Nashville, Tennessee.

Library of Congress Cataloging-in-Publication Data

Reasoner, James.
    Manassas / James Reasoner.
       p. cm. — (The Civil War battle series ; 1)
    ISBN 1-58182-213-8 (alk. paper)
    ISBN 1-58182-008-9 (hardcover : alk. paper)
    1. Manassas (Va.)—History—Civil War, 1861–1865—Fiction. 2. Virginia—History—Civil War, 1861–1865—Fiction. 3. Bull Run, 1st Battle of, Va., 1861—Fiction. I. Title. II. Series: Reasoner, James. Civil War battle series ; 1.
PS3568.E2685M36 1999
813'.54—dc21   98-52494
                                      CIP

Printed in the United States of America.

1 2 3 4 5 6 7 8 9 10—05 04 03 02 01

For Ed Gorman, Martin H. Greenberg,
and Ron Pitkin

Part One

Chapter One

E ASY NOW," William Shakespeare Brannon breathed as he watched the oncoming riders over the barrel of his rifle. "Just keep coming, boys."

Beside Will, his deputy, Luther Strawn, shifted a little, making the brush that concealed them rattle loudly. At least the noise sounded loud in Will's ears. He grimaced and shot a look at Luther, who just raised his eyebrows and shook his head. Under the circumstances, that was as much of an apology as the deputy could make.

Will turned his attention back to the riders. There were six of them coming up the gentle slope of the hill toward the clump of live oaks where Will and Luther were hidden. Beyond the riders a broad, shallow valley fell away into the distance. In the spring the valley would be filled with colorful explosions of wildflowers, and by summer it would be green with thick, lush grass. But now, in late January 1861, it was a mixture of mottled browns and grays.

The riders wore long gray coats, which made them blend into the background to a certain extent. If it came to shooting, that would make it more difficult, thought Will. Why couldn't bandits all wear nice colorful bandannas and give a man something to aim at? His younger brother Titus might be able to shoot the wings off a butterfly at a thousand yards, but Will had never been that good with a rifle. He was much handier with the .36 caliber Colt Navy revolver holstered on his right hip. Though as sheriff he considered it his job to keep the peace, he didn't use any gun unless he had to.

Might just come down to that today.

The riders were still far enough away that he couldn't see their faces very well, shaded as they were underneath the broad-brimmed hats. Will didn't have to see the men to know them: three of them were the Fogarty brothers, George, Ransom, and Joe; two more were cousins of the Fogartys, Marcus and Newberry Paynter; and the sixth and final man was Israel Quinn, whose wife, Margery, was some distant kin of the Fogartys and the Paynters. Will never had been able to figure out exactly how Margery Quinn was related.

Not that it mattered. Nearly all the men in that bunch, be they Fogarty, Paynter, or Quinn, were no-account. Thieves and layabouts. They were the bane of Will Brannon's existence.

Early this morning six men had robbed the general store at Burke's Station. One of them had pistol-whipped old man Burke within an inch of his life for no reason; the storekeeper hadn't been putting up a fight. Luckily, someone had found the old man soon afterward and gotten him to a doctor, and word of the robbery had been sent quickly to Will's office in Culpeper, the county seat. Again, luck was on the side of the law, and Will had been there to get the news. Quickly, he had rounded up Luther Strawn, and they had set out on horseback to get ahead of the robbers.

The Blue Ridge Mountains rose behind the hill where the two lawmen waited. Will knew that the Fogartys and their kin had a hidey-hole somewhere up there in the mountains. He had never gone up there to try to root them out; that would have been out of his jurisdiction as sheriff of Culpeper County. But he could dang sure ride like blazes and get in front of the thieves so that he could stop them before they left his bailiwick. That had been his thinking, anyway. During the long afternoon he and Luther had spent on this hill, Will had begun to fear that they hadn't been in time to head off the robbers after all.

But now they were coming, and Will was ready for them. Sure, it was three-to-one odds, but he and Luther had the high ground and good cover, and if the Fogartys and their kin decided not to surrender when Will called out to them, Will figured he and Luther could sweep three or four of them out of the saddle right quick-like. Luther could get two with that scattergun of his, maybe three if they were bunched up, and Will was good enough with the rifle to take down one man. Then it would be up to that Colt Navy on Will's hip and Luther's old dragoon.

Yep, a few more minutes, and things would really start to rip, Will told himself. Nothing a Brannon loved more than a good fight.

He used the back of his left hand to wipe sweat from his forehead. Funny. It was a cool day. He oughtn't to be sweating so much.

The men on horseback were almost close enough now.

Someone let out a shout.

Will stiffened. He peered through the brush and saw another man riding around the base of the hill. The Fogartys and their companions reined in and turned their horses to greet the newcomer. Will grimaced. Their backs were to him and Luther now. He couldn't shoot somebody in the back, not even a Fogarty. Besides, they were too far away for Luther's shotgun and the handguns to be accurate enough. If any shooting started now, the thieves could just sit back and sieve the hilltop with lead until both Will and Luther were dead.

Will hadn't gotten a good look at the newcomer. Whoever the man was, he was talking to the thieves, and suddenly the whole bunch started riding back the way they had come, away from the hill where Will and Luther were hidden.

"Lordy, now what?" Luther asked in a whisper.

Will thought desperately. The only way he and his deputy would be able to handle the gang was to take them by surprise. That wouldn't be possible now. He and Luther might be able to overtake them, but what then? The Fogartys wouldn't surrender. Will knew that, even though he would have given them a chance to. Going after them now wouldn't accomplish anything except to get him and Luther shot to ribbons.

"Nothing we can do," said Will, not bothering to keep the bitterness out of his voice. "Next time we'll gather up a posse before we start out after them, make the odds more even."

"How do you know there'll be a next time?"

"I know the Fogartys," Will replied heavily. "There'll be a next time."

• • •

HIS FATHER had named him after William Shakespeare. John Brannon had read every play that old Englishman ever wrote, and he had been able to recite big chunks of each one from memory. Will remembered many an evening when he was a youngster, sitting in front of the fire and listening to his father recite Shakespeare. John Brannon always sat in an old rocking chair when he was holding forth. Even now, years later, if Will happened to hear somebody quote a passage from Shakespeare, he could hear in his mind the creaking of that chair as his father rocked back and forth and waved his arms and hollered out the words like he was actually old King Lear, or Hamlet, or Macbeth.

Will's next youngest brother was named Macbeth, but everybody called him Mac. The next brother in line was Titus Andronicus Brannon, and Will had always been glad he hadn't been saddled with that name. Then came Coriolanus Troilus Brannon, also a name Will was thankful he hadn't been given. The youngest son was Henry, probably the luckiest of the bunch when it came to names, and finally Cordelia, the only Brannon daughter, whose name had come from John Brannon's favorite among the plays, *King Lear.* Cordelia had been something of John Brannon's favorite, too, being both the youngest and the only girl in the family. But then John Brannon had died ten years ago when Cordelia was only seven, and now her memories of him were dim. Will knew that, and in a way he felt sorry for her that she had not gotten to know their father for a longer time.

But in another way Cordelia had been lucky, because she remembered John Brannon more as a colorful character and hadn't been old enough when he died to realize what a failure he had been as a husband and father. Will had been eighteen when John Brannon passed on, and he knew quite well what his father had been like.

The road that led through the rolling farmland of Virginia's Piedmont region forked. The left-hand fork led on southeast toward Culpeper, while the right-hand fork ran due south and went past the Brannon farm. It was late afternoon, the sun almost touching the peaks of the Blue Ridge behind them, when Will and Luther stopped their horses at the fork.

"I'm going on home," Will said. "You sure you don't mind seeing to the office?"

"Naw," replied Luther. "Got nothin' better to do tonight."

"All right, then. I'll see you in the morning."

"Sure." Luther hesitated, then added, "Will."

"What?"

"I sure am sorry it didn't work out. Us and the Fogarty bunch, I mean. I know you wanted to get those boys."

"It's not a matter of getting them," Will declared, his voice sharp. "They're criminals, and I was elected to put a stop to such goings-on."

"Yeah. That's what I mean," said Luther. He gave Will a tired smile and pulled on the reins, guiding his horse onto the Culpeper road.

Will sat there in his saddle for a moment, then sighed and rubbed a hand over the dark beard stubble on his jaw. He shouldn't have snapped at Luther, he told himself. What he had said was true enough: it was his job as sheriff to apprehend anybody who broke the law. But Luther had been right, too. Will bore a special enmity for the Fogartys and their kin.

He heeled his horse into motion, sending the rangy line-back dun trotting down the fork of the road that led to the Brannon farm.

By the time he arrived, the sun was behind the mountains and the shadows of dusk were thick. Will turned off the road onto the lane that ran between the house and the barns and the corrals. On both sides of the lane were fields of winter wheat. The land beyond the house and the barns was used as pastureland for Mac's horses at the moment, but come spring much of it would be plowed and planted with corn, potatoes, snap beans, cucumbers, and sweet potatoes. Will would do as much as he could when it came to be plowing and planting time, but his duties as sheriff kept him off the place more than he liked. He was the only one in the family still at home who worked at anything other than farming, and sometimes he worried that his brothers and sister resented that.

But he was good at what he did. He could break up a tavern fight without anybody getting hurt too badly, he was a good tracker, and if it ever came down to serious trouble, he could handle that Colt Navy and folks knew it. Will Brannon had killed one man in his life, a tavern owner who rented out rooms above the tavern and had the bad habit of robbing and sometimes chopping up his guests with an ax, especially when they were travelers nobody was likely to miss. He kept hogs, too, in a pen out back, which made it handy for getting rid of the evidence of his crimes. Eventually, though, he'd been found out, and when Will came to arrest him, the man went mad and came at Will with the same ax he'd used on his victims. It had taken four .36 caliber slugs in the chest to put him down, and even at that, the ax blade had gotten stuck in the tavern floor less than a yard away from Will's feet on the downswing. Will hadn't been sheriff at the time, only a deputy, but when the sheriff decided not to run for re-election, everybody urged Will to try for the job. He had been elected easily. Anybody who'd stand up to a madman with an ax sure didn't spook easy, folks said.

That had been four years earlier, and sometimes Will still woke up in the middle of the night, not scared really, not even sweating, but he could see the twisted face of that man and how the lamplight reflected off the blade of the ax. He was usually awake for a good long spell after that.

This evening the lights of the house glowed yellow through the windows, and Will thought it was a pretty sight. The house was big and solid and sturdy, built of thick planks that got a good coat of whitewash once a year. Will saw to that. His father had built the house, probably the best job of work John Brannon had ever accomplished, but at the time of his death, it was already run down. Will had stepped in and seen to it that the place was fixed up. Later, as they grew older, his brothers had helped, too. That effort had extended into the fields. Stumps that John Brannon was going to get rid of "one of these days" were uprooted and hauled off. Fences that had been leaning were straightened and braced so that they would never again be in danger of falling down. The holes in the barn roof were patched. It didn't matter to Will that he was only eighteen when his father died. He was a man fully grown, and he was going to put things right.

He supposed he'd been trying to do that ever since, both on the farm and as the sheriff of Culpeper County.

He rode into the barn and swung down from the saddle. He didn't need light to get the saddle off the dun, rub the animal down, see that it had plenty of grain and water in its stall. Mac was the horseman in the family, but Will could tend to chores such as these because he'd been doing them all his life.

The last of the day's light was fading as he walked from the barn to the house. A cold breeze was blowing, and Will tugged down his flat-crowned black hat.

He stepped into the warmth of the house and took a deep breath. Ham and fresh biscuits and something sweet and spicy . . . sweet potato pie, that was it. Will grinned as he took his hat off and hung it just inside the door, on the same hook where he hung his gun belt. His mother didn't allow any firearms at the dinner table. That was one of Abigail Brannon's rules, and you didn't break it even when you were the county sheriff and nearly thirty years old.

Will brushed a hand over his thick black hair to straighten it, then stepped across the foyer to the dining room. His sister was setting the table. She looked up at him and smiled. "Hello, Will," she said.

Cordelia was the only one of the children to have inherited John Brannon's fiery red hair. It tumbled in thick masses around her face and past her shoulders. To Will, Cordelia would always be the tomboy with dirt on her face who had followed him and his brothers around all the time, but when he forced himself to step back from being the big brother, he had to admit that she had grown into a beauty. The young fellas hereabouts were certainly aware of that, and if they were, then he had to be, too.

"Did you make the sweet potato pie?" he asked.

Cordelia's smile broadened into a grin. "I sure did."

"I reckon it'll be good, then."

"Don't let Mama hear you say that," Cordelia teased. "She sets quite a store by her sweet potato pie."

"Where is she?"

Cordelia glanced toward the ceiling and the second floor above it. "Up in her room. Resting."

Will nodded. He wasn't certain what their mother did when she said she was resting, but he was pretty certain she wasn't lying in bed taking life easy. More than likely she was sitting in her rocking chair reading the Bible. That was about as idle as she would ever allow herself to be.

"What about the boys?"

"They'll be in directly. I told them supper was almost ready, but Mac just had to take Titus and Henry out to the barn to show them that new foal. He sure is proud of it."

"It's a pretty little thing," Will said. "Well, if they don't get back soon, there'll just be more food for you and me. You need to eat plenty, you're so skinny."

"Be careful. I'll throw a biscuit at you. What did you do today?"

Tried to ambush a gang of thieves and no-goods, thought Will. *Came this close to a shooting scrape where I could've got myself killed, and Luther, too.*

But he said, "Not much of anything. Being sheriff's an almighty peaceful job these days."

"I reckon things won't be peaceful anywhere much longer," Cordelia added. "Not once the war starts." She turned away and took a step toward the door that led to the kitchen.

"There's not going to be any war," Will declared.

"That's not what Titus says."

"Titus is wrong. Just because Lincoln's going to be in office soon doesn't mean—"

He stopped at the sound of a footstep behind him and turned to see his mother in the entrance to the dining room. Her face wore the same stern expression it usually did, the most common expression Will could remember seeing on her for the past ten years.

"Lincoln," she snapped with disapproval. "I swear, that man's going to be the death of us all."

"Now, Mama—" Will began.

"Don't you now Mama me, Will Brannon," she interrupted. "Once he's inaugurated, that man is going to try to ruin everything folks believe in."

Will knew better than to get into this argument. When it came to states' rights, his mother could orate just as long and passionately as any of the politicians in Washington. Instead, Will said, "I'll just go out and see what's keeping the boys."

He stepped past Cordelia and went out through the rear door in the kitchen. As he walked away from the house toward the barns, he heard voices on the night air. The rest of the Brannon brothers, except for one, coming home for the night. Will saw the lantern swinging from the hand of one of them.

"Didn't I tell you she was the prettiest little thing you'll ever see?" That was Mac, talking about the new foal.

"I don't know," began Henry, and Will could tell from the tone of voice used by his youngest brother that Henry was up to some sort of devilment. "I don't reckon Titus thinks any ol' horse could be prettier than Polly Ebersole, now do you, Titus?"

"Hush up," said Titus. "I don't know what you're talking about."

"I'm talking about Polly Ebersole," Henry persisted. "You know, the gal you're in love with."

"Damn it, Henry! You take that back."

"Why should I? It's the truth, ain't it?"

Will stepped forward to meet them and said, "Better quit your squabbling, boys. Supper's just about on the table."

He could see them now, the three of them, his brothers, and he wondered, not for the first time in his life, how they could have all turned out so different. They all shared the same sort of tall rawboned build, but that was where the similarities ended.

Will had the broad shoulders and long arms and knobby fists of a fighter. His hair was dark and already touched with gray in a place or two, despite his not having reached thirty years of age.

Mac, three years younger at twenty-five, was much more slender, with a shock of brown hair that sometimes fell in his face. His hands with their long fingers and gentle touch could calm down almost any horse when they stroked along its shoulder, and his soft voice could win the trust of any animal, no matter how wild it was. Will couldn't remember all the times Mac had brought some sort of critter home from the woods, talking to the animals as if they understood every word he was saying.

Titus, who was twenty-three, never wasted time talking to animals, but he was hell on killing them. The stew pot in the Brannon house never went wanting for fresh meat. Titus could bark a squirrel or a coon or a possum without even seeming to aim, like the rifle was just a part of him and he could use it to reach out and touch whatever he aimed at. Slender like Mac, his hair was as dark as midnight, and he wore it longer than any of his brothers.

Henry was a little shorter and a little stockier than any of the others, and he had grown up practically worshiping his brothers and wanting to do everything they did. He had never been good at any one particular thing, like they were. But he had picked up enough over the years to be able to handle a pistol, like Will, ride pretty good, like Mac, and shoot a rifle, like Titus. Will didn't figure Henry would ever be the equal of any of them at those things, but he was good enough to get along. And he still had that cockiness that went with being nineteen years old and having the world by the tail.

Only Cory, at twenty-one lodged right smack between Titus and Henry, was missing. He was the only one of the family to have left home and also the only one to have inherited much of John Brannon's dreaminess and love of poetry. Six months earlier Cory had announced he was going west to seek his fortune. Will had expected Abigail to lay down the law and tell him he could do no such thing, but to his surprise she had agreed with Cory's plan. Maybe because he had always reminded her too much of her late husband, Will thought.

"Howdy, Will," Henry said now. "We were just talkin' about Titus and Polly Ebersole—"

"I heard what you were talking about," Will cut in before Titus could protest again. "Come on. Let's go eat."

"And you just shut your mouth about Polly," Titus said, unable to resist putting in the last word on that subject.

"No talking about Lincoln and war, either," Will warned them quietly. "We don't want to set Mama off again."

"That's right," Mac agreed. "You know how she can get going on that subject."

Titus snorted. "Just because you don't want to talk about it don't mean it ain't going to happen. You know what happened in South Carolina last month. It's the Second American Revolution, that's what it is."

Will shook his head and said, "Just because those delegates to that convention in Charleston voted to secede doesn't mean it'll actually happen."

"It's *already* happened. That vote was binding. The Union's dissolved, Will, no two ways about it."

"We still don't want a lot of Secesh talk at the dinner table," Mac insisted. "Folks need to think mild thoughts while they're eating. It's good for the digestion."

Again Titus snorted, but that was his only response.

Hoping for the best, Will led the Brannon brothers into the house for their supper.

Chapter Two

ABIGAIL AND Cordelia had supper on the table. Will took a deep breath, enjoying the smell of the honey-cured ham that filled the dining room. After John Brannon's death, there had been some lean times for the family, but for the past few years, as the farm had prospered, there had always been plenty of food on the table. The crops had been consistently good, the hogs were fat, and the milk cows never dried up. The place was a far cry from the huge plantations that grew cotton or tobacco, but Will was happy with the way things had turned out. He and his brothers could handle the upkeep on the farm without having to resort to keeping slaves. In fact the Brannons had never had any slaves since there had been no need for them, nor, while John Brannon was alive, the money to afford them.

Will hadn't ever thought much about slavery. He remembered, though, how his father had come to this country as an indentured servant. John Brannon had hated those limits on his freedom, and Will supposed that being a slave would be even worse. He was just glad he hadn't had to make the decision whether or not to use them on the farm.

"How's that new foal, Mac?" asked Cordelia as the brothers took their places around the table.

"Mighty pretty," Mac said, then shot a warning glance at Henry so that the youngest brother wouldn't start comparing foals and Polly Ebersole again. Will saw the look and was grateful for it. After the tension of the afternoon he'd spent waiting in ambush for the Fogartys, a ruckus here at home was the last thing he wanted.

Will speared a slab of ham with his fork and pulled it onto his plate, then heaped up potatoes and beans around it, topping them with a biscuit. He wondered who the man was who had stopped the Fogarty bunch and kept them from riding into the ambush. Will hadn't recognized him and hadn't been close enough to overhear any of the conversation. He could only speculate, and that was a waste of time.

Wherever the Fogartys and their kin had gone, they had been up to no good. Will was sure of that.

"Come out to the pasture with me tomorrow," Mac said to Cordelia as he poured himself a cup of buttermilk from a porcelain pitcher. "We'll let that foal run a little."

"Can we take a ride, too?" asked Cordelia. She had ridden her first horse when she was barely a toddler, perched on the animal in front of Mac, who kept a big brotherly arm firmly around her so that she couldn't fall off. Ever since then, she had loved to ride.

Mac drank deeply of the buttermilk, then licked away the white mustache it left on his upper lip. "I reckon so," he told her. "That mare of yours needs to stretch her legs. Come winter like this, none of the horses really get enough exercise."

"Titus could take one of them and ride over to Mountain Laurel," suggested Henry with a sly grin.

Mountain Laurel was the plantation owned by Duncan Ebersole, Polly's father. A hardheaded, tightfisted Scotsman who seemed to be living proof of every old skinflint story ever told about the Caledonians, Ebersole ran his family like he ran his cotton plantation: with a firm grip on every little thing.

Will and Mac both glared at Henry while Titus's face darkened. "I told you to shut your trap—" Titus began.

"I don't agree with Duncan Ebersole's religion," Abigail put in. Ebersole was a Congregationalist while all the Brannons were strictly hardshell Baptists. John Brannon had not brought his native Catholicism with him from Ireland to America. "But at least he is a churchgoing man," continued Abigail as she looked around the table at her sons. "That is more than I can say for some."

Will shifted his rear end uncomfortably in his chair under his mother's scrutiny. His duties as sheriff sometimes made it difficult for him to make it to church services. As for Mac, well, Mac had always preferred the outdoors. He would rather be riding and enjoying nature than be shut up in some gloomy church listening to dirgelike hymns. Henry attended church more than either of them did, but that was only during the times of year when the fishing wasn't good. Most any other Sunday he could be found traipsing along the Rapidan River or the little creek called Dobie's Run near the farm. Titus was the only one of the brothers who went to church regularly, and Will had always suspected that was because Titus was such a gloomy cuss to start with. Cordelia attended every Sunday, of course, along with Abigail. Abigail wouldn't have had it any other way.

"Mr. Ebersole says Virginia ought to have itself a secession convention like the folks down in South Carolina," said Titus. "He attended the one in Charleston, you know."

Will bit back a groan. He knew about Duncan Ebersole's visit to the South Carolina convention. The planter had told everyone in Culpeper County who'd hold still long enough to listen about the fiery speeches, the impassioned rhetoric, the vehement calls for the sovereign state of South Carolina to separate itself from the United States. That was exactly what had happened, though it was still unclear just what the government in Washington thought about the declaration.

At the moment Will was more concerned with what his brother Titus had just done. Titus wanted to steer the conversation around the dinner table away from his feelings for Polly Ebersole, and bringing up secession was a sure-fire way of doing it. Will exchanged a look of dismay with Mac, who also knew what was going on.

"Well, if you ask me, Duncan Ebersole is right about that, at least," declared Abigail. "What must be done if we wish to preserve our southern traditions is for more of the states to secede and form a country of their own to stand against the northerners."

Henry laughed. "You sound like a fire-eater, Mama," he said.

"That's a name I'll wear proudly, if it means I am partaking of the fires of liberty."

Cordelia began, "Well, I think—"

"Young ladies of good breeding have no business holding political beliefs," Abigail contended, interrupting her daughter. "You should leave that to the men, dear."

Will thought that his mother had never permitted her sex to keep her from holding—and expressing—opinions on everything under the sun, political and otherwise. But he knew it wouldn't be wise to point that out, so he concentrated instead on the piece of ham he cut off and popped into his mouth. It was good, with just the right touch of sweetness from the honey curing.

"I was thinking," said Mac, "of going over to Richmond next week for the winter fair. Cully Montayne plans to race that chestnut gelding of his against Edward Symington's black."

Henry leaned forward eagerly in his chair, politics and the widening rift between North and South forgotten for the moment. "Are you going to make it a three-way race, Mac?"

"Thinking about it," Mac answered with a smile.

Henry let out a whoop of excitement, a lack of decorum that brought a glare of disapproval from Abigail. "You can beat 'em both, Mac!" he exclaimed. "I'm sure of it. Can I go with you?"

"Well, I don't know if the farm could get along without you for that long." Mac looked at Will. "What do you think, Will?"

"I think we should all go," Will proclaimed, startling himself with the words. He didn't know where they had come from. Now that he had started, though, he plunged ahead. "I reckon a little time away from home would be good for us. I'm sure Luther wouldn't mind coming by to tend to the chores for a day or two, and he can hold down the fort at the sheriff's office. He can get his cousin Jasper to help him. He's been looking to find some work for Jasper."

He saw the looks of excitement and anticipation between Henry and Cordelia and knew that giving in to the impulse had been a good idea. Young folks needed to get out and have a little fun from time to time—and it wouldn't hurt the older members of the family, either.

"I don't know," Abigail began dubiously. "I'm not sure you should all be gallivanting off when there's work to do on the farm." Her mouth tightened into a grim line. "Once you start giving in to temptation, it's hard to stop."

Will knew she was talking about his father. John Brannon had never been the sort to wrestle with temptation; he'd waved a white flag at it every chance he got.

Mac said, "Why, Mama, I figured you'd come with us if the rest of us go. You don't want to stay here by yourself."

"Won't be by myself," Abigail insisted stubbornly. "I'll have my Bible with me, like always."

"Oh, Mama, you have to come with us," Cordelia pleaded. "It wouldn't be the same without you."

"That's right, Mama," added Henry. "Come with us."

Will played the trump card. "I might need you to help me keep an eye on these youngsters, see that they don't get into any trouble."

Abigail conceded slowly, "Richmond's full of sin these days, I expect. Maybe I'd better go along."

Once she had given in that much, all the others assumed that she had decided to accompany them to the state capital. Will leaned back in his chair and grinned. Even though this trip was a spur-of-the-moment thing, he was already looking forward to it.

"Besides," said Titus, "you'll want to go hear Governor Letcher speak on the secession issue. He's supposed to give a talk at the fair. I heard about it at the general store in Culpeper a couple of days ago."

"There's to be a secession rally?" asked Abigail.

Titus shrugged. "That's what I've heard."

Suddenly Will wasn't so sure that traveling to Richmond was such a good idea. The idea of secession provoked strong feelings, both for and against, and if there was to be a rally supporting it, those opposed would naturally turn out, too. Could be trouble in the making, he thought.

But it was too late to back out now. And besides, he wanted to see Mac race one of their horses against Montayne's chestnut and Symington's black. Maybe that long-legged, mouse-colored two-year-old Mac was so fond of. That horse could flat-out *run*.

"It's settled, then," Abigail announced with a nod. "We're all going to Richmond."

Will drank from his cup of buttermilk and hoped he hadn't made a mistake by suggesting the trip.

• • •

THE STARS were bright overhead, pinpricks of brilliant light against the deep black background of the winter sky. Will and Mac stopped at the edge of the pasture, both of them enjoying the crisp coolness of the air on their faces. They took out their pipes and tobacco pouches and began to fill the briars.

"Mama sure got more enthusiastic about going to Richmond once Titus mentioned that rally," Mac commented.

"Yep. Henry's right: she's a fire-eater at heart."

"Maybe it's going to take eating some fire before everything's put right."

Will glanced over at his brother. Mac was taking a lucifer from a small packet of them he carried. He scratched the soft sulphur match into life against the sole of his boot, held the flame to the bowl of his pipe, and puffed until he got it burning good. In the glow of the match, Will got a good look at Mac's face, lean but not gaunt, mostly planes and angles like Titus's but not quite as sharp. It was a good face. Will said, "Got another match?"

"Sure."

When Will had his pipe going, he blew out a cloud of smoke and asked, "What do you think, Mac? Is there a war coming?"

"I don't feel good about it," Mac replied with a sigh, "but it's sure starting to look like it, what with South Carolina voting to secede."

"Over something like slavery?"

"That's not all of it, and you know it," said Mac. "Folks in New York and all those other Yankee states don't have any right to hold us down and tell us how to live. Is that what you want?"

"Hell, no. But I wish we didn't have to fight over it."

Mac shrugged. "So do I. The last thing I want to do is go off to war—"

He stopped short, and his hand shot out to grip Will's arm. "There!" Mac exclaimed. "Did you see it?"

"See what?"

Mac pointed with his other hand. "There, on the other side of the pasture."

Will stared into the starlit darkness and after a moment caught a faint movement on the far side of the pasture. "What am I looking at?" he asked. "Some sort of varmint?"

"Not hardly," breathed Mac. "It's a horse."

So it was, Will realized. Now that he knew what to look for, he could make out the shape of the animal. It was a good-sized horse, too. He could tell that much even across the width of the pasture. The horse was walking slowly along the edge of the trees that bordered the open ground.

"Is that one of ours?" Will asked with a frown.

"Nope. But he's been here before."

The two brothers watched as the horse paced along the edge of the pasture. Will couldn't tell exactly what color the horse's coat was, but in the starlight it appeared to be a sort of silver gray. When he asked his brother about it, Mac said, "I've never seen him in daylight, only at night. But I think you're right, Will. Silver gray, that's what he is."

"Where'd he come from? How did he get over the fence on the other side of those trees?" For some reason, Will kept his voice pitched low.

Mac answered in the same quiet tones. "A horse like that wouldn't have any trouble jumping that fence. He can probably sail over that top rail like it's not even there."

"What does he want?"

"I don't know. At first I figured he was after our mares, but he hasn't called them to him or tried to get to them. He just comes there to the edge of the trees and paces back and forth for a while, then disappears back into the woods."

"And you've never tried to catch him?"

"Catch him?" Mac sounded shocked. "Why would I want to do that?"

"Well, he must belong to somebody, probably one of our neighbors. And I'd wager whoever it is doesn't know that he's getting out at night."

"That horse doesn't belong to anybody but himself," Mac declared emphatically.

"You can't know that."

"Yes, I can. All I have to do is look at him."

Will glanced at his brother. Mac had always been like that, acting as if there was some sort of mystical bond between him and the animals. Will supposed that maybe he was too hard-headed, but he had never put any stock in such things. He believed in things he could see and hear and touch, and that was about all.

"Well, I think we ought to try to catch him. If he doesn't belong to any of the neighbors, then we'd have ourselves another good horse."

"You couldn't catch him," scoffed Mac. "Might as well reach up and try to gather in a handful of those stars in the sky."

"Watch me," Will declared. He started walking toward the far side of the pasture, moving at a steady pace, not too fast, not too slow. Mac hissed at him to stop, but Will kept moving.

He would have been the first to admit that Mac knew more about horses than he did, and if anybody was going to catch this mysterious creature, Mac would have a lot better chance than Will ever would. Yet the horse was on Brannon land, and Will felt as if that gave him certain rights. He veered to the left, intending to circle wide around the horse before coming up on it.

He heard footsteps and looked around to see Mac going the other way, heading to the right as he crossed the pasture. Mac might not believe that Will could catch the horse, but he'd be damned if he would stand by and watch while there was the slightest chance that might happen. If anybody was going to lay hands on that horse, Mac would want it to be him. Will smiled and tried not to chuckle at the thought.

The horse had stopped its pacing, Will saw. Now it was standing still, about the middle of the pasture's edge. Its head swung slowly one way, then the other. The blasted animal was watching them, Will realized. And if it was as smart as Mac seemed to think it was, it probably knew what they were up to. Will kept going anyway, walking in a wide circle until he had almost reached the grove of trees. Then he turned toward the horse and started to move in. Across the way, Mac did the same thing.

The horse bolted, but not the way Will might have expected. Instead of whirling around to dash back into the woods, the horse suddenly lunged forward into a ground-eating gallop. In what seemed like only a couple of strides, while Will and Mac stood flatfooted in surprise, the horse had crossed half the pasture.

"He's headed for the barns!" Will shouted.

Mac broke into a run, but it was hopeless. The horse was moving like a streak of light. Already it had reached the far side of the pasture. Will started to run after it, too, knowing that he would be too late.

The horse galloped into the wide yard between the barns and the house. It went straight to the big double doors of the largest barn, where the brood mares were stabled. Rearing up, its forelegs lashed out, the hooves slamming into the doors.

The doors opened outward, so the horse couldn't kick them open. He might have battered his way through them, given enough time. Will and Mac didn't intend to give him that much time. Shouting and waving their arms, they ran after him, and the commotion caught the attention of the others in the house. The front door slammed open and Titus and Henry ran out into the yard. Seeing what was going on, Henry ran toward the barn, shouting and waving like Will and Mac in an attempt to drive the horse away. Titus ducked back into the house.

Will and Mac were closing in now. The horse was still kicking at the barn door, but it finally stopped as the two men ran from the pasture and Henry approached from the other direction. Over the shouts, Will heard the shrill whinnies of the mares inside the barn. The big silver-gray stallion hadn't made a sound that Will had heard, but the mares knew he was just outside the barn.

The horse wheeled around, and Will yelled, "Look out, Henry!" Henry stopped short and reeled back a step as the horse reared up again. It didn't try to kick at Henry, but the sheer size and obvious power of the animal was enough of a threat to make any man back off.

With Henry driven back for the moment, the horse turned its attention to Will and Mac. Its hooves came back down to the ground, and in a smooth continuation of the same motion, it was running again, only this time its gallop carried it straight toward the two onrushing brothers.

Mac let out a yelp of surprise and fear and threw himself to the left to avoid being trampled. Will went diving in the other direction. Both of them landed hard and sprawled on the ground as the horse thundered between them and took off again across the pasture.

Once again, the horse's speed was evident. It was putting distance between itself and the house and barns at an amazing rate. Will and Mac picked themselves up and started trying to brush some of the dust from their clothes.

Footsteps thudded on the boards of the porch as Titus hurried out of the house and ran into the yard. He was carrying his favorite rifle, a Sharps .52 caliber. Abigail and Cordelia came out of the house right behind him, Abigail calling loudly, "My lands! What's all this commotion out here?"

Nobody answered her. Titus was too busy cocking and aiming the Sharps, and Will and Henry just stared at him, seemingly unable to comprehend what he was about to do. Only Mac leaped toward him, grabbing the barrel of the rifle and forcing it down toward the ground.

"Stop it!" Mac demanded. "What the hell do you think you're doing?"

Titus jerked the rifle loose from Mac's grip. "That's a wild horse," he said coldly. "If we don't kill him, he'll keep coming after our mares until he's stolen all of them."

"You can't just shoot him!"

Titus looked out across the pasture and made a noise of disgust. "Not now I can't. He's gone."

Will followed Titus's gaze and saw that the stallion had indeed disappeared, no doubt galloping back through the trees and leaping the fence that marked the boundary of the Brannon farm. "You couldn't have hit him anyway," he pointed out to Titus. "Not at that distance, aiming by starlight."

"Well, we won't ever know, will we?" fumed Titus.

Will gave a little shake of his head. He didn't like the way he had frozen up for a moment when Titus started taking aim at the horse. As sheriff, he had faced his share of tight spots. He wasn't supposed to just stand around and gawk while violence was about to unfold right in front of him. He had left it up to Mac, arguably the gentlest member of the family, to intervene and prevent Titus from shooting at the horse.

Frowning darkly, Will wrapped his thoughts around the matter in the only way that he could make it make sense.

"That horse may belong to somebody, Titus," he said. "It was on our land, but it's still probably better that you didn't kill it. We could've found ourselves in court."

Titus tucked the Sharps under his left arm. "That's all you care about, ain't it, Will?" he retorted. "Keeping things all nice and legal-like?"

"I *am* the sheriff of Culpeper County."

"Yeah. Glad you reminded me." Titus turned and stalked back toward the house.

Will started to make an angry comment of his own about how the only reason Titus was mad was because he'd missed a chance to show off how good a shot he was, but as he took a deep breath, he thought better of it. No point in throwing more fuel on the fire.

Besides, his mother had a blaze of her own going. Abigail crossed her arms and looked at the three of her sons still standing in the yard, but her sharp-edged words were directed at only one of them.

"Macbeth Richard Brannon," she said ominously, "did I just hear you curse?"

Chapter Three

MAC ENDURED the scolding his mother gave him in stoic silence. He hadn't meant to take the Lord's name in vain, and as far as he could see, he hadn't actually done that. All he'd said was "hell." But that was just as bad where his mother was concerned.

It seemed, though, that a man who was twenty-five years old ought to be able to say just about anything he wanted to without worrying what his mama would think about it. Some things a fella just never got over, Mac supposed, and one of them was the way he would always feel about five years old whenever his mother was around, especially when she was frowning in disapproval.

"You'd better do a bit of praying tonight, young man," Abigail concluded. "You've got a lot to get straight between you and the Lord."

"Yes, ma'am," Mac agreed. "I'll do that."

"See that you do." Abigail turned and went back in the house, followed by Cordelia, who gave Mac a quick, sympathetic glance before she went in.

Henry sauntered up beside Mac and observed with a grin, "Boy, she laid down the law to you, didn't she, Mac?"

"I'll live."

"Good thing Mama never heard what you said the time that old milk cow stepped on your foot. I never heard of some of those words before."

Will laid a hand on Henry's shoulder. "That's enough," he said. "Don't go threatening your brother."

"Me?" Henry asked innocently. "I didn't threaten him, Will."

"You were about to suggest that Mac might want to do some of your chores for you for a while, lest you accidentally let it slip about him cussing when that cow stepped on him."

"You know I wouldn't do that—"

Mac interrupted, "I know that if you did, I'd have to tell her about what I caught you doing out in the barn that day—"

Henry leaped at him, catching hold of his shoulders. "You just shut up!" he exclaimed. "I told you I wasn't doin' a thing, not a damned thing—"

"Now there *you* go cussing," Will said with a grin. "Sounds to me like you're the one who needs to get right with the Lord, Henry."

Henry gave Mac a hard shove and then turned to stomp away, muttering under his breath. Mac tried not to laugh, knowing that would injure the youngster's pride that much more. But he and Will couldn't help but grin at each other.

"Let's take a look at the barn doors," Will suggested. "See how much damage that brute did with its hooves."

They got an oil lantern from the small storage room just inside the barn and then examined the doors once the lantern was lit. The flickering yellow glow showed that some of the boards had cracked under the driving impact of the silver-gray stallion's hooves.

"We'll need to replace those boards," Mac noted. "I thought he was going to kick his way right through there."

"He tried hard enough," said Will. "Was it my imagination, or did that horse wait until it had lured us out there in the pasture, then make a beeline for the barn?"

"That's what happened, all right," agreed Mac. "Funny thing, wasn't it? Almost like he knew exactly what he was doing."

"I've seen some smart horses in my time, but I don't know if I ever saw one that could think like that."

"And you thought you were going to catch him."

Will laughed ruefully. "Not really. I just wanted to see what he'd do."

"Well, we found out, I reckon."

They blew out the lantern and put it back in the storage room, then went into the house. Henry was still up, sitting in a rocking chair near the fire that was burning low in the fireplace, but Titus, Abigail, and Cordelia had already gone on to bed. People who lived on farms generally turned in pretty early.

Some of Henry's natural cockiness had returned. "Ready to do that prayin', Mac?"

"I'll worry about how I get along with the Lord, and you tend to your own business," Mac told him.

"Just wouldn't want you burning in all that fire and brimstone. You're my brother, after all."

"And you're my *little* brother, and I'm telling you to get on up to bed. Time you were asleep."

"I'll second that motion," Will said. "Good night, Henry."

Grudgingly, Henry got up and headed for the stairs. "G'night," he said. Before he was halfway up the stairs, he was stifling a yawn.

Mac took the chair where Henry had been sitting, while Will pulled up another. They settled down in front of the fire, and Mac observed, "I thought I saw something on your face at supper, Will. Something happened today, didn't it?"

Will grunted. "You'll hear about it soon enough, I suppose. Half a dozen men robbed old man Burke this morning. Pistol-whipped him pretty bad."

Mac sat forward and asked, "Will he be all right?"

"The doctor thought so," Will replied with a shrug. "Hard to say, though."

"Who'd do such a—" Mac stopped, realizing that he already knew the answer to the question he'd been about to ask. "The Fogartys," he said heavily.

"That's what I think. I saw them later in the day, together with the Paynter boys and that Israel Quinn. That makes six," Will said.

"Where'd you see them?"

"Up in the northwest part of the county." Will hesitated, then added, "Luther and I were laying for them."

Mac leaned forward again. "What happened?"

"They almost rode right up to us. I was about to holler at them to throw down their guns . . . then some other fella came along and talked to them, and they all rode off together. Luther and I never had a chance to get the drop on them."

"That's a shame," Mac noted with a shake of his head. "If there's anybody in the county who's liable to be guilty of robbing old man Burke, it's the Fogartys."

Mac had never liked the Fogartys. Even though the origins of the friction between the Brannons and the Fogartys was lost somewhere in the past, Mac had a good solid reason for disliking them. He had been riding along the road from Culpeper one day when he'd come across Ransom Fogarty, the middle brother, savagely whipping a team of horses that had been pulling a wagon. The wagon's rear axle was broken, something that was certainly no fault of the team, but Ransom was taking his fury out on them anyway, cursing them and holding tightly to the reins as he slashed at them with a whip. Mac had watched and listened to the brutality for a couple of minutes as he rode by.

That had been a couple of minutes too long. He turned his horse around, rode back, took the whip away from Ranse Fogarty and broke it, then used his bare hands to beat Ranse black and blue.

It had felt damned good to do it, too.

Ranse hadn't been carrying a gun that day, which was undoubtedly lucky for Mac, because he'd been unarmed, too. As Mac rode away, Ranse's shouted threats to kill him had followed him. Mac didn't worry too much about the threats; he knew Ranse wouldn't do anything without the approval of his older brother George, and it seemed unlikely that George would want Ranse gunning for the brother of the county sheriff. George Fogarty hated all the Brannons, but he had enough sense not to want Will Brannon coming after him and his brothers for a killing that didn't even make them any money.

Sure enough, nobody had tried to bushwhack Mac, but he got some mighty hard looks from all the Fogartys any time he happened to see them in town.

That was all right with Mac. He was used to having the Fogartys hate him.

"Well, one of these days, I'm going to catch them with the proof of something they've done," Will was saying. "They probably had the money they stole from old man Burke on them today, if I'd had a chance to search them."

"Next time," said Mac.

"I hope. Like I told Luther, where the Fogartys are concerned, I know there'll be a next time." Will yawned, covering his mouth with the back of his hand. When he was through, he stood up and stretched. "Reckon I'll go on up, too. You coming?"

"I think I'll stay down here a little while longer."

"All right. But those cows are going to want milking mighty early in the morning."

"Don't worry. They'll get milked."

"I know they will," said Will, and it made Mac feel good to hear the confidence that his brother had in him. Just like a fella could never really consider himself completely full-grown while his mama was yelling at him, he never lost the good feeling that came with meeting the approval of his older brother, either.

When he was alone in front of the fireplace, Mac leaned back in the rocking chair, steepled his hands together in front of his face, and stared over the tips of his fingers at the flames. The fire leaped and danced, and in the ever-constant motion of the flames he saw something else, something sleek and powerful and silver gray, something that ran like the wind.

Funny. Before tonight, Mac had seen the stallion maybe half a dozen times, pacing there on the edge of the pasture, and not on any of those nights had he felt the urge to catch the horse.

But now, he wanted to lay his hands on that silver-gray hide, feel the smooth warmth of it and the play of powerful muscles beneath the skin. He wanted to tangle his fingers in the slightly darker mane and swing up on the back of the horse, wanted to feel it stretching out and running beneath him, the wind of its speed cold in his face.

"Damn it, Will . . . ," Mac whispered.

Before tonight, he had been content to watch and admire.

Now, he had to know for himself.

• • •

THERE WERE four bedrooms on the second floor of the Brannon farmhouse. One was Abigail's, of course, and another was Cordelia's. Will and Mac shared a room, as did Titus and Henry.

Titus was already snoring loudly as Henry came quietly into the room they shared. A bit of starlight shone through the gap in the curtains over the room's single window. That was enough illumination for Henry to find his way around. He didn't need to light a candle to get around in the room that had been his home all his life.

He sat down on a narrow ladderback chair and took off his boots and socks. A moment later, stripped down to his long underwear, he slid into the large four-poster bed, reclaiming some of the quilts from Titus so that he could pull them over on his side.

Henry rolled onto his right side, facing away from his brother. The room was cold. Warmth from the fireplace downstairs never made it all the way up here to the second floor. He was grateful for the heavy quilts as he wrapped them around him.

Despite his tiredness after a day of working around the place, he found himself unable to fall asleep right away. Instead he lay there and stared into the darkness of the room and thought.

He was nineteen years old. It was time he started to give some thought to finding himself a wife and settling down. Will and Mac could be old bachelors if they wanted, and Titus was convinced he was going to marry Polly Ebersole—not likely, Henry thought, but he supposed stranger things had happened. He didn't care what his brothers did. He wanted to get married.

Only thing was, who was going to marry him?

Not that there weren't plenty of unmarried young women in Culpeper County. There was a good crop of them, in Henry's opinion. But none of them seemed to want to have much to do with him. He supposed he must be ugly. His ears stuck out a mite, and he had that scar on his forehead he'd gotten when he fell off the barn when he was eight years old. Those didn't seem like such awful flaws to him, but he reckoned they were enough. Otherwise he wouldn't have had so much trouble finding a girl who was willing to have him court her.

Of course, it might have helped if he'd actually asked any of them if they were willing . . .

That had been some horse Will and Mac had chased up from the pasture tonight. Henry's musings leaped from women to horseflesh without a second's hesitation. He liked to ride, and he'd even thought that he might like to take part in a race sometime, like Mac often did, but he couldn't even imagine how it would feel to be on the back of a mount such as that big silver-gray stallion. Henry wouldn't have admitted it to save his life, but just the thought of doing such a thing made him a little scared.

Titus let out a particularly loud snore, and Henry reached over and dug an elbow into his brother's ribs. "Hey!" he said. "Some of us are tryin' to sleep here."

Titus snorted, mumbled something incoherent, and rolled over onto his side. He was silent and probably would be for a while, until he started up again.

Henry pulled the covers tighter around him and closed his eyes, determined to take advantage of the quiet and doze off.

It was awhile, though, before the dizzying spiral of horses and women that filled his thoughts receded enough to let slumber claim him.

• • •

ACROSS THE hall, in Cordelia's room, the young woman shared the restlessness that seemed to have invaded the house tonight. Her feet were cold, even though she was wearing socks and was bundled under several layers of covers. She wished spring would hurry up and get here. Winter was all right, but Cordelia liked the warmer weather better. Summers were magnificent, when you could go barefooted and feel the grass between your toes and lie beneath the shade of a big tree and let the breeze carry all your troubles away.

In the winter you couldn't stretch out. You had to hold it all in and save all the warmth you could.

Cordelia remembered a day last summer when she had gone traipsing off down the creek looking for berries, and once she was out of sight of the house, a wicked thought had occurred to her. She had taken off her dress and her shift and sprawled out nude on the grassy bank of the creek, loving the way the fiery fingers of the sun had caressed her body. She hadn't stayed like that for long—someone could have come along and seen her, and besides, it was just too sinful—but the memory had remained with her. Maybe this summer, if there was a chance for her to do that again . . .

And if there wasn't a war going on by then . . .

She shivered underneath the covers, but it wasn't from the chill in the room. She had listened to the talk of secession at the supper table tonight, as well as all the other times over the past few months, and whether her mother thought it was unladylike for a young woman to hold political opinions or not, Cordelia hadn't been able to keep from forming them.

She hated the Yankees. Why couldn't they just leave the southern states alone? Cordelia didn't want to own any slaves; she wasn't even sure if she believed in slavery. But that didn't give the northern states the right to dictate to the rest of the country. If they wanted to preserve their precious Union, then they ought to realize that not everybody was going to believe the same way.

But even more than the anger she felt toward the North, she felt fear. If a war came—and all it would take would be for somebody to fire the first shot—then her brothers would be liable to go off to the fighting and get themselves killed and never come back. Cordelia had to bite her lip to keep it from trembling as she thought about that. Corey had already ridden off, headed west to become a rich man—or so he claimed. Having him gone was hard enough. She didn't know if she could manage to survive if anything ever happened to Will and Mac and Titus and Henry . . .

She closed her eyes and prayed, "Lord, let it be summer again, and without any old war . . ."

• • •

FAIRS WERE usually held in the summer, but for the past few years, Richmond had held one in the winter, too, to break up the monotony of the long chilly season. At this time of year, there were no fruits and vegetables to show, so dances and parties and horse races and political rallies took the place of them. Mainly, it was just an excuse for folks to come into town and get together for a few good times before spring arrived and the year's real work got underway.

On this night, as Will tried to go to sleep, he found himself looking forward to the fair but worrying about it at the same time. Luther was a good man, and Luther's cousin Jasper could be depended upon as long as the chores didn't require too much energy or initiative, but Will was still somewhat concerned about leaving them in charge of not only the farm but the whole county's law enforcement as well.

That was how a deputy learned, Will reminded himself, by shouldering responsibility. He'd done his share of it, back when he was a deputy. And the lessons he had learned, especially during moments such as the one during which he had faced that crazy tavernkeeper with the ax, had stood him in good stead since he'd pinned on the sheriff's badge. Luther would do fine.

And Luther probably wouldn't even have to worry about the Fogartys, Will reminded himself, because they would likely travel to Richmond for the fair, too.

Will was already excited about the race. Mac was sort of tall and gangly, not like most of the men who rode their horses in competition, but that didn't seem to matter. The bond Mac shared with whatever mount he happened to be riding made up for any extra weight the horse was carrying. Horses seemed to *want* to win for Mac, and they would run their hearts out if he would let them. But of course, he never would. Mac cared too much about them for that.

What worried Will was the possibility of trouble at that Secessionist rally. If the Secesh forces gathered together, there were bound to be some abolitionists there, too, yelling and hollering about slavery. The Secesh bunch would yell and holler back, and then somebody was liable to throw a punch, and that was all it would take to start a riot. If everyone was lucky, nobody would pull a gun and light the fuse that would turn a riot into a massacre . . .

But all that was sheer speculation, Will reminded himself. Maybe there wouldn't be any trouble at all, just some arguing. Not all abolitionists were damned lunatics like that fella John Brown, who'd gotten himself hanged for trying to capture the Federal armory over at Harpers Ferry and use the munitions there to start a slave revolution.

Will sighed and punched the pillow, bunching it up under his head. If he and Mac could catch that stallion, Mac could ride it to victory against Montayne and Symington. Will was sure of it. But they didn't know if the horse would ever even return to the Brannon farm, let alone allow itself to be caught. For a horse to have that much speed and power and intelligence was a downright dangerous combination, Will thought. Trying to lay hands on it would be almost like trying to capture a man who didn't want to be caught.

Maybe that was the key, Will told himself. He had captured fugitives by putting himself in their place and trying to think like they were thinking. Maybe he and Mac could do the same thing where that horse was concerned. If they were going to catch him, they would have to outwit him, because they sure couldn't outrun him.

They only had a week, though, before the fair. That wasn't long enough. It would take time and planning, and probably a lot of both those things, to ever dab a loop on that stallion.

But there would be other fairs and other races. It wasn't like this was their last chance . . .

• • •

ABIGAIL BRANNON knelt beside her bed. Despite the thick rug, the floor was still hard on her knees. She endured the pain as she clasped her hands in front of her bowed head and prayed.

She had been there like that for almost half an hour, whispering softly as she talked to her Lord. There was a lot to pray about tonight, just as there was every night: the farm, the children, the war that was bound to come. Mostly she prayed for the children, prayed that the Lord would keep them all strong and safe from harm, both physically and spiritually. She knew they had their own crosses to bear: Will and the violence in him that made him strap on a gun each and every day of his life and sometimes use that gun in anger when his fists weren't enough; Mac and the idleness that sometimes made him stop whatever work he was doing and stare off into the distance like he was looking into a dream, fertile ground for Satan to sow temptation; Titus and the dark thoughts that often claimed him, coupled with his desire for a girl whose station in life was so far above him that he was doomed to disappointment and more brooding; Henry, full of the mischief of a boy, unwilling or unable to grow up, a pure vexation to both his mother and the Lord, though Abigail would never be so presumptuous as to believe she was privy to the thoughts of Jehovah on any subject, even one of her own children; and Cordelia, beautiful, innocent Cordelia, the only one Abigail didn't have to worry about because she knew that Cordelia would never do anything to bring down the wrath of God on her head.

And Corey, of course, her lost sheep.

John Brannon had given her the children, and to this day Abigail was grateful to him for that. She truly was. But that was all he had ever given her other than pain and regret. He had been so charming at first, coming into her life and sweeping her off her feet, taking her away from the little Tidewater town where she had grown up the daughter of a ship's chandler. They had come here to the Piedmont and started the farm, and it hadn't been long before Abigail realized what a mistake she had made. John Brannon was a man with all sorts of unholy appetites, mostly for whiskey and the words of Shakespeare. Abigail had wanted to name the children after the writers of the Gospels, but John Brannon had insisted that they honor the man he called the Bard of Avon. That was always his way, to put man before God.

Nearly all that was bad in John Brannon, he had passed down to his children. Will had gotten his temper, the quick, explosive rages that often led to violence; Abigail no longer remembered how many times her husband had come home from some tavern brawl with bruises and bloody scratches and a big grin on his face. Mac had fallen heir to the tendency of drifting off into waking dreams; many was the day Abigail had gone out into the fields with John Brannon's lunch and found him leaning on the plow, the mules motionless while their so-called master stared off at things only he could see. To Titus had gone the legacy of vaulting ambition and overweening pride; John Brannon had actually believed that he was as good as anyone else and that someday everything would be much better for his family. Corey had been cursed with the same rootlessness as his father that had led him to wander far from home; without that he would still be here on the farm where he belonged, rather than off in Kentucky or Missouri or wherever he was. Henry had his father's charming smile and ready laugh and quick wit so that he could talk almost anyone into doing almost anything; an ability like that could make a young man neglect his work and think he could get by on less than his absolute best effort.

Abigail took a deep breath, pausing briefly in her prayers as she gathered her thoughts, "And be with the South, Lord. Give us Your strength as we struggle with the forces that would destroy our way of life. Lead us away from the paths of war if such is Your wish, but if war comes, be at our side as we lift the banner of liberty and crush those northern Yankees!"

She breathed a long sigh, then whispered, "We ask these things in Jesus' name. Amen."

Chapter Four

RICHMOND WAS a city of between thirty-five and forty thousand souls, sprawled on the small hills alongside the James River. The center of town was dominated by the large, pillared state capitol. Half a dozen church steeples thrust up at various points around the city. Several trestles spanned the river, since Richmond was the major hub for railroad transportation in the state. Hundreds of thousands of pounds of tobacco and cotton moved through here on their way to the shipyards at Norfolk. Richmond might not be as large as some of the cities up north, such as Boston and New York and Philadelphia, but it was plenty big enough for a country boy like Will Brannon.

Will sat on the high seat of the wagon next to Mac, who was handling the reins of the team of mules. Titus, Henry, Abigail, and Cordelia sat in the back of the wagon, Abigail in a cushioned rocking chair that had been lifted into the wagon bed. She didn't have to rock; the motion of the wagon itself did that for her.

Henry and Cordelia sat cross-legged, leaning against one of the sideboards. They were singing a hymn, their voices clear and sweet. Henry had wanted to sing "For the Love of Barbara Allen," but Abigail had told him to stick to hymns instead. They were a more pleasing sound to the Lord, and therefore to her, she had explained.

The day was cold, and the mules' breath made little clouds of steam that wreathed their heads. The members of the Brannon family were wrapped in coats and blankets, and the thin, watery sunshine cast a little warmth on them. Mac followed the wagon road that led into town from the northwest. When he reached a crossroads, Mac swung the team into a turn that took them onto the other road, which skirted around the northern edge of the city. Their destination was the large circular racetrack laid out on a tract of flat open ground just outside Richmond.

Will turned his head and looked back over his shoulder at the horse tied to the wagon's tailgate. Mac had chosen the mouse-colored two-year-old to run against Montayne and Symington, as Will had thought he would. The animal wasn't the most physically impressive specimen of horseflesh Will had ever seen, but it was capable of an opening burst of speed that often took other riders by surprise and left them unable to catch up. Mac had led many a race from start to finish, as long as the distance wasn't too great.

"Too bad that's not that stallion back there," Will said. "I reckon you've got a good chance as it is, but on that horse, Montayne and Symington would really be eating your dust."

Mac grunted. He had been out to the pasture every night since the silver-gray stallion had lured him and Will out there and then made its dash for the barn. So far he hadn't seen even a glimmering of the stallion. He was afraid it was never coming back to the Brannon farm.

"You can't catch what you can't see," he responded, a little bitterness creeping into his voice. "I never should have rushed things by trying to walk up on him that night."

"Sorry."

"Not your fault," said Mac with a shake of his head. "I ought to have followed my instincts."

Will knew what he meant, and he also knew that Mac never would have dreamed of trying to tell him how to perform his duties as sheriff. Will had intruded, and it had maybe cost Mac his only chance to lay hands on that stallion.

But that was in the past. Nothing he could do about it now. Instead, he waited until Henry and Cordelia had finished the hymn they were singing, then turned to them and said, "Sing 'Camptown Races.' Seems appropriate, considering where we're going."

Henry and Cordelia looked at their mother, and after a moment, Abigail gave a little nod. "All right," she conceded. "They're not as good as hymns, but I enjoy Mr. Foster's songs, I suppose."

Henry broke into a grin and lifted his voice, joined immediately by Cordelia. When he got to the "doo-dahs," he dropped his pitch as low as he possibly could, making both Will and Mac chuckle. Cordelia laughed out loud and kept singing. Even Abigail smiled slightly at Henry's foolishness.

Only Titus showed no change of expression. He stayed where he was, sitting in the rear of the wagon with his knees drawn up. He stared out to the side as he swayed back and forth a little to the motion of the vehicle. His Sharps rested on the wagon bed beside him. He seldom went anywhere without the rifle.

There was more traffic on the road, especially as the Brannon wagon approached the racetrack. The flatness of the ground around the track made it a good place to camp as well, and many of those who came into Richmond from the country would pitch their tents there during the fair. Men on horseback, families in wagons, and couples in buggies converged on the place. There was a large barn near the track, and a dance was to be held there tonight.

Will kept his eyes open, scanning the faces of the growing crowd for the familiar visages of the Fogartys or any of their kin. Of course, it was difficult to know just who was who in that bunch, since it was rumored that the Fogartys didn't always pay much attention to family ties when it came to fornicating. So far Will hadn't seen any of them, but he was certain George and Ransom and Joe would be here. They wouldn't pass up a chance to get drunk and kick up their heels.

"Look there," observed Mac, pointing up ahead to where a large ring of poles had been driven into the ground. Brightly colored pennants were attached to the tops of the poles, and they fluttered in the chilly breeze. "They've marked off the course this year."

He was right. Usually the racetrack was just a circle of plowed and smoothed ground, but this year someone had gone to the trouble of putting up the poles. "More colorful," Will said.

Mac was frowning slightly. "Yeah, but if a fella was to fall off his horse and run into one of those poles, it'd be liable to bust him up pretty bad. A horse could run into them, too."

"Well, at least you don't have to worry about that."

"Why not?"

"How long has it been since you fell off a horse, Mac? What were you, five years old?"

The memory brought a smile to Mac's face. "Four, I reckon."

"You sit a saddle better'n anybody in the state of Virginia. You won't be falling off."

Mac didn't argue, and a few minutes later he swung the mules into another turn that took them off the main road and down a path to the spot where they usually camped when they came to Richmond. It was a field alongside a small trickle of water that ran into Shockoe Creek, which flowed on through the main part of the city to join the James. The easy availability of water made it a prime campsite.

Which was why several tents were already set up in the field, with wagons parked next to them. Will looked over the inhabitants closely, but none of them appeared to be Fogartys. That came as no real surprise. When the brothers reached Richmond, they would head straight downtown to the saloons and whorehouses. They might spend the whole trip deep in debauchery and not even come out to the racetrack.

Mac brought the wagon to a stop. "This good enough?" he asked.

Will nodded and said, "Fine." He swung down easily from the high seat and went around to the back of the wagon to help his mother get down. He had suggested on previous trips that Abigail just wait in the wagon until they had the tent set up, but he knew by now she wouldn't do that. She had to be down on the ground, supervising everything that the rest of them did.

Henry and Cordelia had already hopped out as soon as Mac halted the wagon. Cordelia spotted a friend from earlier fairs at the next campsite and waved at her. The girl waved back enthusiastically and came over to the Brannon wagon. She had rosy cheeks and a tumbled mass of strawberry blonde curls, and she gave Henry a big smile. "Hello, Cordelia," she greeted her. "Is this that handsome big brother of yours you told me all about last summer?"

"All my big brothers are handsome," Cordelia replied with a laugh, "but this is Henry, if that's who you're asking about."

"It is indeed," the girl acknowledged. "Hello, Mr. Henry Brannon. I am Miss Katherine Grange. But you can call me Katie."

"Uh, hello," Henry said. "I'm right pleased to make your acquaintance, Miss Katie."

"Not Miss," she insisted. "Just Katie."

Mac came around the other side of the wagon and saw Henry and Cordelia talking to some girl from another camp. Henry was blushing furiously and looked like he could use some rescuing. Mac reached into the wagon and picked up a heavy bundle of folded canvas that would serve as ground cover for the tent. He announced, "Here you go, Henry," and shoved the awkward bundle into his brother's arms. "You can take care of that."

"Thanks, Mac . . . I mean, all right. I will." Henry hurried off to spread the ground cover while Cordelia and the other girl laughed. Mac just shook his head.

Standing beside the tailgate, Will reached up to his mother. He took her right hand in his left, then cupped his right hand under her left elbow. Abigail leaned on him for support as she stepped down from the high gate. When both feet were on the ground, she brushed her hands together as if she were brushing dust off them, then looked around. "Where's Titus?"

"He was here a second ago," said Will. He glanced around the field and spotted Titus standing on the bank of the little unnamed creek. His Sharps was tucked under his left arm, and he was looking off to the south, toward downtown Richmond.

Mooning over the Ebersole girl again, more than likely, thought Will. Duncan Ebersole and his daughter would have come to Richmond for the fair like most everybody else in the region, but he and Polly wouldn't be camping out. They would be staying in the most luxurious hotel downtown and attending all the fancy-dress balls . . . places where a Piedmont dirt farmer such as Titus Brannon wouldn't be welcome at all.

Will felt a pang of sympathy for his brother, but it came and went quickly. Titus knew he had no chance to marry somebody like Polly Ebersole. He was just torturing himself by hanging on to such a dream. But that was his own decision to make. Will strode over to him and said, "Come on, Titus. Best get busy setting up camp with the rest of us."

Titus gave Will a narrow-eyed glance, then shrugged and followed him to the wagon. He laid the Sharps inside the bed and reached in with Will to heft the heavy tent.

Mac untied the two-year-old from the wagon and led it over to the stream to drink. As the horse dipped its muzzle in the water, Mac rested a hand on its flank. He liked what he felt there: good breathing and a sense of power and strength just waiting to be unleashed. The horse would run a good race; Mac was sure of that.

He became aware of a commotion elsewhere in the camp and turned to see a man leading another horse toward the creek. The horse was long legged, with a sleek black hide that seemed to gleam in the winter sunlight. It walked with a nervous, almost prancing gait, as if it could barely contain itself.

The man leading the horse wore a leather vest over a heavy woolen shirt. He had a tight cap of brown curls under a beaver hat. Though he was small, a full head shorter than Mac, the sleeves of his shirt bulged with muscle, and he had no trouble handling the massive horse. As the horse began to drink, the man looked over at Mac and nodded. "Howdy, Brannon," he said.

"Hello, Edward," replied Mac. Edward Symington wasn't a farmer; he owned a successful hardware store in the settlement of Manassas, up north of here. But his real occupation was taking that black horse of his all over the state and racing it. Symington was a good rider, but it didn't take much skill to win when you were on the back of a horse like that.

"Going to be running in the race tomorrow?" Symington asked casually.

Mac knew the attitude was a pose. "Yep, I plan to," he acknowledged.

"Where's your horse?"

"Right here," Mac said, patting the shoulder of the two-year-old.

Symington gave a skeptical snort. "That animal? I figured you'd hitched him to the wagon along with the rest of the mules."

Mac smiled and kept a tight rein on his temper. Symington was an unpleasant fellow most of the time, but Mac figured that was pretty much a facade. Symington just liked to get under the skin of his opponents in the hopes of rattling them into making a mistake when it came time to ride against him.

"This fella can run a mite faster than any mule," Mac answered, stroking the two-year-old's shoulder. "You'll see that tomorrow."

"Oh, we'll see, all right," said Symington. "We'll all see."

"Cully around?" Mac asked, in hopes of changing the subject.

Symington shook his head. "Haven't seen him. You know Montayne. He likes to show up late. I reckon he thinks that'll help him somehow." Symington laughed and added, "It won't help him in this race. He'll be eating my dust, just like the rest of you."

"How many horses are going to be running?"

"Counting yours, six, last I heard."

Mac nodded. Six was a good field, not too large but not too small. "Who else is here?"

Symington named three other men, all of whom were known to Mac. He had raced against them before. He asked, "Do any of them have anything new?"

"Naw, just the same old nags."

Barring something unforeseen, that meant the real race would be between Cully Montayne, Symington, and himself, thought Mac. He knew the other riders, knew their horses, knew they wouldn't provide any serious competition. Symington, in his arrogance, probably felt the same way about Mac and the two-year-old.

Mac's horse was through drinking. It was nosing around through the sparse dead grass on the creek bank. Mac pulled its head up and said, "Come on, boy. We'll get you some grain."

"Good luck tomorrow, Brannon," Symington called after him mockingly. "You'll need it."

"You, too," replied Mac.

When he got back to the wagon, he found that Will and Titus had the tent up. Henry and Cordelia were carrying their supplies inside. Abigail's rocking chair had been lifted down from the wagon, and she was sitting in it beside the tent, holding court as it were. Several old friends had already stopped by to say hello.

Will came over as Mac was filling a feedbag with grain and then strapping it on the two-year-old's nose. "Saw you talking to Symington," he commented quietly. "He still as annoying as a bluebottle fly?"

"Every bit," said Mac. "But he'll be singing a different tune tomorrow."

Will grunted. "We can hope so." He was about to say something else when suddenly somebody yelled angrily a couple of campsites away. Will turned to see what was going on, and as he did so, a woman screamed.

That was more than enough for Will. His lawman's instincts took over, and he broke into a run, heading straight for the trouble. Mac was right behind him.

They darted around another wagon, this one with a tall canvas cover that blocked their view. As they came around it, they saw a woman struggling with a man. She was trying to get away, and he was determined to hold on to her. Will caught a glimpse of a bruise already forming on the woman's terrified face. He lunged forward and grabbed the man's shoulder, jerking him around and throwing a punch at the same time.

Will's fist crashed into the man's jaw and sent him staggering back against the covered wagon. "Damn you!" the man yelled as he caught his balance and started clawing at the butt of the gun holstered on his hip.

Will palmed out his Colt Navy and brought it up in one smooth efficient motion. His thumb was looped over the hammer, and he eared it back as the barrel came level. A jolt of surprise went through him as he stared over the sights at the man, recognizing him as Joe Fogarty. For a split second, Will thought about lifting his thumb from the hammer and driving a bullet into Joe's face. It would have been a legitimate case of self-defense, since Joe had reached for his gun first.

But Will controlled the impulse and ordered loudly, "Stop it, Joe. Take your hand away from your gun."

Joe was unsteady on his feet, but it wasn't from the blow he had just received. He was drunk, Will realized. But after a tense moment, Joe moved his hand away from the butt of his pistol. "Sheriff Brannon," he said with a leer. "I might of knowed it. You got to follow us all the way down here just to make life miser'ble for us?"

"I don't see the other two, Will," Mac said quietly.

"Where are your brothers, Joe?" Will demanded.

"Left 'em in a crib downtown. Hell, they're drunk."

As if he wasn't, thought Will. "What are you doing out here?"

"Came to see my pretty lil' Sareybeth. I been courtin' her."

"He has not," exclaimed the young woman who had been struggling with Joe. "I don't want nothin' to do with him."

Joe belched. "Aw, now, Sareybeth, you got no call to go talkin' like that. You know you love me."

Will recognized the young woman now. She came from a family that farmed some acreage in the southern part of Culpeper County. "Where's your folks?" he asked her.

"They went to buy some supplies and left me here to watch over the camp." She sent a scathing glance at Joe. "That's when he showed up. I reckon he was watching and waiting for them to leave."

"I reckon you're right," said Will. He lowered his gun a little but still kept it pointing at Joe. "You get on out of here, and if you come around bothering this girl again, I'll have you thrown in jail, Fogarty."

"You can't do that," protested Joe. "You ain't no lawman here. This ain't Culpeper County."

"I'll go to the local law. They'll believe any charge I swear out against you."

"Yeah, you're prob'ly right," Joe snarled bitterly. "You badge-totin' bastards stick together, don't you?"

Once again, Will thought about how easy it would be to simply lift his thumb from the hammer. "Get out," he ordered again, and this time his voice shook a little from the strain of controlling himself.

Joe Fogarty glanced around, no doubt seeing that a crowd had gathered, and none of them looked overly friendly toward him. He shrugged and turned away from the wagon. Stumbling a little, he walked over to a horse that stood nearby with its reins dangling to the ground. He caught hold of the reins, got his foot in the stirrup on the second try, and awkwardly swung up into the saddle. "You think you're a big man, don't you, Brannon?" he sneered at Will. "One of these days you'll find out differ'nt. You'll find out just how puny you really are."

"Not as puny as somebody who'd pistol-whip an old man on top of robbing him," Will shot back, and he could tell from the way Joe's eyes widened for a second in surprise that his thrust had gone home. Then Joe jerked the horse around and kicked it into a gallop, forcing several of the bystanders to scurry to get out of the way before they were trampled.

Carefully, Will lowered the hammer of his revolver and slid the gun back into its holster. The young woman came over to him and started thanking him effusively. Will broke into her words by saying, "Did you give that young fella any encouragement, Miss Sarah Beth?"

"Never!" she declared a little resentfully. Then, after a moment, she added, "Well, not really. Not after the first time or two he came callin', anyway. Once I'd got to know him. But he *is* a mite handsome."

Will supposed a young woman might think so. Joe Fogarty had a wide mouth, with the upper lip scarred a little on one end, but the girls didn't seem to mind that. They liked his heavy-lidded eyes and his shock of brown hair. To Will he just looked like trouble.

"You'd best tell your pa about this," he told Sarah Beth. "He won't want to leave you alone again on this trip."

"Well . . . all right. But I don't reckon Joe would've really hurt me." She lifted her fingertips to the bruise on her cheek and touched it gingerly. "He just got a mite overwrought."

Will gave her a nod and touched a finger to the brim of his hat, then turned away. Mac said, "Miss Sarah Beth," and tipped his own hat before falling in alongside his brother. Will was taking long strides, but Mac had no trouble keeping up with him.

"It'd sure be nice to live in a world without any Fogartys in it," Will commented.

"There'd just be somebody else causing a ruckus," Mac pointed out. "'Man is born to trouble.' You've heard Mama quote that Scripture often enough."

Will nodded. "I suppose so. But that gal never should have led Joe on in the first place."

"What do you expect? She's young, and she thinks he's handsome. Some snakes are right pretty, too, until you go to pick them up. But folks have to learn that for themselves."

Will couldn't argue with that.

When they got back to their campsite, they found Abigail deep in conversation with a man wearing a dusty black broadcloth suit and a broad-brimmed black hat. Mac nudged Will in the ribs with an elbow and nodded toward the stranger. "Fella dressed like that has got to be either a preacher or an undertaker."

Henry was close enough to overhear the comment, and he noted quietly, "He's a preacher, all right. And he's preaching the gospel of secession."

Chapter Five

QUICKLY, WILL moved closer and heard the man in the black broadcloth suit saying, ". . . be there tonight to hear the Lord's Word, ma'am?"

"Oh, yes, indeed, Pastor," Abigail assured him. "My whole family will be eager to hear your message."

Will stepped around the preacher and rested a hand on the back of his mother's rocking chair. "Howdy," he said with a polite nod. "I'm Will Brannon."

Abigail glanced up at him sharply, as if she were annoyed by his interruption, but the man in black just smiled broadly and stuck out a hand. "Pleased to meet you, son," he responded heartily. "Your ma's just been tellin' me about you. You'd be the lawman?"

"That's right," said Will as he shook the man's hand. "County sheriff, up in Culpeper County."

"Been there many a time spreadin' the Word of the Lord. I'm Pastor Vickery, Obadiah Vickery."

"Where's your church, Pastor?" Will asked. "Here in Richmond?"

"My church? Where's my church, you say?" Vickery spread his arms to indicate the field around them. "The whole world is my church, son! I don't believe in tyin' the gospel down and lockin' it away behind walls and doors. No, sir!"

Vickery's loud, booming voice carried well, drawing the attention of several other families who were making their camps in the field between the racetrack and the creek. The preacher was a physically imposing man as well, tall and broad-shouldered with a craggy face and thick white hair under his black hat. A long white mustache drooped over his mouth.

"Pastor Vickery is going to hold a rally here tonight," Abigail explained to Will. "I've promised him that we'll all attend."

"What sort of rally?" Will asked, even though he already knew the answer.

"Why, I'll be speakin' about that abomination in the Lord's eyes known as abolition, young Will. And I'll be prayin' for the souls of those godless Yankees who want to strip us southern folks of our rights as citizens of these here United States."

Titus stepped up and interjected, "Like the right to secede from the Union."

Vickery clapped a hand on his shoulder. "That's right, son, that's right. Sometimes when folks just can't get along, it's best for them to go their separate ways. That's what we got to do with the North."

"That's the truth, Pastor," agreed Titus with a nod. "Those Yankees can't tell us what to do."

Will's fingers tightened on the back of his mother's rocking chair as he heard the fervor in Titus's voice. It could be that some of Titus's anti-abolition sentiments came from listening to Duncan Ebersole. Whenever the owner of Mountain Laurel was in Culpeper, he usually wound up at the general store, surrounded by a group of men as he loudly expressed his opinions of the North and the growing crisis that had been aggravated by the election and coming inauguration of Abraham Lincoln. Titus chimed in on the choruses of agreement that always followed Ebersole's pronouncements. How much of that was because Titus actually agreed with the plantation owner, and how much was prompted by his desire to curry favor with Ebersole, Will didn't know.

"There'll be a bonfire tonight and some good ol'-fashioned preachin'," Vickery went on. "I hope to see all of you folks there."

Abigail nodded. "We will be, Pastor. You can count on it."

Vickery smiled and moved on to personally carry his message to the other families camped in the field, even though only those who were hard of hearing could have missed what he had said to the Brannons. Abigail watched him go with admiration shining in her eyes.

"It's a shame none of my boys ever heard the Lord's calling," she lamented. "It would have been so nice to have a preacher in the family."

Will and Mac exchanged wry glances. Somehow, neither of them could imagine any of the Brannon boys being a minister. Titus was the only one who might have leaned in that direction, but early on he had found his true calling in black powder and lead.

"Well, I just hope the pastor doesn't stir up any trouble," said Will. "Most folks have come here to have a good time, not to argue about abolition."

"If there's any stirring up of trouble, it'll be by those Yankees," Abigail contended. "I hear tell they've got agents all over down here, just primed and ready to get folks all upset." She turned her head and looked up at Will. "By the way, what was that commotion I heard earlier? Somebody was doing a bunch of hollering and screaming."

Will shook his head. "Nothing for you to worry about, Mama. Just some folks getting rowdy."

Just Joe Fogarty beating a woman, he thought. Unfortunately, there was nothing unusual in that.

Abigail nodded as she rocked, then announced, "Cordelia! You'd better get some beans on to cook, girl."

• • •

BY THE time night had fallen, the field was full of tents and wagons. Small cook fires were scattered all around the area, so numerous that they almost looked like reflections of the stars in the sky above. But at the edge of the field, next to the road, men had piled brush for a larger fire. When the time was right, Obadiah Vickery strode over to the pile, a blazing torch in his hand, and set it alight. The winter-dried wood caught fire quickly, and as Vickery stepped back, flames leaped up and spread their reddish yellow glow all around in a big circle.

Within minutes people began to walk over from their camps to form a large ring around the bonfire. The Brannons were among them. The three-day trip from their home had been a tiring one, and Will would have rather turned in for the night, but Abigail had insisted that they attend the pastor's rally.

Abigail led the way, with Cordelia just behind her, flanked by Titus and Henry. Will and Mac brought up the rear. Leaning close to his brother, Will muttered in a low voice, "See any sign of Joe or the other Fogartys?"

Mac looked around at the faces of the crowd lit by firelight. He shook his head. "Nope. I'm sure Joe went back to the place he left George and Ranse."

"Yeah, but he could've brought them back here. He won't forget how I hit him."

Mac grunted. "If he's smart, he won't forget how close he came to getting a bullet through the head."

"Saw that, did you?" Will asked with a rueful smile.

"I saw you come close. Reckon I might've done the same thing myself."

"No. Not you, Mac. You wouldn't shoot a man in cold blood, not even a Fogarty."

"Well . . . I might *want* to."

But Will was right, and Mac knew it. He wouldn't gun down anybody. It wasn't that he didn't believe in killing. It just seemed to him that there had to be some other way to solve things.

"Brethren and sisters, welcome!" boomed Pastor Vickery. "Praise God, praise God! You've come to hear the Word of the Lord, and I plan to oblige you!"

Vickery held both hands in the air. A Bible was clutched in his left hand while his right was clenched in a fist. He threw his head back and began to pray, bellowing the flowery words up at the star-dotted sky as if that would make it easier for God to hear them.

Mac stood with his family, head bowed and eyes closed, but after a few minutes of Vickery's long-winded prayer, his attention began to wander. With his eyes open only in narrow slits, he peered around at the large group. He spotted Edward Symington about a third of the way around the circle. Symington was holding his hat in his hands and looking very pious. Next to him was his wife, and around her was their brood of five or six children. Mac couldn't remember how many youngsters Symington had, and the way they were hiding in their mother's skirts, he couldn't get an accurate count of them, either. Not that it mattered. Either way, Symington had plenty of mouths to feed.

As Vickery droned on, Mac looked in the other direction. He saw Cully Montayne, a small, round, pink-cheeked fellow who looked more like a store clerk than a horse trader and trainer. Cully knew more about horses than anyone Mac had ever met, with the possible exception of, well, himself. Mac liked Cully, and he hoped that if he couldn't win the race tomorrow, that Montayne would. Cully would be riding a three-year-old chestnut gelding, a good horse that rated somewhere between Symington's magnificent black and Mac's unimpressive gray-brown two-year-old when it came to looks. When it came to speed, though, Mac knew Cully's horse could give Symington's a run for the money.

He hoped that his two-year-old could do the same.

Mac realized the prayer was over, so he lifted his head. Vickery was still droning on, welcoming his makeshift congregation. Nearly every sentence was punctuated by a shouted "Amen!" from the crowd.

While Vickery was speaking, several men began to circulate through the group that had gathered. Each of them carried a stack of papers, and they pressed the sheets into the hands of anyone who would take them. One of the men came by the

Brannons, and both Henry and Titus reached out to snag one of the documents.

They were handbills, Mac saw by reading over Titus's shoulder. In bold print, they announced DOWN WITH THE ABO-LITIONISTS! DOWN WITH THE MINIONS OF SATAN! SMITE THEM WITH THE HAND OF RIGHTEOUSNESS! SECEDE! SECEDE! SECEDE! UP WITH THE GLORIOUS SOUTHERN CONFEDERACY!

Mac had seen handbills like that before, tacked up on trees and posts in Culpeper and the surrounding country. They never stayed up for very long, though, because abolitionists came along and tore them down, replacing them with their own handbills. It seemed to Mac to be a waste of paper, but he supposed the war of words made both sides feel that they were doing something to further their cause.

And better a war of words, he reminded himself, than a war of bullets and bayonets. When folks were just yelling at each other in print, at least they weren't spilling blood.

"Now the Lord says, folks, that we are to have dominion over the animals," Vickery said, still waving his Bible in the air. "I ask you, what are the Negroes if not animals? Highly developed animals, mind you, but still animals! Now, would you take a mule or a pig or a cow and say to them, 'Go on and get out'a here, you're free now? Just go on and take care of yourself, 'cause a bunch of folks from up north say that you're free.'" He paused and looked around, then continued, "Of course not! That mule, that pig, that cow, they can't just go out and fend for theirselves, because they've been domesti-cated! It's our Christian duty to take care of 'em, just like it's our Christian duty to take care of our niggers! Why, they'd be lost without somebody to tell 'em where to go and what to do and when to eat. You know that. You all know that."

More shouts of "Amen!" and "Tell it, Pastor!" came from the crowd.

Vickery slapped his free hand against the battered leather cover of his Bible. "But the folks up north, they don't care about what's in here! They don't care about the Good Book! They think they know better'n God, who gave the white race dominion over the earth an' everything on it! It ain't enough for them that they got all the factories, and the banks, and the shipping lines! Naw, sir, that ain't enough! They think they're so all-fired smart that they got to come down here and tell us southern folks how to live our lives and run our own sovereign states! They say we ought to do away with our whole way of life!"

"It's an evil way of life! Abe Lincoln says so!"

The shout cut through the approving murmur of the crowd and caused a silence to fall abruptly over the gathering. For a moment, the only sound was the crackling of the flames.

Then somebody shouted, "Who said that? Damn it, who said that?"

Vickery held up his hands. "No need to indulge in profane language, my friend, though I can understand how upset you are that a follower of that Illinois ape has wormed his way into this congregation of God-fearin' folks."

The same tension that gripped the crowd had affected the Brannons as well. Abigail was looking around like nearly everyone else, searching for the source of the catcall. Titus shared his mother's reaction, while Cordelia just looked worried, like Will and Mac. Henry seemed excited, as if he was halfway hoping that a fight would break out.

Suddenly, shoving erupted on the far side of the bonfire. Several men began waving handbills, but not the ones that Vickery's followers had been distributing earlier. One of the men shouted, "Cast your lot with the Lord! The Union forever! Down with slavery!"

"That's it," Will muttered under his breath to Mac. "That's all it's going to take."

He was right. Another member of the crowd sprang forward and swung a punch at the abolitionist, ignoring Vickery's shouts of "No, brother, no! No violence!"

It was too late for that. Fist cracked against bone, and the brawl was underway.

Will grabbed hold of his mother's arm, while Mac took Cordelia's hand. "Come on," Will urged Abigail. "Let's get you back to the tent."

A whole knot of men were now struggling on the edge of the crowd. Arms flailed as wild punches were thrown. Handbills for both sides went flying into the air. Women screamed, men shouted angrily, and kids darted happily underfoot as the melee spread. Politics meant nothing to the youngsters; this was just an opportunity to run and yell and have a high old time.

But it was deadly serious business, and Will knew it. He shepherded his mother back to the camp, glad that Abigail didn't put up a fuss about leaving the rally. "Those . . . those abolitionists!" she sputtered. "They ruined a perfectly good sermon by Pastor Vickery!"

Will hadn't been all that impressed by the pastor's rantings, but right now he was more concerned with getting his family to safety. He glanced over his shoulder, saw Mac leading Cordelia by the hand, and asked, "Where's Titus and Henry?"

Mac jerked the thumb of his free hand toward the bonfire. "Last time I saw them, they were back there."

Will gritted his teeth against the curse that wanted to come from his mouth. Both of those boys were hotheads, each in his own way, and Will would have bet that they had found some-body by now who was just as hotheaded and ready to fight.

As they reached the wagon with the tent pitched beside it, Will ushered his mother into the canvas structure, then turned to Mac and Cordelia.

"Stay here," he told them. "I'll get Titus and Henry."

"You're liable to need help," Mac began. "Cordelia can look after Mama."

Will shook his head. "I don't think the fighting will spread this far, but if it does, I want a man here. Blast it, just do what I tell you, Mac!" He was accustomed to his orders being obeyed, and he let his exasperation slip out in his harsh words.

Mac blinked in surprise, stared at his brother for a second, then nodded. "All right," he agreed. "I'll stay here."

"Good," Will said curtly. He started back toward the brawl, moving in a loping trot.

He could feel Mac watching him for a few yards and knew he had spoken too sharply to his brother. After all, Mac wasn't one of his deputies. Will had no right, save that of being the older brother, to go barking orders at Mac.

He could apologize later, he told himself. Right now, he wanted to find Titus and Henry before those boys got into more trouble than they could handle.

• • •

TITUS FELT a fierce exultation burning through his veins as he waded into the fight. He didn't care that much either way about slavery, but it was the southern states' right to continue with that peculiar domestic institution if they so desired. All Titus really wanted at the moment, though, was to hit somebody.

Beside Titus, Henry let out a loud whoop and yelled, "Down with the abolitionists!" A man with a dark, narrow face under the brim of a slouch hat heard him and turned to throw a punch at his head. Henry saw the blow coming and ducked to the side, letting the man's fist go past his head. He shot out a hard, straight right, landing the punch squarely in the man's belly. The man doubled over, and Henry shoved him away.

Titus spotted one of the men who had been trying to force abolition handbills on the crowd. The man was being jostled this way and that, and he still clutched a wad of the papers in his hand. He was yelling something, but Titus couldn't hear his words above the angry noise of the crowd. Titus stepped closer, clubbed his hands together, and swung them at the man's face. They landed with a force that sent a satisfying shiver of impact up Titus's arms. The abolitionist went down hard on the ground, and several other men began to kick him.

The man would be lucky, Titus knew, if he didn't wind up being stomped to death.

Before he could spend any time worrying about that, someone hit him from behind, knocking his hat off and sending him staggering forward. Desperately, Titus caught his balance and stayed upright. No matter which side a man was on, going down in this mob would be dangerous and likely fatal. Titus was pragmatic enough to know that a bootheel didn't stop to ask a man's political views before it knocked his teeth out.

Despite the danger, it felt good to take part in this struggle. It was a fight for a way of life, a fight for the rights of a whole people, for men Titus admired . . . men like Duncan Ebersole.

As he stood toe to toe with one of the abolitionists and slugged it out with the man, he wondered if Polly would be impressed with his bruises the next time he saw her.

Elsewhere in the struggle, somebody knocked Henry into another man. The man turned and caught hold of his shoulders, and Henry found himself looking up into the craggy features of Pastor Vickery. "An abomination!" roared Vickery, spittle flying from his mouth and striking Henry in the face. "An abomination unto the Lord!" One big fist drew back.

"Pastor!" Henry shouted. "It's me, Henry Brannon! I'm no abolitionist, Pastor!"

Vickery was caught up in a frenzy of righteous anger, though, and clearly didn't comprehend anything Henry had said. Henry tried to twist out of the preacher's grip, but Vickery was too strong. His knobby fist started down toward Henry's head.

A long arm came over Henry's shoulder, and strong fingers caught hold of Vickery's wrist, stopping the blow before it could fall.

Henry twisted his neck and saw his brother Will standing behind him. It was Will who had grabbed Vickery's wrist, Will who now struggled with the preacher. Henry finally tore himself loose from Vickery's grasp and stumbled to the side.

Seeing that Henry was safe, at least for the moment, Will shoved Vickery back and let go of the pastor's wrist. Vickery's chest was rising and falling rapidly as he breathed deeply, but he seemed to have regained some control of himself. "Brother Brannon," he said. "What . . . what have I done?"

Will glanced around at the brawl and thought that was a mighty good question the preacher had just asked.

Suddenly, a pair of shotgun blasts split the night. Will turned quickly, afraid that the fight was turning into a gun battle, but instead he saw several men in gray uniforms striding through the crowd, holding scatterguns pointed toward the sky. "Richmond militia!" one of the men shouted. "Everybody stop this fighting! *Now!*"

Already, the punches had stopped flying. Knots of struggling figures untangled. Forgotten handbills from both sides were crumpled underfoot as men shuffled around uneasily.

Several sprawled shapes on the ground did not get up. Moans of pain came from some of the fallen men, while others lay silent and motionless, unconscious—or worse.

The man who seemed to be in charge of the militia shouted, "All you people go back to your camps! This is over!"

As the crowd began to disperse, some of the other militia members checked on the injured men. The leader, though, fastened his gaze on Will and Vickery and strode over to them.

"Might've known you had something to do with this, Pastor," he greeted Vickery.

"The violence was none of my doin'," Vickery contended. "It was Yankee agitators who started it, Colonel."

The militiaman nodded. "I believe you, Pastor. Can you point out any of them?"

Vickery looked around for a moment, then shook his head in disgust. "They've already slunk away like the dogs they are."

The colonel looked Will up and down and asked, "Who might you be?"

"Will Brannon. Sheriff of Culpeper County."

That made the colonel cock a bushy gray eyebrow in surprise. "Sheriff, eh?" he noted. "You're a mite out of your bailiwick, Sheriff."

"I'm not here as a lawman," explained Will. "My family just came to enjoy the fair and the horse race."

"Brannon," the colonel mused. "You have a brother who rides in the races sometimes?"

Will nodded. "That's right. My brother Mac."

"I've won some money by betting on him from time to time. Don't reckon I will tomorrow, though. Symington's black will win."

"We'll see," said Will. He didn't much like this militia leader, even though the man and his troops had broken up the riot.

The colonel swung his attention back to Vickery. "I don't want any more trouble, Pastor."

"I have to spread the gospel, Colonel. The law of God comes before the law of man."

"I'm just askin' you to be a little reasonable. There's a rally downtown tomorrow night, and there'll be plenty of police on hand to make sure things don't bust out like they did here. Save your sermon until then."

Vickery glared for a moment, then nodded grudgingly. "All right. But only because there'll be a bigger crowd down there."

"Indeed there will. More people to hear your message." The colonel looked at Will again. "Tell your brother I said good luck. He'll need it against Symington."

Will nodded but didn't say anything. The colonel turned and walked off to gather up his men, now that the trouble was over.

"Colonel Stevens is a good man," Vickery observed, "but I'm afraid he doesn't realize just how evil those Yankee abolitionists really are. They'll stop at nothing to work their unholy will on us good southerners."

Will just grunted. He didn't want to encourage Vickery to get started again, nor had he forgotten how the man, in his frenzy, had almost struck Henry.

That reminded Will of his brothers, and he looked around for Henry and Titus. He spotted both of them standing not far away. Henry looked to be in pretty good shape, but Titus's face was already starting to swell up and turn black and blue from the punishment he had absorbed. *He must have gotten in a real punching match with one of the abolitionists*, thought Will.

"Come on, you two," he said. "Let's get back to camp. We've all had enough excitement for one night."

Chapter Six

AMAZINGLY, NO one had been killed in the fighting the night before, and when the sun rose the next morning, the only signs of the violence that had taken place were a few broken tree limbs lying around, pieces of wood from the bonfire that had been picked up and wielded as clubs, then thrown aside when the Richmond militia arrived.

Gray clouds were moving in, so the sunshine didn't last long. As Mac ate breakfast, he looked up at the sky and observed, "Liable to rain later. I hope it holds off until after the race."

Henry paused in stuffing large bites of johnnycake in his mouth long enough to say, "You can win even if it's raining, Mac."

Mac shook his head. "I don't know. I never ran this horse in mud before."

Abigail was sitting in her rocker with a plate of food in her lap. She predicted, "It won't rain until this evening, at least."

Titus looked up from where he sat cross-legged on the ground beside her. "How do you know that, Mama?"

"My bones haven't started aching yet. Once they do, it'll be about eight hours before the rain starts."

"I hope you're right," said Mac. "I'll feel better about my chances on a dry track."

He waited until everyone had finished eating and Cordelia was cleaning up before catching Will's eye and inclining his head toward the creek. Will gave a small nod, then strolled over to the stream a few minutes later just as Mac was doing the same thing.

The brothers stood side by side on the bank. Mac asked in a low voice, "Got any money down yet?"

"Nope. Thought I'd take care of that this morning."

A grin stretched across Mac's lean face. "I'm not sure how fitting it is for a sworn lawman to be gambling."

Will returned the grin and noted, "We're not in Culpeper County, little brother. Here I'm just a citizen like anybody else . . . a citizen who wants to do a little wagering."

"Well, don't let Mama catch you at it. She'd skin you alive."

Will chuckled. "I know. I'll be careful." He looked over at Mac and asked, "You reckon you can actually win?"

"Is that any way to be? You ever known me to lose a race?"

"Yeah," said Will. "Lots of times."

"Well, today won't be one of 'em," Mac declared. "Symington's overconfident, as usual. I can outride him. And I can beat Cully just on speed."

Will clapped a hand on his brother's shoulder. "All right, then. I'll go see what sort of interest I can drum up."

He moved off to circulate through the field, while Mac returned to the wagon and took a curry comb from his gear. He began brushing the two-year-old, speaking softly to it as he did so. The words, whatever they might have been, were strictly between man and horse.

While Mac was doing that, Titus and Henry walked over to the racetrack, where a crowd was already beginning to gather. Since there were no grandstands from which to watch the race, the spectators could stand anywhere they wanted, as long as they were well clear of the track itself. Some families were already spreading blankets and quilts on the ground inside the circle of the track. Buggies had begun to arrive, carrying wealthy onlookers from Richmond and well-to-do visitors from other parts of the state. Their drivers parked near the track, angling the vehicles so that the passengers would have a good view of the race.

As they came closer to the growing crowd, Henry nudged Titus in the ribs and said, "Look there. Isn't that Mr. Ebersole's buggy?"

Titus looked and saw a fancy black buggy with a lot of expensive silver trim. Hitched to the buggy were a matched pair of blood bays, the silver trim on their harness sparkling even under cloudy skies. The horses were high-stepping along under the expert guidance of the black man in servant's livery who was handling the reins from his perch on the driver's seat. The slave maneuvered the buggy into an opening and then brought it to a stop in a prime location for viewing the race.

"That's them, all right," Titus answered, feeling his heart begin to beat a little faster in his chest.

"Didn't say nothing about who was inside," Henry noted with a grin. "I just asked wasn't that Mr. Ebersole's buggy."

Titus ignored his little brother's gibe and started walking quickly toward the black buggy. The driver climbed down quickly from his seat and hurried to help a young woman step out of the vehicle. She wore a coat with a thick fur collar over a long dark blue dress that brushed the tops of her shoes. A hat the same shade as the dress was pinned to an upswept mass of thick blonde curls. The driver kept his eyes downcast as he lightly gripped her arm to help her down. As soon as she had both feet on the ground, he let go of her and stepped back.

A man followed the young woman from the buggy. He wore a gray tweed suit under a long canvas duster. A broad-brimmed planter's hat sat squarely on his head. Gray hair that retained a touch of its original reddish color fell to his shoulders. His neatly trimmed beard was a shade darker than his hair. He stepped up beside the young woman and took her arm, revealing in the process that he was slightly shorter than she was. He walked with the confident bearing of a much larger man, though, as he led the woman toward a pavilion that had been set up next to the racetrack. The large, tentlike structure, open on the sides, was where most of the wealthy and influential spectators were gathering.

Titus started toward the pavilion, too, but he had only gone a step when Henry grabbed his arm. "What do you think you're doin'?" Henry exclaimed. "You can't go in there!"

"Why not? There's nothing to stop me."

"Nothin' but the fact that all those folks are rich as blazes, and you're just a poor dirt farmer from Culpeper County."

"We're not poor," snapped Titus.

"Compared to Mr. Ebersole and his friends, we are. Listen, Titus, he may not mind that you show up every time he has a party at Mountain Laurel. We're neighbors, of a sort, and he's got to be neighborly. But down here at Richmond, it's different."

Titus stared at his younger brother. "What's the matter with you?" he demanded. "I figured if anything you'd be eggin' me on, hoping that I'd make a fool of myself in front of Polly so you could get a good laugh out of it."

Henry shrugged and shook his head, saying, "I don't know, Titus. I know I been raggin' you a lot about Polly, but . . . I just think it'd be better if you didn't go over there."

"Well, it ain't any of your business, is it?" Titus turned and stalked toward the pavilion without giving Henry a chance to say anything else.

Henry watched him go, then turned and started looking around for Will, just in case there was any trouble.

Titus felt his nerves growing more taut as he approached the pavilion, but he forced himself to keep walking. He glanced down at himself. He was wearing clean clothes, and even though the elbows of his shirt were patched, nobody could see that under his coat. He had washed his hands and face this morning, ignoring the shock of the cold water against bruised flesh that had made him wince, and he'd even knocked the dust off his hat and boots. He figured he looked imminently respectable.

Still, he found himself wishing he was carrying his Sharps, instead of leaving it back at the wagon. He didn't need it here, of course, but somehow it always made him feel better to curl his fingers around the smooth wood of the stock.

He paused and drew in a deep breath as he reached the edge of the pavilion. Then he stepped underneath the canvas cover and made his way toward the Ebersoles, ignoring the stares and looks of disdain aimed in his direction by some of the wealthy spectators who had gathered for the race.

"Howdy, Mr. Ebersole," Titus said as he came up to the planter. "Glad to see you could make it." He was vaguely aware that he was interrupting a conversation Ebersole was having with someone else. He rushed the words out anyway, knowing that if he didn't, they might choke him to the point he couldn't even talk.

Duncan Ebersole slowly turned his head and looked at Titus. His eyes glittered with annoyance at first, but as he saw the swollen, bruised countenance of the young man, a smile tugged at his mouth.

"Good Lord, lad, what have ye been doin'? Tha' face o' yours looks like it's been kicked by a mule."

"Got in a fracas with a bunch of abolitionists," Titus said proudly. "They look worse than I do, Mr. Ebersole, I can promise you that."

"Well, then, good work," Ebersole said. "Dinna ye think so, Polly?"

Polly was standing beside her father, her hand still tucked in the crook of his arm. She smiled at Titus and said, "I think you should wear those bruises like badges of honor, Mr. Brannon."

Titus. Call me Titus, he wanted to say. But that would have been too forward, so he just blushed and nodded and said, "Thank you, ma'am."

Ebersole slid a case from his vest pocket and took out a cigar, then replaced it without offering one to Titus. He put the cigar in his mouth and chewed it without lighting it. "I heard there was a bit o' trouble out here last night," he commented.

"Colonel Stevens of the Richmond militia said it was nigh on to a riot."

Titus shook his head. "Not really. Just a bunch of us had to put some damned abolitionists in their place." He glanced at Polly. "Beggin' your pardon, Miss Polly."

"No need to apologize, Mr. Brannon. You're just speaking the truth about those awful Yankees, after all."

Ebersole slipped an arm around Titus's shoulders. Titus tried not to stiffen in surprise. He realized that the man's other arm was still linked with Polly's, so Ebersole's touching him made a connection of sorts between him and Polly. At least, Titus wanted to think of it that way.

"Listen, lad," Ebersole said in a confidential tone, "is that brother o' yers runnin' a horse in today's race?"

"Yes sir. One of our two-year-olds. It's a good horse."

"Ah, but can it win against Ed Symington's black?"

"Of course it can," Titus answered without hesitation. Familial loyalty would let him say nothing else, even though he didn't really know all that much about horses. Fact was, Mac had probably forgotten more about horses than Titus had ever known.

"Yer sure?"

"Yes sir."

"So if I was t' place a small wager on yer brother, I could feel certain that I'd collect some winnin's?"

"If I had the money, sir, I'd sure bet it on Mac," Titus proclaimed.

"All right then." Ebersole pulled his arm back and reached inside his coat. He took out a wallet and opened it, plucked out a wad of bank notes and stuffed them into Titus's hand. "Take this an' wager it for me. I'm countin' on ye to get good odds, though, lad."

Titus stared down at the bills in his hand and felt his mouth go dry. He had never seen so much money at one time before, had certainly never held that much. And Duncan Ebersole was trusting him to place bets on the race with it!

"I . . . I'll do my best, sir," he managed to say.

"Go on wi' ye, then. I'll see you after the race this afternoon, when ye bring me my winnin's."

Titus nodded. He practically stumbled out of the pavilion, his head swimming with the responsibility with which he had been entrusted.

Behind him, Polly frowned and said to her father, "You gave Titus that money just to get rid of him, didn't you?"

Ebersole's teeth clenched tightly on the cigar. "I'll not have some farmer wi' dirt under his fingernails sniffin' around you, Polly. Brannon shouldn't be pushin' in where he don't belong."

"Do you really think his brother's horse will win?"

Ebersole shrugged. "I dinna care one way or the other. All I'm bettin' is money."

• • •

SEVERAL MEN brought out their fiddles, and the country folk spent their morning dancing and singing and visiting with friends they hadn't seen in a while. More pavilions were set up, and the wealthy businessmen from Richmond and the plantation owners strolled among them. Slaves poured drinks and began unpacking the dinners they had brought out for their masters in large wicker baskets. It was a good time, a pleasant, convivial time, and despite the gray skies, the rain held off, just as Abigail Brannon had predicted.

By early afternoon, almost everyone was eating. Beans, pone, fried chicken, black-eyed peas, thick slabs of ham brought from smokehouses all over the state, and every kind of pie and cake you could think of. The food was simple but good and filling.

Mac didn't have any appetite, even though the air was full of delicious aromas. He left the rest of the family at their campsite and walked off along the stream, following it all the way to the point where it joined Shockoe Creek. From there he could see most of Richmond spread out in front of him along the banks of the James River. He heard a train whistle in the distance. The air was heavy and moist, even without any rain. He didn't like it. A horse couldn't run as fast in air like this.

But the air would be the same for all the horses, he reminded himself. He was just looking for things to worry about. The last little while before a race always found him nervous like this.

A step behind him made him look around. Will stood there, a chicken leg in one hand. "You ought to eat something, Mac. One drumstick won't weigh you down too much."

Mac smiled faintly and shook his head. "That's not what I'm worried about. Just don't feel much like eating right now."

"You're going to win. You know that."

"Depends on what Symington does." Mac hated to say it, but honesty forced the words out. "That black of his is faster than our horse."

"How much faster?" asked Will.

Mac shrugged. "Not much."

"Well, there you go. In a close race, it's the man in the saddle who decides it, not the horse. You've told me that yourself. And I know you're twice the rider Symington is."

"Thanks. I just hope I don't let you down."

"You never have," Will said.

"What about the bets? If I lose—"

"Hell. It's only money." Will held out the chicken leg. "You sure you don't want to eat?"

Mac shook his head.

"Well, I hate to see good food go to waste." Will took a bite, then said, "Come on. Time to get saddled up."

• • •

THE HUBBUB of voices in the air grew louder as the time approached for the beginning of the race. People crowded around the track, some in the open, some under the gaily striped canvas of the pavilions. The Brannons took their place near the track. The wind had picked up, and the pennants atop the poles marking the race course were fluttering and snapping. Abigail pulled her coat more tightly around her and announced, "It'll be raining by tonight. I feel it in my bones now."

"We'll be snug in our tent," Will replied. "Roads'll be muddy when we start home tomorrow, though."

"We shouldn't have come. This is all foolishness. Folks should keep to home."

Will didn't argue with his mother. Abigail would feel different in a few minutes. Will knew from past races that she would get just as excited as everybody else once the horses started thundering around the track. And she would cheer just as loudly for Mac as the rest of the family did.

Will saw a man in a sober black suit and top hat standing with several other dignified-looking men near the line that would mark both the start and finish of the race. He recognized the governor of Virginia, the Honorable John Letcher. The governor would start the race with a pistol shot in the air, and one of the men with him appeared to be checking the pistol that would be used.

Cheers and shouts went up as the horses were led out to the track. Despite the chilliness of the day, the riders had all discarded their coats and were in shirtsleeves. Will whistled and hooted and clapped as he spotted Mac leading the two-year-old. Beside him, Titus and Henry did the same, while Cordelia settled for waving a scarf in the air and calling a more ladylike, "Hurrah for Mac Brannon!"

Mac must have heard, because he glanced over at them and grinned. He looked calm, and so did his mount. The same couldn't be said for Symington's black. The horse was skittish, and Symington had to pull down hard on the reins to keep it under control. Cully Montayne wasn't having that trouble with his chestnut, nor were any of the other riders.

The horses formed a line, ragged at first, then straightening as the riders swung up into their saddles and urged the animals more into position. Symington was on the inside end, the best place to start. Montayne was next to him, then one of the other men, then Mac. The other two riders took the two outside positions.

Governor Letcher climbed onto a stool that one of his aides had set up for him. His politician's voice rolled sonorously over the large gathering, welcoming all the spectators to the race. Then he said wryly, "But I know you're not here to listen to a speech. You've come to watch these fine horses run. So . . ." He turned to face the riders and lifted the pistol. "If you gentlemen are ready . . . ?"

Curt nods from Mac and the others.

"Very well, then." The governor thrust the pistol into the air above his head and pulled the trigger. The gun went off with a sharp crack.

Instantly, the horses leaped ahead from the starting line. A huge shout went up from the crowd. Will was yelling as loud as anyone else as he saw Mac take the early lead with a burst of speed from the two-year-old that no one except the Brannons had expected.

One of the other riders was in second place, followed by Montayne, Symington, and the final two riders. Symington's black had jumped a little sideways at the sound of the gun, which had slowed down its start considerably. But the horse was making up ground now, and Symington quickly drew even with Montayne. Neither of them, however, could pass the second horse, and by now Mac was well out in front.

Mac felt the two-year-old running easily underneath him. He leaned forward along the horse's neck. Wordless communication flowed between man and animal. Mac sensed how exhilarated the horse was, how excited to be running like this. They swept through the first turn together and headed down the far side of the track. The faces of the cheering spectators flashed by, nothing more than a meaningless blur to Mac. The only things that existed for him at this moment were the horse and the track.

The second turn, a dash up the backstretch, the starting line looming in front of them and then falling behind as they flew past it. The track was a quarter-mile long, the race a mile and a half. One lap finished, five to go.

Mac felt a prickling on the back of his neck and turned his head to look behind him. The horse that had held on to second place ever since the start of the race was making a move, surging forward gallantly under the urging of its rider. It drew almost even . . . then Mac saw the break in its stride, so tiny as to be almost invisible, but it stood out boldly to Mac's experienced eyes. Sure enough, a moment later the horse began to drop back. Its rider had tried to pull ahead too early. He should have waited.

But it didn't really matter, Mac knew. Even if the other rider had waited, the horse would not have had the speed to catch up and take the lead.

Mac turned his eyes ahead and leaned over slightly in the saddle as his mount swept around another turn.

By the time the race was at the halfway point, some members of the crowd had become too hoarse to keep cheering. Others made up for it, though, bellowing their lungs out in support of their favorite. The field of horses had gotten stretched out by now, with Mac still in the lead on the two-year-old, Symington now in second place with Montayne close behind him, and the other three riders trailing far behind. Will craned his neck to see over the top of Cordelia's head. She was standing in front of him and jumping up and down in excitement. Titus and Henry both crowded forward, pumping their fists in the air every time Mac rode past. Abigail had her hands clasped together in front of her as she watched raptly, and Will thought she looked like she was praying, even though he knew she would deny that she would ever take something as unimportant as a horse race to the Lord. But still she called out softly from time to time, "Come on, Mac! Come on!"

The starting line fell behind Mac for the fourth time. Two more laps to go. His horse was still running smoothly, with no sign of effort. But even though the horse did not appear to be tiring, Mac's instincts told him that the hooves were not flashing quite as fast now, the stride was not quite as long as it had been. The horse might not feel fatigue, but it was setting in anyway.

A glance back told Mac that Montayne and Symington had swapped places. Montayne's chestnut was running in second now. Mac felt a tingle of surprise. He had thought that the black would pull away from the chestnut by now. Maybe Symington was having trouble with the horse. That was the way with high-strung animals: everything had to be right for them to perform at their best. The least little thing could sometimes throw them off their stride.

Montayne was closing in as they reached the far side of the track. The chestnut was barely a length behind Mac's horse now, but Mac tried to concentrate on what was ahead of him, not behind him. Ride your own race, he told himself, and let the others ride theirs. But that was easier said than done, and he found himself glancing back again.

Half a length now. That was all that separated the chestnut from the mouse-colored two-year-old.

Wordlessly, Mac urged more speed from his mount. The horse responded, but still Montayne drew closer. The chestnut's nose drew even with the rump of Mac's horse. It forged ahead relentlessly.

And again, as the chestnut was about to draw even, it faltered, just as the other horse had done. A second challenge had failed. Mac felt like whooping in triumph as the chestnut began to fall back. He rode past the starting line and into the final lap. The line would be the finish line the next time he saw it in front of him. The horse stretched out, into the turn.

Symington galloped past him, the black running faster than Mac had ever seen a horse run.

Mac let out a cry of agonized surprise. He had been concentrating on the duel with Montayne and had forgotten all about Symington. The merchant from Manassas had played him for a fool, waiting back there while Mac and Montayne had expended their mounts' energy on each other. Mac leaned forward in the saddle, yelling now, digging his heels into the flanks of his horse, but it was no use.

By the time the horses reached the finish line, Symington's black was three full lengths in front. Mac crossed second, followed by Montayne and the other three riders bringing up the far rear.

A ball of sickness rolled around in Mac's stomach. He had lost. Will had bet on him, and he had lost. He had let the family down. He felt so ashamed that it was all he could do not to just keep riding, so that he wouldn't have to face them.

Instead, he slowed the horse to a stop, then turned it and walked it back toward the spot where the rest of the Brannons were waiting.

Chapter Seven

WILL LOOKED over at his brothers as Mac rode toward them. Henry wore a disappointed expression, but Titus looked absolutely devastated. His mouth hung open, and his eyes were wide with horror.

"Stop your gawping," Will hissed at him. "Don't you reckon Mac feels bad enough about losing without you looking like somebody just shot your dog?"

"But . . . but you don't understand," Titus practically wailed. "I told Mr. Ebersole that he'd win. I promised him, Will!"

Will put a hand on Titus's shoulder, and in a low voice so that Abigail wouldn't hear, he said, "Right now I don't give a damn about Duncan Ebersole, and you shouldn't, either. Now straighten up and behave, blast it!"

A shudder ran through Titus, but he managed to stiffen himself and square his shoulders.

Cordelia ran forward to meet Mac as he brought the horse to a stop and stepped down from the saddle. She threw her arms around his neck and exclaimed, "Oh, Mac, you rode so good! I thought you were going to win, I really did!"

A rueful smile touched Mac's lips as he lifted a hand and stroked Cordelia's red hair. "So did I," he replied.

His brothers crowded around him. Henry put a hand on his shoulder and said, "You really gave 'em a run for their money, Mac. That was a fine race. Yes sir, a fine race."

At the mention of money, Mac and Will looked at each other, and an unspoken message passed between them. Will's shoulders rose and fell less than an inch in a minuscule shrug. Sure, they had lost their bets, Will seemed to be saying, but it wasn't the end of the world.

"Symington fooled me," admitted Mac, feeling the need to explain it to himself as much as to the others. "I thought he was having trouble with his horse. When Cully passed him, I thought all I had to do was beat the chestnut, and I knew I could do that. But that's what Symington wanted me to think."

"You can't win every race," Henry pointed out. "You'll get him next time, Mac. I'm sure of it."

Mac just shook his head. Right now, he didn't feel that he could ever be certain about anything again.

"Well, now that all this racing foolishness is over, maybe we can get on about our business." That was Abigail's voice, and it made her children step aside to form a path for her as she came up to Mac.

Will protested, "Mama, we didn't come to Richmond on business. We came to have a good time." *And so far, what with Mac losing the race and the near-riot the night before, that goal hadn't worked out too well,* thought Will.

"I intend for us all to attend that rally tonight," Abigail declared. "Pastor Vickery will be speaking again, and I want something worthwhile to come out of this trip. It'll do you all good to listen to what a man of God has to say."

"We already heard everything Vickery's got to say," Will said. "We heard it last night."

"And there's bound to be trouble again tonight," Mac pointed out. "Could be even worse, since the crowd will be a lot bigger."

"I'm not afraid of what any of those no-count Yankee agitators might do," Abigail insisted stubbornly. "We're going to that rally."

Will sighed, knowing it wasn't going to do any good to argue with her. She might have been easier to deal with had Mac won the race, but without the excitement of that to distract her, her attention had turned back to the growing rift between North and South.

"All right, Mama," he conceded. "We'll go."

In the distance, thunder rumbled.

• • •

As soon as he could, Titus slipped away from the others and went looking for Duncan Ebersole. The pavilions were being taken down, and some of the fancy carriages and buggies were already on their way back into town. The black-and-silver Ebersole buggy, however, was still parked near the racetrack, and Titus hurried toward it. He walked around the vehicle, expecting to see Ebersole and Polly sitting inside it, no doubt waiting for him.

Instead, Polly was sitting there alone, and Titus stopped short at the sight of her. After a second, he reached up to tug his hat off. "Miss Polly," he began. "I . . . I was, ah, looking for your father . . ."

"Papa is around here somewhere, Mr. Brannon," Polly answered. "I was so sorry that your brother's horse didn't win the race."

"Yeah, me, too," said Titus. "I mean, I, ah, share that sentiment, ma'am."

Polly smiled at him. "You don't have to put on a bunch of highfalutin airs for me, Mr. Brannon. You can talk any ol' way you want to. I don't care."

"Well, ma'am, I aspire to speak as correctly as possible."

"So I won't know that you're a farmer?" Polly leaned toward him. "Well, I'll let you in on a little secret, Mr. Brannon. I don't care that you're a farmer. I like you just fine no matter what you do."

Titus felt himself staring at her and tried not to. His mouth opened and closed, but no words came out and he knew he looked like a fish. He forced himself to get a grip on his rampaging emotions and replied in a relatively calm voice, "I like you, too, Miss Polly. And I wish, uh, I wish that you'd call me Titus."

"All right . . . Titus. And you can call me Polly. Just plain Polly."

"Oh . . ." He swallowed hard. "There's nothing just plain about you, Polly."

She laughed and said, "Why, you're flirting with me, Titus!"

Before he could respond, he heard his name called from somewhere behind him. "Brannon! Titus Brannon!"

Titus turned and saw Duncan Ebersole striding toward him. The planter didn't look particularly happy to see him, but at least Ebersole spoke in a civil tone as he went on, "I dinna expect t' see *you* after the race, Brannon, since ye dinna have any winnin's t' deliver t' me. I assume ye wagered tha' money on yer brother's horse like I told ye to?"

Titus nodded miserably. "Yes sir, I sure did. I only wish Mac had won, like I told you he would. He came mighty close—"

"Three lengths, it looked like t' me."

"That was just at the end. He led nearly the whole way."

"The end is wha' counts, laddie." Ebersole waved a gloved hand negligently. "But pay it no mind. I can certainly stand t' lose tha' much money, and much more if need be. Perhaps I'll recoup my losses next time."

"That's right," Titus agreed eagerly, seizing on this chance. "There'll be another race in the spring, and then several this summer, and I'm sure Mac will win all of them—"

"There ye go again, assumin' too much." Ebersole's voice sharpened. "'Tis one o' the faults of people like yerself, Brannon. Ye assume too much." He stepped past Titus toward the buggy. "Good day t' ye."

It was obvious from Ebersole's tone that Titus was being dismissed. He glanced again at Polly and thought he saw a flicker of sympathy in her eyes, but then she looked away. With her father right there, she had to be careful what she said and did. Titus understood that, and yet, it hurt when she turned her face away from him.

He started to back up awkwardly, tugging on the brim of his hat as he did so. "Good day to you, too, sir," he called, but

Ebersole ignored him. The driver seemed to appear from out of nowhere and stepped up to the seat, taking the reins and flicking them to start the pair of blood bays moving. The buggy rolled briskly away.

Titus watched it go and wondered if everybody was right. Maybe he had set his sights too high. Maybe he ought to just forget about Polly Ebersole.

But he knew his heart wouldn't let him do that. They were all wrong: she *did* like him. She had been flirting with him just a few minutes ago, for God's sake!

Sooner or later, she was going to be his, and then everybody would see how wrong they had been about her, and him, and everything.

• • •

THE RAIN started late in the afternoon, just a soft mist at first, then strengthening into a steady drizzle. With the thickening overcast, night fell early. The temperature was well above freezing, so there was no worry about the rain turning to snow or sleet, but Will would have almost preferred that. If conditions had been worse, he might have been able to dissuade his mother from her determination to attend the political rally to be held in front of the capitol. But Abigail insisted that a little rain wasn't going to keep her from hearing Pastor Vickery's speech.

The Brannons had already driven downtown in the wagon before the rain started, joining the throngs gathering in the streets of Richmond. They ate supper in a small restaurant on a side street, an extravagance that Abigail deplored but didn't try to talk them out of. The capitol was only a couple of blocks away, and when they had eaten, the family walked in that direction. Everyone else in town seemed to be heading that way, too. The rain might have kept a few people in, but not many. Everyone was wearing slickers and hats, and many people carried umbrellas to help protect them from the drizzle.

Will shivered a little from the chill in the air as he and the others rounded a corner and saw the huge crowd in the plaza in front of the capitol. Torches were burning on the gallery under the portico that was supported by thick white pillars. The evening's speakers were gathered there, protected by the overhang so that they were out of the rain. Will saw Governor Letcher, Pastor Vickery, and about a dozen other men. He looked around the crowd and wondered how many of them were Yankee agitators and abolitionists, planted there to make trouble once the rally started.

The Richmond militia was in attendance, too, several ranks of them lined up along the base of the broad steps that led up to the capitol. Others were scattered along the edges of the crowd, their neat gray uniforms and cockaded hats not looking as impressive as usual because of the damage done to them by the rain. Each man carried a musket, the locks wrapped in oilcloth to keep out the dampness, and the mist in the air beaded on the blades of the bayonets fastened to the barrels of the guns.

Just having the militia around might help keep order, Will thought. Even the most fervent abolitionist would think twice about disrupting the rally if he was afraid he might get a bayonet in the belly for his trouble.

There were certainly all sorts here, from the fanciest dressed merchants and planters—they had slaves holding their umbrellas, keeping them dry—to the lowliest poor white farmers and those in between, like the Brannons. Chances were, nothing would be said tonight that these people hadn't heard many times before, but everybody wanted to be here anyway.

Almost everybody. Will would have preferred being back in the tent, snug and dry, and he figured Mac felt the same way. Titus and Henry and Cordelia, however, seemed to be getting caught up in the excitement that was in the air as surely as the rain was. And Abigail was waiting for things to get underway with an expression of anticipation on her face.

The mayor of Richmond got the evening started. He stepped up onto a podium that had been erected at the edge of the capitol's front gallery and held up his hands for quiet. The murmuring of the crowd gradually died away, leaving only the soft hiss of the rain. The mayor's voice boomed out, easily overwhelming the sound of the rain.

"Welcome, everyone! We're glad you turned out despite the weather, because what you'll hear tonight is mighty important. Yes sir, mighty important!" He paused to let that sink in, then resumed, "We have just received word that Federal troops have moved from Fort Moultrie to Fort Sumter and barricaded themselves there in hopes of closing off Charleston Harbor!"

A roar of outrage came from the crowd at this news. Will tried to recall what he had read and heard about the situation in Charleston. There were three forts there, he seemed to remember, but only Sumter, isolated on an island that commanded the entrance to the harbor, would be easy to defend. The new Confederate government had been making noises about occupying the forts since, according to South Carolina, the Federal troops no longer had any right to be there. But now it appeared that the government did not intend to allow that to happen. Will frowned. For the Federal troops to occupy Sumter was an act of defiance, a slap in the face to the newly founded Confederacy that was not likely to be ignored.

The mayor had turned the podium over to Governor Letcher, who was urging calm. "This crisis can still be resolved by peaceful means," he proclaimed, but the angry shouts of the crowd almost drowned him out. Letcher took off his top hat and used a handkerchief to mop his face. He was out of the rain, so he must have been sweating, unlikely as that might have seemed on such a cool night. Will thought the governor had looked much more comfortable at the racetrack that afternoon than he did here tonight.

With a shake of his head, Letcher relinquished the podium. More cheers rang out as someone in the front of the crowd broke out a Palmetto flag, the unofficial emblem of the Secessionists, and began to wave it in the air. Pastor Vickery stepped to the podium, Bible clenched in his fist, and thundered, "The time has come to separate ourselves from those godless northern interlopers! I'm callin' on the governor to ask for a vote of secession in the legislature!"

Standing off to the side, Letcher made no response other than to mop his face again. The crowd in the plaza in front of the capitol certainly agreed with the fiery pastor, though. The building almost seemed to shake from the force of the cheers.

The band began playing "Dixie." Abigail started clapping her hands together softly in time to the music, and her lips moved as she sang along. Titus and Henry and Cordelia began to sing, too, and even Mac and Will felt themselves getting caught up in the emotion of the moment. A man, a sovereign state, a new nation . . . all could be pushed only so far. Maybe it *was* time to stand up to the North, thought Will. He had hoped that the growing conflict could be settled without any full-scale violence, but the North would probably never understand just how serious the South was unless they were forced to. If secession was what it took to get that message across, then perhaps that was what ought to be done.

Will found himself clapping and singing "Dixie" along with the thousands of other people clogging the street. He had forgotten about the drizzle, no longer caring that drops of rain were falling from the brim of his hat. He glanced around, wondering what had become of all the northern agitators he had been so sure were lurking in the crowd. He saw no abolitionist banners or U.S. flags being waved. No fights were going on. Everyone here on this rainy night seemed to be united in their belief in the noble cause of the South.

If there had been Yankees here earlier, Will thought, they must have slipped away when they saw how things were going. Even a Yankee would be smart enough to see that nothing could stand before the tide that had been launched here tonight. It was a tide that would sweep all the way to ultimate victory and peace. Will was sure of it.

The crowd reached the end of the song and began it again.

• • •

BY THE time Mac guided the wagon up to the field where they had made camp, the road was muddy and the field itself was worse. "We won't be staying here tonight," Mac called to the rest of the family over the wind, which had gotten stronger in the past few minutes. The rain lashed harder at them. "If I pull the wagon out into the field, it'll be stuck for days!"

"Stay here," said Will as he vaulted down from the back of the vehicle. "Titus, Henry, come with me. We'll pack up everything and haul it over here. Might as well start on back home tonight, if you think you can stay on the road, Mac."

Mac nodded. "I can keep the wagon on the road, all right. Maybe if we keep moving, we'll get out of this rain."

Abigail and Cordelia huddled in the back of the wagon under slickers. Darkness was thick around the place. Most of the other visitors who had camped here were already gone. Any who remained were inside their tents. Mac looked around and saw no fires or lanterns burning anywhere. Looking into the rain was like peering into a black curtain. He would have to drive by feel as much as by sight.

Titus and Henry grumbled about it, but they both worked hard as they helped Will break camp. Henry carried what was left of the family's supplies back to the wagon, while Will and Titus took down the tent, folded it, and then gathered up the canvas ground cover as well. The wet canvas was heavy, and they staggered as they hauled the stuff over to the wagon and piled it in the back.

When everything was loaded, Titus and Henry climbed into the wagon bed while Will stepped up to the driver's seat next to Mac. "Let's go," Will announced to his brother at the reins.

Mac got the mules moving again, though it took quite a few slaps to their rumps with the reins and even more shouting. The iron-tires of the wagon wheels slipped in the mud as the vehicle lurched into motion, and Mac held his breath for a second, hoping the wagon wouldn't slide off the road. But the wheels finally caught, and the wagon began to roll smoothly again. He glanced back and saw the mouse-colored two-year-old plodding along, head down, at the rear of the wagon. The horse didn't like traveling in this weather any more than the rest of them.

Maybe they should have tried to find room in a hotel, Mac mused. But that would have been mighty difficult, as crowded as Richmond was right now, and besides, the cost would have been an extravagance that would have scandalized his mother. Abigail never would have allowed it.

Well, rain fell on both the just and the unjust, Mac told himself, then tried to remember where that saying had come from. Was it the Bible or Shakespeare? The Bible, he decided after a moment, one of the Gospels, though he couldn't recall which one. Rain or no rain, he hoped the Lord would figure he was one of the just, not one of the unjust.

"Turning into a real toad-strangler," Will commented.

"Yeah. I'm just glad the road's as good as it—"

Even over the wind and the sound of the driving rain, Will suddenly heard the pounding of hoofbeats. They came from behind the wagon, and as he turned his head he saw something the likes of which he had never seen before, something like a vision out of a nightmare.

A group of riders was galloping toward them, and they carried torches that burned despite the rain, probably because they had been dipped in pitch. The garish glare they cast revealed that the riders were wearing long dusters. Their hats were pulled down over their eyes, and the rest of their faces were obscured by bandannas. Cordelia saw them, too, and let out a scream.

"What the hell!" Will exclaimed as he twisted around on the seat.

"Down with slavery! The Union forever! Kill all the slaveholders!" the riders shouted, closing in on the wagon by now. One of them threw his torch at the vehicle. The burning brand spun through the rainy darkness. Cordelia screamed again as the torch fell into the back of the wagon and bounced once to come down close to her lap.

Luckily, her dress was too sodden to catch fire, and Henry was able to snatch the torch and stand up to fling it out of the wagon. By then, the riders had reached them, and one of them swung at Henry's head with the torch he was carrying. Titus grabbed his younger brother's coat and yanked him down, out of the way of the torch.

"Slavers! Slavers! Kill the slavers! The Union forever!"

Mac had brought the mules to a stop out of sheer shock at the sight of the riders. He realized now he should have tried to whip them up to a faster speed. But that wouldn't have done any good, because the horsemen would have caught up with them anyway. There was no way the wagon could have outrun them, especially on this wet road.

Beside Mac, Will felt fury course through him, burning every bit as bright and hot as those pitch-soaked torches. These damned abolitionist ruffians had come after his family strictly because they were southerners. The Brannons didn't own any slaves, had never owned slaves. But because they came from Virginia, that made them targets for some people's hatred.

Will Brannon was one target who could fight back.

He reached under his coat and curled his fingers around the butt of his Colt. He would have to fire quickly, before the rain made the gun useless. The riders were circling the wagon now, still slashing at the occupants with the torches. Titus and Henry were shielding Abigail and Cordelia with their bodies, all of them pressed low to the bottom of the wagon bed.

"Kill 'em!" shouted one of the abolitionists.

That was enough for Will. He drew the Colt and began to fire as quickly as he could manipulate the hammer and trigger. The gunshots rolled out like thunder. The rain and the flickering glare of the torches made aiming difficult, but Will's instincts guided his hand. The first slug slammed into the shoulder of one of the riders and rocked him back in the saddle. The second drove into the belly of another man, doubling him over. Will's third shot missed, but the fourth broke the arm of another man.

At the same time, Titus slid his Sharps out from under the oilcloth that had been protecting it and thrust the barrel over the sideboard. The big rifle was loaded, and all Titus had to do was cock and aim and pull the trigger. The boom of the Sharps was louder than any thunder. At this range, the .50 caliber slug that struck one of the raiders in the chest and flung him completely out of the saddle was powerful enough to punch a fist-sized hole all the way through the man.

That was enough for the rest of the abolitionists. They turned tail and ran, dropping their torches in the mud as they rode back toward Richmond. The burning brands continued to sizzle and pop for a few moments before the thick mud extinguished them. Only one of the men was left behind, the one Titus had killed. Will suspected that at least one other was mortally wounded, too.

Cordelia was crying softly as Henry hugged her and murmured, "It's all right now, sis. They're gone. It's all over. They won't bother us again."

Cordelia shuddered and pressed her face against Henry's chest. "Why?" she asked raggedly. "Why would anybody want to hurt us?"

"Because we're southerners," Titus spit out bitterly. "That's all those damned Yankees care about. They don't really give a damn about the slaves. They just want us all dead!"

Will suspected there was a grain of truth in what Titus said, at least where some northerners were concerned.

"Titus!" snapped Abigail. "There's no need for profanity here! No matter how angry we are at those Yankees, that doesn't give us the right to break the Lord's Commandments."

"We broke one of 'em, all right," muttered Titus as he looked over the side of the wagon at the motionless shape sprawled in the mud. "'Thou shalt not kill.'"

"The Bible also says an eye for an eye," Will noted, "and they were trying to kill us." Mac started to get down from the seat, and Will put out a hand to stop him. "Where are you going?"

Mac looked back at his older brother in surprise. "To tend to that man. We'll have to put him in the wagon and take him back to Richmond."

"We're not putting that son of a—we're not putting that man in the wagon with our mother and sister and brothers," Will declared grimly. "Leave him lay there."

Mac blinked. "You're sure? You're a lawman, Will."

"Not here, I'm not. I'm just a fella who wants to protect his family, and I say we leave him."

"Will's right," Titus put in. "And I'm the one who shot the miserable, no-good Yankee, so I reckon it ought to be up to me what we do with him."

Mac looked at Abigail. "Mama?"

For a long moment, she didn't say anything. Then, "Any man deserves a Christian burial, even a Yankee." Her chin came up. "So let's pray his friends come back and give him one. Let's go home."

Mac shrugged, unwilling to continue the argument against his mother and the rest of the family. Besides, he remembered how close those torches had come to hitting Abigail and Cordelia, and he couldn't summon up much real sympathy for the dead man, either.

"Right," Mac said, taking up the reins. "We're going home."

• • •

A LOUD POUNDING on the door of the sitting room in the luxurious hotel suite made Duncan Ebersole stumble out of the bedroom, knotting the cord of a silken dressing gown around his waist. His long hair in disarray, he jerked open the door and confronted the man who stood there. "What in blazes do you want?" he demanded angrily. "I already paid you—"

The man stepped into the room, forcing Ebersole to move aside. He was wearing a long duster and a broad-brimmed hat. The bandanna that had been over his face earlier was now pulled down around his throat, revealing rawboned, beard-stubbled features. He swung around to confront the planter and said, "You didn't pay us enough. Those damned farmers fought back. Hell, one of 'em used a pistol like a professional, and another blew a hole in Ruell with a rifle that sounded like some sort of cannon!"

"Blast it, keep your voice down!" Ebersole hissed at his visitor. "I don't want you to wake Polly."

"You said they were just a bunch of dirt farmers who wouldn't put up a fight. I didn't ask why you wanted 'em dead, or why you wanted us to act like Yankees while we were gettin' rid of 'em, but I don't care. I got a dead man, a wounded man who probably won't live, and another with a busted arm who ain't no good to me no more." The man leaned closer to Ebersole and growled, "You got to make that right, mister."

"All right, damn you," Ebersole shot back. "How much do you want?"

The hired killer spat on the sitting room's fancy carpet. "I reckon another hundred ought to do."

"Stay here. I'll bring you your money."

"See that you do."

Ebersole was shaking inside as he went into the other room to fetch the money. This had been a damned expensive day. First there was that money he'd lost wagering on the Brannons' plow horse, then the gold coins he had given to his visitor earlier in the evening, when he'd hired the man and his gang of ruffians to kill Titus Brannon and the rest of the family. Now he was going to be out this extra money, and Brannon was still alive. Still alive to humiliate his betters. Still alive to come sniffing around Polly like he was a hound and she was some sort of bitch in heat.

He went back into the sitting room and tossed a small pouch full of coins to the gunman. "I don't suppose you managed to kill any of them," Ebersole said scornfully.

"Like I said, they fought back. You got what you deserved for lyin' to me, mister, nothin' more." The man left, tracking mud on the carpet and slamming the door behind him.

Ebersole took a deep breath and tried to calm himself. He had not gotten what he deserved, not yet, but sooner or later he would. He always did.

And so would Titus Brannon.

Part Two

Chapter Eight

ON FEBRUARY 18, 1861, Jefferson Davis was sworn in as president of the Confederacy, elected as a compromise candidate by Secessionist delegates meeting in Montgomery, Alabama. Immediately, Davis issued a call for peace, a plea for the North to let the South go its way without plunging the separated nation into war.

Less than a month later, on March 4, Abraham Lincoln echoed his southern counterpart's plea for peace in his own inaugural address. Just as Davis had done, Lincoln pledged that his side would not be the aggressor in any conflict.

In Charleston Harbor, at Fort Sumter, the Federal troops under the command of Maj. Robert Anderson tightened their belts a little more each day. They were bottled up tightly, and neither supplies nor reinforcements could get through. A northern ship, the *Star of the West*, had already tried to reach Sumter, only to be turned back by some warning shots from Confederate batteries on Morris Island and at Fort Moultrie, which had been occupied by Secessionist forces as soon as the Federal troops had retreated from it to Fort Sumter. Even if the Confederate attack that the U.S. soldiers feared was inevitable never came, they still might soon be forced to either starve or surrender.

Word of these developments reached Culpeper County, of course, sometimes quickly, sometimes at a more leisurely pace. Like everyone else, Will Brannon was concerned that things were inching closer to war.

But he was more worried about the fact that the Fogarty brothers and their kin were still raising hell.

On a fine spring morning in the middle of March, Will was sitting in his office in Culpeper with Luther Strawn when the two lawmen heard a commotion coming from outside. Will

121

122 • *James Reasoner*

exchanged a glance with Luther, then stood up from behind his desk and hurried toward the door.

"Sounds like trouble of some sort," Luther said as he joined Will at the doorway. "Folks are sure yellin' and carryin' on."

Will jerked the door open and stepped outside. The sheriff's office and jail were housed in a two-story stone building less than a block from the square where the county courthouse was located. The streets in this part of town were paved with flagstones, and Will's boot heels rang loudly on them as he strode toward the source of the disturbance. Several covered wagons parked in front of the courthouse were surrounded by angry people talking loudly. Some of them were shouting curses.

Will raised his voice so that it cut across the hubbub. "What's going on here?" he demanded.

A couple of dozen faces swung toward him. Young and old, male and female, all shapes and sizes. They were immigrants, Will realized as he looked at the strangers and their wagons.

One of the men stepped forward. He was tall, slender to the point of scrawniness, with a gray spade beard. "We're lookin' for the law hereabouts," he said, then his eyes fastened on the badge pinned to Will's shirt. "Are you him?"

"I'm Sheriff Brannon," Will announced. "What seems to be the trouble?"

"No 'seems' to be about it," snorted the gray-bearded man. "We been robbed, and a couple of us been shot."

One of the women let out a wrenching sob. "They murdered my husband! Shot him down in cold blood, just like he was a dog!"

Some of the other women from the wagon train moved in around the distraught woman, hugging her and patting her on the back and speaking in low tones. The gray-bearded man gestured at the women and said to Will, "See? See what they done?"

"Maybe you'd better start at the beginning," Will said to the one who seemed to be the leader. "What's your name?"

"Meader, Wilfred Meader," responded the gray-bearded man. "We're from down in the Tidewater, headin' for the Blue Ridge to start some farms there."

"What happened to your places in the Tidewater?"

Meader shrugged. "Lost 'em, to taxes mostly. A farmer just don't hardly stand a chance in this world."

Those who were willing to work got by all right, thought Will, but he kept the comment to himself. He didn't know these people, didn't know much of anything about them except where they were from. He had no right to sit in judgment of them. At the moment his only concern had to be the crime they were reporting.

"And you say you were robbed?"

Meader nodded and continued, "They come at us out of nowhere, whilst we was goin' through a little draw."

"How many of them?"

"We only saw three."

Will looked over the party of travelers. There were six wagons and at least two dozen people in the group. "You're saying a good-sized bunch like you couldn't fight off three men?" he asked. He wondered suddenly if these people were Quakers. He didn't think so, even though the men wore dark, sober suits and the women long black dresses and sunbonnets.

Meader glared at him. "I said we *saw* three men. There were other bandits we never saw. They were perched on the hills to either side of the trail. They shot at us, made us stop." His voice shook slightly with anger at the memory of the holdup.

"So it was the bushwhackers hidden on the hills who killed the two men?"

That question drew a wail from the woman being comforted, and Will realized maybe he shouldn't have been quite so blunt about it. But blast it, if he was going to do these people any good, he had to know what had happened.

"No," replied Meader slowly, "the men on the hills just fired in front of our teams and made us stop. It was the three men who rode out of the trees . . . they pointed pistols at us and told us we'd have to turn over all our money and valuables to them. Then Alvin . . ." He turned to glance at the sobbing woman. "Her husband. He yelled out at 'em, told 'em they couldn't take everything we had in the world. So one of 'em lifted his gun and he . . . he shot Alvin right off the wagon."

Not surprisingly, that brought more anguished cries from the grieving woman. Will said quietly, "What about the other man who was shot?"

"Fella named Fred Cummings. Not much more'n a boy. He didn't have any folks, but he was friends with Alvin. He run forward carryin' a ax when Alvin was shot, and one of the other robbers gunned him down." Meader shook his head. "They didn't care about nothin', those three. You could tell it by lookin' at 'em. They'd've killed all of us if they had to, to get what they wanted."

"What else could you tell by looking at them?" Will asked.

Meader frowned at him and said, "What do you mean?"

"What did they look like? How were they dressed? I'm trying to figure out who could have done this, Mr. Meader, so I can go after them. I reckon that's what you want?"

"Damn right it's what we want! They're thieves and murderers! It's up to the law to catch 'em."

"I'll do my best," vowed Will, "but I need a place to start."

"Well . . . like I said, there was three of 'em in the bunch that we saw. But there were at least two more men with 'em, because we got shot at from both sides of the trail by those fellas who was hid out."

"And the ones you saw?" Will prompted.

"We couldn't tell much about them. They was white, not niggers, I'm sure of that. They was wearin' long coats and had their hats pulled down and cloths over their faces."

The description reminded Will immediately of two separate incidents. One was the attack on him and his family on their way back from Richmond. But that had been carried out by abolitionists. The other incident was the robbery of the store at Burke's Station and the pistol-whipping of old man Burke. Those thieves had been dressed like the men Meader had just described. Will was convinced the Fogartys and their kin had been behind that crime.

He was equally convinced that George and Ransom and Joe had had something to do with this one, too.

In the days following the family's return from Richmond, Will had pondered long and hard about what had happened. He remembered his clash with Joe Fogarty over the young woman at the camp, and he considered the possibility that the men who had attacked them had not been abolitionists at all, but the Fogartys instead. Finally, he had discarded the idea because he had heard the voices of several of the men and had not recognized any of them. Besides, it wasn't the way of the Fogartys to strike back at an enemy in secret. They would have wanted the Brannons to know who was attacking them.

But the Fogartys could have easily been behind this latest holdup and the two killings. The casual brutality with which the two men had been murdered struck Will as something they would do. He said to Meader, "Where did this happen?"

"'Bout six miles east of here. Place where the road goes 'twixt a couple of big pines, then dips down into a draw."

Will nodded. He knew the location. "My deputy and I will ride out there, see if we can pick up their trail." Will looked at the group of immigrants and addressed them. "If any of you men want to ride along, we'll try to come up with some horses for you."

Several men shuffled their feet and looked as if they were about to step forward, but then the women with them clutched their arms to stop them. One woman had already lost a husband today; none of the others wanted the same thing to happen to their men. One by one the pilgrims looked down at the ground, unable to meet Will's gaze.

"All right," he said after a moment, not bothering to hide the scorn in his voice. "Luther and I will see what we can do."

"We're much obliged, Sheriff," said Meader. "We're simple folk, farmers. We ain't any good when it comes to things like this. That's your job."

Will didn't need anybody to tell him his job. Keeping a tight rein on his temper, he gave Meader a curt nod and said to his deputy, "Come on, Luther."

Luther hurried to keep up with Will's long-legged strides as he walked back toward the sheriff's office. In a low voice, Luther recalled, "I thought you said we'd take a posse with us the next time we went after the Fogartys."

"So you figured out it was likely them, too." Will grunted. "You saw how much luck I had raising a posse from that bunch."

"Some of the men from town would go with us if we asked, I reckon."

"We may not even be able to pick up the trail," Will cautioned. "If we do, that'll be soon enough to send you back here for reinforcements."

"Oh. Yeah, I reckon that makes sense."

They went into the office and got their hats. Both lawmen were already wearing holstered handguns, but Will took his rifle and Luther's scattergun from the gun cabinet on the wall. He handed the greener to the deputy, then took a box of ammunition from the desk drawer. He glanced again at the now empty gun cabinet. Luther had made it. It was good work, well put together, the wood sanded and polished until it had a shine to it. Luther was a good carpenter and probably should have followed that line of work instead of packing a badge. Maybe one of these days Will would suggest that to him.

The livery stable was a block away, on one of the unpaved streets. Will and Luther walked over there, and the hostler saddled their horses. They rode out of Culpeper a few minutes later, following the road east out of town.

The countryside was gorgeous with new growth. Trees were budding out, wildflowers were blooming amidst the newly green grass, and the sun was warm, even though a slight chill in the air was enough to remind Will that winter wasn't all that far behind them. Still, if he was going to be out in the country, he would much rather have been able to enjoy it instead of having to concentrate on finding the men responsible for two murders. At least two murders, he reminded himself, because he had suspected for a long while that the Fogartys were behind some of the other killings that had plagued Culpeper County from time to time.

It took less than an hour for Will and Luther to reach the site of the robbery. There was little to show that a bloody tragedy had taken place here. Meader and the other immigrants had loaded the bodies of the dead men into the wagons and taken them on into town. Will saw a couple of dark splotches on the road that could have been dried blood, and there was a welter of tracks in the dirt, too, revealing where the mules and oxen pulling the wagons had stood while they were halted. Will spotted other tracks and knew that in all likelihood they had been made by the horses of the robbers. He backtracked off the road and into the trees. While Will was doing that, Luther rode up to the tops of the hills that flanked the trail and looked for signs there.

Will was able to follow the tracks through the trees, because the hoofprints were visible in the soft carpet of pine needles that had fallen over the winter. Gradually he became aware that he was not only backtracking the thieves, but that they had left the scene of the crime this way, too, retracing their route. He emerged from the trees on a small rise, and Luther came riding over to join him.

"Look there," Luther said as he pointed at the ground. "The fellas who was hid on that hill rode over this way and joined up with the bunch you're trackin', Will."

Will nodded and added, "Yeah, and I imagine the men over on the other side of the trail circled around and joined this group somewhere up ahead." He looked toward the line of hills in the northwest, hazy with distance. "They're headed for the Blue Ridge again."

"We're less'n three hours behind 'em. Reckon we could get ahead of 'em again, like last time?"

"No, last time we were able to cut them off because we were following them at an angle," Will said with a shake of his head. "This time they'd be straight ahead of us. But I might be able to catch up."

"You mean *we* might could catch up."

Will glanced over at his deputy. "I thought you were going back to Culpeper to gather up some men."

"Look, Will, if I do that, it's goin' to take a long time. And I might not be able to find you. Why don't we track those sons of bitches together as far as their hideout? Then I could go back and fetch help, whilst you kept an eye on 'em."

Will considered the plan for a moment. Luther had a point. If they separated, it might be difficult for Luther to find him again. This way, they would at least have a chance of discovering where the Fogartys hid after committing their crimes.

"All right," Will said after a moment. "We'll do it your way, Luther. Come on." He heeled his horse into motion and followed the rise toward the northwest.

The tracks were easy to follow most of the time. The ground was soft after the recent rains and held hoofprints well. Occasionally the two lawmen hit a stretch of rockier ground and lost the trail for a short time, but by casting back and forth they were always able to pick it up again. They pushed their horses hard, trying to make up some of the lead that the Fogartys had on them. Will thought of their quarry only as the Fogartys now; he was that convinced they were behind the robbery of the wagon train.

The sun reached its midday height and then began its long afternoon descent. Will and Luther rode on, pausing only to rest their mounts. They chewed biscuits Will had in his saddlebags and washed them down with water from the numerous little creeks in the area when they stopped to let the horses drink.

Will wasn't the best tracker in the world—or even in his family; Titus had that honor—but he thought the tracks he and Luther were following looked a little fresher, as if the men they were after weren't so far ahead of them now. He knew from the terrain that they had ridden north of the town and left it far behind. The Blue Ridge was looming closer. Officially, that was Rappahannock County, and Will wouldn't have any jurisdiction. But he was damned sick and tired of letting the Fogartys run rings around him. He was going to stick to their trail like a burr this time, no matter where it led, and if that caused any trouble between him and the sheriff of Rappahannock County, that was just too bad.

The country was getting more rugged. It wasn't all rolling hills and farmland anymore. Now there were brush-choked draws and rocky bluffs thrusting up from the landscape. The trail was harder to follow, and Will wished he had Titus with him. Titus could track just about anything; that skill was part of his natural ability for hunting. But he and Luther managed to stay on the trail, and Will was certain now that they were closing in on their quarry.

"Keep your eyes open," he advised Luther. "We don't want to ride up right on top of them without any warning."

"You reckon we're that close?"

"Don't know," Will said with a shake of his head. "How do those tracks look to you?"

Luther reined in and bent over in the saddle to study the tracks they had been following. "Edges look pretty clean," he said after a moment. "Could be they're not more'n half an hour ahead of us."

Will nodded. "That's what I thought, too. Come on."

They had just started riding forward again when they heard the sudden rustle of brush from a thicket up ahead. Will jerked back on his horse's reins with his left hand and brought his right to the butt of his Colt Navy. Luther brought his horse to an abrupt halt, too, and nodded toward the thicket.

"You hear that?" he asked in a whisper.

"Yeah," Will said. "Let's slip up there quiet-like."

He and Luther swung down from their saddles and let the reins dangle on the ground so their horses wouldn't wander too far. Will left his rifle in the boot attached to the saddle, preferring his revolver at close quarters like this. Luther brought the scattergun with him, though. At short range it was a devastating weapon.

Will palmed the Colt from its holster and eared back the hammer, hoping that the clicking sound wasn't too loud. He and Luther cat-footed forward, veering away from each other so that they would be two separate targets in case any shooting broke out. They approached the thicket from both sides. Will had not heard any more noises from it since that first rattling.

Suddenly, though, as Will and Luther closed in, the brush was loudly disturbed again. It sounded like something was thrashing around in there, and Will wondered if one of the Fogartys was hurt. Or maybe the thing making the noise wasn't one of the Fogartys at all. Suddenly the thought raced through his mind, *Maybe it wasn't even human . . .*

At that instant the brush seemed to explode outward and a huge black bear lurched into the open. The bear was reared up on its hind legs, and it threw its head back and let out a terrifying growl as it spotted the two men with its weak, piggish eyes. Of course, it was bound to have scented them long before now.

Luther let out a yelp of surprise and fear and scuttled backward. Will stayed where he was, knowing he would draw the bear's attention less by remaining still. The bear swung around toward Luther, and Will thought it was about to charge the deputy. "Get up a tree, Luther," he shouted. That might not do much good, because bears could climb trees, too, but sometimes they wouldn't. Often, they were content just to chase whoever they were after up into the boughs of a tree and leave them there.

The bear hesitated at the sound of Will's shout, then started to lumber after Luther, who had turned and broken into a full-fledged run toward a stand of oak trees.

Luther had only gone a couple of steps when a sharp crack sounded and he stumbled. Will thought at first his deputy had stepped on a branch and broken it, but then he saw Luther pitch forward, a dark stain showing on the back of his shirt.

Will's instincts threw him aside, even as his brain was still struggling to realize that Luther had just been shot.

Something whipped past his ear, making a flat, ugly sound. He knew it must be a bullet. Landing hard, he let his gut keep telling him what to do and started rolling toward the thicket from which the bear had emerged.

The bear had stopped short when Luther fell, seeming to be as surprised by what was going on as Will was. It let out another deep, growling, rumbling roar, so loud that Will couldn't hear the shots that were seeking him out. He saw dirt suddenly kicked into the air near his head, however, and knew that a slug had just plowed into the ground. He threw himself into a final lunge that carried him all the way into the thicket.

Branches clawed at him, ripping his shirt and his skin as he plunged deeper into the undergrowth. The ground slanted down, and he hugged it as he crawled ahead. The brush shook and rattled above his head, and some of the newly budded leaves floated down around him, knocked loose by the bullets tearing through the growth.

Will's heart was pounding heavily in his chest. *Someone had shot Luther.* That thought shouted in his brain. He stopped crawling and lay still, trying to take stock of the situation. Guilt gnawed at his insides. He had gone running for cover and left Luther out there with not only whoever had shot him but also that bear.

The rational part of Will's brain told him that he had seen the way Luther had flopped on the ground. That loose-limbed sprawl could mean only one thing. Luther had been killed instantly by the shot that had struck him in the back. Will knew that logically, but at the same time, he felt a growing shame at the way he had abandoned his deputy, not to mention rage at the men who had gunned him down.

Will turned around carefully, trying not to make too much noise or disturb the brush. He didn't hear any more shots now, and the bear was quiet as well. Using his toes and elbows, he began pulling himself toward the edge of the undergrowth. Will had to be certain there was nothing he could do for Luther. He owed the deputy that much.

Within minutes, Will had reached a spot where he could cautiously part the branches that grew thickly around him and peer out into the open. The first thing he saw was Luther's body, still lying facedown and motionless. Luther hadn't moved. The dark, reddish-black stain on the back of his shirt was even larger now.

Movement caught Will's eye, and he saw the bear lumbering away from the thicket, away from Luther's body. The way Luther was lying there so still must have spooked the animal. Will could tell that the bear hadn't touched Luther. Instead, it was leaving.

Luther was dead, all right. Will was close enough so that he could see the deputy wasn't breathing. Chances were, Luther had never known what had happened to him. The bullet that had struck him had likely blasted him clear on into whatever was on the other side of death. That knowledge didn't make Will feel any better, though. Instead, a red-hot knife of sorrow and anger plunged into him. Whoever had done this would pay. He would see to that.

And chances were, he would get his opportunity to do just that real soon, because he suddenly heard the sound of horses approaching.

The bushwhackers had killed Luther and driven Will into the brush, and now they were coming to finish the job.

Chapter Nine

MAC CALLED, "Whoa!" to the mules and brought the team to a stop in front of the high porch of Davis's General Store in Culpeper. He stood up and stepped directly from the wagon seat onto the porch. Michael Davis, the slender, fair-haired proprietor of the emporium, was standing in the doorway watching a couple of his employees load sacks of flour and sugar and salt into another customer's wagon. Davis grinned and nodded at Mac, saying, "Howdy there, Brannon. What can I do you for?"

"Need a keg of nails," Mac told him. "We're building a shed onto one of the barns. And as long as I had to come into town anyway, I figured I might as well replenish the rest of our supplies."

Davis nodded. "Glad to fix you up. Come on inside. We'll get started totin' up your order whilst the boys finish loadin' Mr. Saunders's wagon."

Mac followed the man into the cool dim interior of the store. The place was crowded with shelves, and the aisles between them were narrow. Just about anything a person might need could be found here, though, from nails to pickles to ladies' undergarments.

Davis went behind the long counter that ran across the rear of the store and picked up a piece of brown paper and a stub of a pencil to write down the things Mac needed. Before Mac launched into the list, however, he commented, "I saw some covered wagons parked down the street. Strangers in town?"

"Yep," replied the storekeeper. "Bunch of pilgrims from down in the Tidewater headin' for the Blue Ridge. Reckon they couldn't make a go of it where they were, so they figure to start over somewheres else. Leastways, that's what I heard tell about 'em. They ain't off to a very good start, though."

"Oh? Why's that?" Mac knew how talkative Davis was and also knew that he might be delaying getting the supplies by asking questions, but he was in no real hurry. It wouldn't hurt anything for him to listen to the storekeeper ramble on for a few minutes.

"Well, they ran into some bad luck on the way here, or so I'm told," drawled Davis. "Seems some fellas stopped the wagons, robbed ever'body, and killed two of those pilgrims."

"Killed two men?" Mac repeated in surprise.

Davis nodded solemnly. "Shot 'em down. Bad business, if you ask me. I wish such things wouldn't happen around here so frequently."

Mac put his hands flat on the counter and leaned forward, his leisurely attitude of a moment earlier completely forgotten now. "Does Will know about this?"

"Why, sure he does. He talked to that fella Meader, the leader of the bunch, and heard all about it. That's why him and that deputy of his rode out to look for those killers."

"When was this?"

"This mornin'. 'Bout ten o'clock, I reckon."

"Did Will and Luther go alone?"

"Yep. Your brother asked those immigrants if any of 'em wanted to go with him, but none of 'em volunteered."

One of Mac's hands clenched into a fist and thumped softly on the counter. "And no one from town went with them, either?"

Davis shrugged and said, "Will didn't ask anybody else. I guess he figured it was up to him, him bein' sheriff and all."

That was exactly how Will would figure it, thought Mac. "How many of the robbers were there?"

"Nobody knows for sure. Five or six, maybe more."

The Fogartys and their kin. Mac leaped to that conclusion as Davis told him the rest of the gossip about the robbery and the shootings, and he knew Will would have thought that, too. But it didn't really matter who the thieves and killers had been. Will would have gone after them regardless.

Mac turned and headed for the front door of the store. Behind him, Davis called out, "Hey! What about those nails and your other supplies?"

"I'll get them later," Mac called back over his shoulder. "Right now, there's something else I have to do."

He hurried outside and stepped from the porch back into the wagon. Snatching up the reins as he sat down, he pulled back on them and started the mules backing up. Then he turned the team and sent the wagon rolling briskly down the main street of Culpeper.

He was headed back to the Brannon farm to fetch Titus and Henry. Will might have started after those outlaws with just Luther Strawn with him, but if Mac had anything to do with it, the two lawmen would have reinforcements before the day was over.

• • •

WILL SLID back several feet, then lay as still as possible in the brush. The horses came closer, and he heard the vague mutter of men's voices. He couldn't recognize any of them, though.

Abruptly, gunfire roared through the still afternoon air. Will ducked his head, pressing his face to the ground. He tasted dirt in his mouth and suppressed the impulse to spit it out. Bullets stormed through the brush around him. One of the slugs actually burned across the back of his hand as it lay there on the ground, causing him to jerk his hand toward him. The bullet had left a red streak on his skin.

The shooting went on for what seemed like forever, even though Will knew it couldn't have been more than a minute or two. When it was over, the silence that fell sounded eerie to his ears. He stayed where he was, hoping the bushwhackers would be convinced that he must be dead, so that they would ride away.

Convinced or not, they weren't taking any chances. A few moments later, he heard a crackling noise, and a tendril of acrid, stinging smoke drifted past his nose.

They had set the thicket on fire.

Will tried to fight down the feeling of panic that welled up inside him. No doubt they were sitting out there just waiting for him to come bursting out of the brush. If he gave in to panic and did that, they would shoot him down.

The crackling of the burning brush grew louder. Will slithered backward, less concerned about stealth now because the sound of the fire covered up any noise he was making. He twisted his head, looking from side to side in an attempt to locate the blaze. He saw that they had fired both sides of the thicket. Red leaping flames were closing in quickly from both right and left, greedily consuming the branches. Yet, because it was spring and the brush had a lot of new growth on it, the fire didn't move quite as rapidly as it might have otherwise. Those few seconds gave Will a chance he might not have had.

He was moving backward down the slope when he became aware that his feet and legs were wet. He turned to look behind him and saw that the ground formed a natural bowl here. Water had collected in that bowl, forming a small stagnant pond that was not visible from outside the thicket.

More than half of the brush was on fire now. Flames were leaping high in the air, and a column of black smoke spiraled up from the conflagration. Inside the thicket, a terrible heat battered Will. Sweat bathed his face, and when he gasped for air, it seemed to sear his lungs. Air was what he had to have, though, so he drew in several deep breaths of it, then slid the rest of his body into the pond. It was deep enough to cover him completely. The dirty green water closed over his head.

His eyes were squeezed shut, but even if they had been open, the water was too thick with scum for him to have seen anything. He lay there, sinking into the mud at the bottom of the pond, as the fire consumed more and more of the thicket.

He could hear his own heartbeat, as loud as a drum. The water and the darkness seemed to close in on him, and he felt a tightness growing around his chest until it threatened to squeeze the very life out of him.

But at least here in the pond, he had escaped the awful heat of the fire. The water was already hot and growing hotter, but it was nothing like the inferno up above.

He could survive the fire by lying here underwater. He knew that. But would the gunmen still be waiting for him when he surfaced? Or would they look at the blaze, figure that no one could have survived that, and ride away before the fire burned itself out? Did they know the pond was hidden in here?

Will had no answers. All he knew was that he had to have air. He rolled over and lifted his head until his nose and mouth broke the surface. He gulped down some of the superheated air and then sank again, the tightness in his chest easing a little.

The relief didn't last long. Within seconds, he needed to breathe again. Stubbornly, he held out, fighting down the urge to open his mouth and let the brackish water flow into his mouth and throat and lungs, filling him until he would never rise again.

The air didn't seem quite as hot when he pushed himself to the surface after an unknowable amount of time. Nobody shot at him, either, as far as he could tell. He went down again, stayed under as long as he could, then rose to gulp more air and lifted a hand to wipe pond scum from his eyes.

The fire was burning itself out. The bushes around the pond were bare now, all their leaves consumed. The branches looked like black, skeletal fingers clawing at the sky. A few flames still flickered here and there, but mostly Will saw just sooty ashes.

What was more important was what he didn't see. No one was waiting there to kill him.

He sat up and looked around, wiping more of the mossy scum from his face. He couldn't see Luther's body from where he was, so he stood up and half-walked, half-staggered up out of the bowl. Luther still lay where he had fallen, but as Will stumbled over to the deputy, he saw that someone had shot Luther again. In fact, it looked like someone had fired several bullets into the back of Luther's head, almost blowing it away.

Will fell to his knees and let out a low moan of sorrow and rage. "I'm sorry, Luther," he whispered raggedly. "I'm so damned sorry." Water dripped from his hair and blended with the tears welling from his eyes. The Fogartys would pay for this, he vowed to himself. By God, they would pay!

A series of shudders shook Will, but when they finally faded away, he felt a little stronger. His lungs burned with every breath he took, but at least he was still breathing. He had survived. The men who had left him here had made a terrible mistake. They hadn't waited to make sure he was dead before they rode away.

He pushed himself to his feet and looked around for the horses. They were gone, of course. Men who would ambush a pair of lawmen wouldn't think twice about stealing a couple of horses. That meant Will had lost his rifle, too.

He found his hat, though, lying on the ground where it had fallen off his head when he first leaped for cover as the ambush began. He picked it up, knocked some of the dust off it, and settled it on his head, then realized how absurd his actions were. He was soaking wet and covered with green pond scum from head to toe, and here he was knocking dust off his hat before he put it on. A laugh that was edged with hysteria came from his mouth.

After finding a rock on which to sit, he took his boots off and drained as much of the water from them as he could. Then he removed his socks and wrung them out before spreading them on the rock to dry. He had a long walk in front of him, and wet feet would only cause more blisters to form.

He wasn't sure where he was, somewhere northwest of Culpeper. It was past the middle of the afternoon, and he knew he couldn't walk all the way back to town before night fell. But he might be able to find a farm, or a small crossroads settlement, where he could seek shelter for the night and perhaps borrow a couple of horses so that he could come back for Luther's body. In the meantime, he dragged the deputy into the burned-out thicket, hoping the smell of the ashes would keep animals away from the body.

With that done, he put his socks back on—they were only slightly damp now—and pulled the boots on over them. He checked the sun and then started walking as straight a course as he could figure for home.

• • •

"I DON'T KNOW how you expect to find Will out here in the middle of nowhere," Titus complained as he rode beside Mac.

"That's why I brought you along," explained Mac. "I've heard you brag about how you can find just about anything in the woods."

From behind them, Henry laughed. He was bringing up the rear of this little procession consisting of the three brothers on horseback. "Titus can find 'most anything, all right," Henry commented, "except what he really wants. And gals like Polly Ebersole don't ever go in the woods, do they, Titus?"

Titus flushed angrily, but at least he didn't tell Henry to shut up. Mac was grateful for that. He didn't want a lot of arguing going on while they were looking for Will.

Something told him, some instinct, that Will needed their help. His life might even be in danger if they didn't find him in time.

But Titus was right: they had no real idea where to look for Will. All they knew was that he had ridden out to the site of the robbery and killings and that he hadn't come back to Culpeper. To Mac that meant he was on the trail of the outlaws. Since the robbery was the only starting point they had, once he had fetched his brothers from the farm, they had ridden out to the place, too.

Titus had been able to pick up the trail, which pointed them northwest toward the Blue Ridge. Mac remembered what Will had said about the Fogartys having a hideout somewhere up there in the mountains. Since he felt that they had already wasted enough time, he had decided they would ride straight toward the Blue Ridge without slowing down to follow the tracks. They ran the risk that way of not finding Will at all, Mac knew, but he was unwilling to spend any more time than necessary on this pursuit. He wanted to catch up to Will as soon as possible, and being more cautious might mean they would be too late.

It was a gamble either way, and Mac preferred to restrict his gambling to an occasional horse race.

Come to think of it, he had lost the last race. They couldn't afford to lose this wager.

So late afternoon found the three of them trotting their horses through country that was gradually turning more rugged. They wouldn't be able to get back home tonight, Mac thought, but that was all right. They had brought bedrolls and enough supplies with them to camp out one night. Cordelia had packed a whole saddlebag full of sandwiches made from slabs of roast beef and thick slices of bread. She had wanted to come with them but had to settle for helping with the provisions. Abigail wouldn't hear of Cordelia riding after a bunch of thieves and killers, and Mac hadn't wanted the responsibility of looking after her, either.

But she had sure been mad when they told her she couldn't come. She'd been practically spitting nails. It wasn't often that Cordelia's temper lived up to that red hair of hers, but when it did, it was best to watch out.

Titus suddenly reined in, and Mac and Henry followed suit. "Look there," Titus noted, leveling an arm and pointing up ahead. "Something's been burning."

Mac looked where Titus indicated, and sure enough, he saw a brownish haze in the air where a cloud of smoke had for the most part dispersed. He might have overlooked it himself if Titus hadn't pointed it out.

"What do you reckon it means?" asked Henry.

Titus shrugged. "Something's been burning," he said again. "That's all I know."

"Could have been a settler burning off some brush," Mac mused. "Looks like it was a good-sized fire."

"We're heading pretty much in that general direction. We can go take a look," Titus suggested.

Mac nodded, reaching a decision quickly. "Let's go," he urged as he heeled his horse back into a trot.

About a quarter of an hour later, as they crested the top of a small rise, Titus spotted a figure trudging toward them on foot across the broad shallow valley that opened up before them. The man was several hundred yards away, but Titus jerked his horse to a halt and exclaimed, "That's Will!"

"Where?" asked Henry, trying to see what Titus had seen.

"Right there," Titus said, pointing.

Mac saw the distant figure now, too, and he kicked his horse into a run. "Come on!" he called over his shoulder.

The man on foot must have seen them coming, because he stopped to wait for them to gallop up to him. Mac recognized Will, just as Titus had, but as they came closer, they all saw that Will had been through the wringer. His face was dark with what looked like soot, and his clothes were muddy and stained. His hat was the only thing about him that wasn't filthy, and he took it off and held it at his side as he waited for them.

"You boys are about as welcome a sight as any I've ever seen," Will called to them as they brought their mounts to a halt. He smiled tiredly.

Mac swung down from the saddle and hurried forward to grip his older brother's arm. "What in blazes happened to you?" he inquired anxiously.

146 • *James Reasoner*

"Blazes," Will said. "That's a good word to describe it."

"Where's Luther?" asked Henry.

"Dead," Will answered hollowly. His voice was raspy and hoarse, and he flinched a little as he spoke, as if every word hurt him.

Mac held out his canteen to his brother. "You need something to drink," he said. "Then you can tell us about it."

Will drank the cool water gratefully and then sat beneath a nearby tree and related the day's events to his three brothers. They sat wide-eyed with horror.

"Damn, Will," Henry said in a hushed voice when his oldest brother had finished the story, "they like to killed you."

A grim smile tugged at Will's mouth. "Yep, I reckon so."

"Was it the Fogartys?" Mac asked.

Will blew out his breath in a long sigh. "I don't know," he said. "I honestly don't know. I never saw them, never heard their voices well enough to recognize any of them." He looked up at Mac. "But my belly tells me it was them. Holding up that wagon train, gunning down those pilgrims . . . that's something they'd do."

Mac nodded his agreement.

"And ambushing us like that, then setting fire to the brush to make sure I was dead, that sounds like George Fogarty to me," Will continued.

Henry lifted the rifle he had brought with him. "Then why don't we go kill us some Fogartys?"

"I don't have any proof, damn it!" Wearily, Will scrubbed a hand over his soot-stained face. "I'm still sworn to uphold the law. I can't just go around shooting Fogartys because I feel like it."

"Well, I'm no lawman," Titus practically shouted back. His brothers all looked at him and knew exactly what he meant. He could lay for the Fogartys and kill them one by one without having to get closer to them than a few hundred yards. He was that good with the Sharps.

Will shook his head. "No, Titus. I sure as hell don't want to have to arrest my own brother for murder."

Titus spat and fumed, "Wouldn't be murder to shoot down some mad dogs, now would it?"

"Forget it," Mac said. "Will's right."

"Well, then," pressed Henry, "what *are* you going to do, Will?"

"Try to find some proof that the Fogartys are responsible for those killings. Maybe if some of those immigrants see them again, they'll recognize them, or maybe we can catch them before they have a chance to sell our horses."

"So you're going to arrest them?" asked Titus.

Will nodded. "I reckon."

"They may not come along peaceable-like."

Will shrugged and said, "I'll deal with that when the time comes." He pushed himself to his feet. "Right now, I want to go back there and get Luther's body. We can tie it onto one of the horses, and the rest of us can ride double."

"That'll be slow going," Mac pointed out.

"I'm in no hurry. And neither is Luther."

• • •

WHEN THEY reached the burned-out thicket, they found that Luther's body had not been disturbed, just as Will had hoped. Mac and Titus would have tended to lifting the body onto one of the horses and lashing it in place, but Will told them he wanted to take care of that chore himself. He owed that much to Luther, he said, for getting the deputy killed like he had. Mac didn't care for the sound of that. The way he saw it, whichever of the bushwhacking Fogartys had pulled the trigger was to blame for Luther's death, not Will.

They rode several miles back toward Culpeper before stopping to make camp for the night. Will ate a couple of the sandwiches Cordelia had packed and drank several cups of coffee. He seemed to feel a little better after that.

None of the others knew it when Will's eyes snapped open in the middle of the night, visions of flames still searing in his mind. That wasn't the only thing he had seen in his nightmare, though. Luther had been there, too, bullet-blasted head and all, jumping and capering just like the flames, a big grin on what had once been his face.

Will sat up, shivering and sweating at the same time. He breathed deeply, relishing in a way the pain he felt in his seared lungs. It told him he was still alive.

After a long time, he lay down and went back to sleep, and thankfully no dreams haunted him this time.

In the morning they placed Luther back on one of the horses and rode double on the other two. By noon they were nearing the Brannon farm. "We'll stop at home," Mac said, "and you can stay there while the rest of us take Luther's body on into town."

"I can't do that—" Will began.

"Yes, you can," Mac told him. "Ma and Cordelia will want to fuss over you, and if you don't let them they're liable to make all of our lives miserable. You know that."

Reluctantly, Will nodded. "I know. But it doesn't matter. I'm the sheriff, and Luther was my deputy. I'm taking his body in. It's my job."

"Then we'll ride around the farm," Mac stated. He glanced at Luther's corpse. "I don't want the womenfolk seeing that."

"Neither do I," Will agreed.

The four of them swung wide around the farm and hit the road leading into Culpeper. It was early afternoon when they entered the main street and began to make their way to the undertaking parlor, which was just down from Will's office and the jail. People on the sidewalks saw the body draped over the back of the horse and followed along, curious about the violence that had obviously occurred. Will had draped his coat over Luther's head, not wanting to subject his deputy and friend to the stares of the townspeople.

The riders pulled up in front of the undertaking parlor. The undertaker, a jolly-looking Dutchman named Van Zandt, came hurrying out. He was short and fat, with wispy blond hair, and though his natural expression was a big smile, he forced his face into a look of sorrow when he saw the body.

"Such a shame, such a shame, ja, ja," he commented as he watched Titus and Henry untie Luther's body and carry it inside. Will allowed them to handle the chore this time. Van Zandt went on, "It is the deputy, ja?"

"His name was Luther Strawn," Will said heavily. "I'll want that carved on a good marker, hear?"

"Oh, ja, the finest marker, Sheriff. That he will have, I swear."

Several of the townspeople came up to Will, and the boldest of them asked, "What happened, Sheriff? Did you find those outlaws?"

Will ignored the question. "That wagon train still in town?" he asked instead.

One of the townies nodded. "Yeah, they're still here."

Turning to his brothers, Will told them, "I'd better go talk to Meader again."

"I'll go with you," Mac volunteered as Will started along the boardwalk.

"You don't have to."

"I know. I'll come anyway."

Will looked at Mac and gave a curt nod. "Thanks."

They headed toward the square. That was where the immigrants' wagons would be parked. They were only halfway there when Will stopped short and stared across the street into Davis's General Store.

"What is it?" asked Mac.

"I just saw Joe Fogarty go in there," said Will, and he reached for the Colt Navy holstered on his hip.

Chapter Ten

WILL'S FINGERS had curled around the butt of the Colt Navy and lifted it halfway from the holster before he paused and cursed. He jerked the gun the rest of the way out of the holster and stared down at it. The weapon was crusted with dried slime from the pond. It would have to be completely taken apart and cleaned before it would be of any use again.

Will shoved the Colt into Mac's hand. "Give me your gun," he demanded.

"Wait a minute," Mac began. "What are you going—"

"I'm going over there to arrest Joe Fogarty," snapped Will. "Now give me your gun, blast it!"

The mood he was in, Will was ready to knock Mac down and *take* his brother's gun if it came to that. But after a couple of seconds ticked by, Mac pulled the revolver from the holster on his hip and extended it butt-first toward Will. "Take it," Mac said. "You're liable to need it."

Will frowned at the disapproval in Mac's voice. He took the gun, but he asked, "You think I shouldn't go over there?"

"I think you shouldn't go in there intending to kill Joe," Mac advised. "You said it yourself, Will. You're sworn to uphold the law. You'll have to give him a chance to surrender peacefully. Not only that, but there's liable to be innocent folks in that store. If any shooting starts, some of them could get hurt."

Mac was right, and Will knew it. But that didn't mean he had to like it. Right now, he was burning up with his desire for revenge on the Fogartys. He could start with Joe.

"All right," he relented. "No shooting. Unless Joe starts it."

"I can't argue with that," Mac agreed. "Let's go."

"You don't have to come with me."

"The hell I don't." Mac turned and beckoned to Titus and Henry, who had come back out onto the porch of the undertaking parlor. "We're all going."

Will grimaced. He hadn't meant to draw all three of his brothers into this feud with the Fogartys. But Mac and Titus and Henry were part of it now, and Will knew he couldn't get them out of it. He turned and headed across the street toward Davis's store, followed by his brothers. Will held the gun he had borrowed from Mac down beside his leg, not bothering to put it in the holster.

There were steps at the end of the porch in front of the general store. Will climbed them, and as he reached the top, Michael Davis stepped out of the building. Davis stopped short when he saw the dirty, grim-faced lawman striding toward him. His eyes widened in surprise.

"Will—" he said.

"Is Joe Fogarty in there?" demanded Will.

"Uh, yeah, Joe came in a few minutes ago," Davis admitted. "He's buying powder and shot."

"So he and his brothers can kill more people." Will moved toward the door, and Davis stepped aside. Will paused to ask, "How many other people are in there?"

"I don't rightly know. Half a dozen, I'd reckon, counting my clerks."

"Any of them Fogartys or Fogarty kin?"

Davis shook his head.

"There shouldn't be any trouble, then." Will pulled open the screen door and stepped into the store. Mac, Titus, and Henry were right behind him.

Will's eyes had a little trouble adjusting to the dimness inside the building after being in the bright afternoon sunshine outside. Squinting, he swept his gaze around the store, then focused on the rear counter, where a man stood talking to one of the clerks. Will strode toward him and called out, "Joe Fogarty."

Joe, who had been standing with one elbow resting negligently on the counter, straightened and turned quickly toward Will. Will's vision was better now, and he saw clearly the surprise on Joe's face. "Brannon!" Joe exclaimed. "But I thought you were . . . how did you—?"

The shock Joe expressed at seeing him was all the proof Will needed. Joe had thought he was dead, and the only reason he'd have to think that was if he had been there, shooting up that thicket and then setting fire to it.

"You and your brothers left too soon, Joe," Will answered calmly. "You should've made sure I was dead in that brush."

The clerk behind the rear counter was already scurrying off to the side, well away from Joe. Will heard soft voices behind him and knew that his brothers were shooing out the store's other customers. He was left facing Joe at a distance of about twenty-five feet. Will's legs were spread just slightly, his feet planted firmly on the planks of the floor. He was still holding the gun down alongside his right thigh.

Joe shook his head and tried to brazen it out. "I don't know what you're talkin' about, Sheriff. I just didn't figure on running into you in town today."

"Because you thought I was dead," repeated Will. "You thought you and your brother and your cousins killed me yesterday when you killed my deputy, Luther Strawn."

"Luther's dead?" asked Joe, feigning ignorance. "Sorry to hear that. Luther was a good old boy."

It was all Will could do not to put a bullet in Joe's mocking face. With effort, he announced, "You're under arrest, Joe."

"What for?"

"Murder and robbery."

Joe shook his head. "I ain't killed nobody, nor stolen anything. And you can't prove otherwise, Brannon."

"You sound mighty sure of that."

"I am," Joe said smugly.

"Why? Because your brothers and the rest of your kin will lie for you and say you weren't anywhere near that wagon train that got held up?" Will took a step toward Joe. "Those pilgrims are still in town. Maybe you didn't know that. I'm going to take you down there and let them listen to you talk. Maybe they'll recognize your voice. Maybe some of them got a good enough look at you so that they'll recognize you without that duster and bandanna you were wearing. You want to take that chance, Joe? All I need is one of those immigrants to say that they think you were one of the robbers, and two minutes later you'll be behind bars."

"Damn it, this ain't fair—" Joe burst out.

"As fair as what you did to Luther." Will took another step. "You boys've been running roughshod over folks around here for a long time. Once you're locked up, what do you think a jury will do when you come up for trial?"

Joe licked his lips. He knew the answer to that. Unless he had a better alibi than his relatives lying for him, he'd be convicted. And he couldn't have a better alibi, Will knew, because he'd actually been there. Joe and the other Fogartys had held up that wagon train and murdered those pilgrims, had shot Luther Strawn in the back, and had done their best to kill Will as well. Those were facts, and there was nothing Joe could do to change them.

"I won't go to jail," he declared.

"You're under arrest, Joe," Will repeated. "Come along peacefully now."

"Damn it, no!" Joe tensed, quivering with the threat of violence.

Another step. "Yes," Will demanded.

Joe's hand flashed toward his gun.

The youngest of the Fogarty brothers was fast, no doubt about that. Faster than Will, more than likely. But Will already had a gun in his hand, and as he lifted it, his thumb looped over the hammer and cocked the revolver so that it was ready to fire as soon as it came level. Joe had already cleared leather, and the barrel of his gun was tipping up. Will lifted his thumb.

The gun boomed and bucked against his palm. The bullet smashed into Joe's body and drove him back against the counter, but it didn't put him down. Joe was able to instinctively finish his draw, and he fired as Will was cocking the pistol for a second shot. Joe's bullet smacked into the floor beside Will's left foot. Will extended his arm and aimed better this time, then fired again. The noise in the store was deafening, and powder smoke clogged the air, making it difficult to see and breathe.

Will's second shot caught Joe in the chest and threw him back halfway over the counter behind him. His gun slipped from his fingers and thudded to the floor. He straightened, pawing at the holes in his chest that leaked crimson, then pitched forward to land facedown on the floor. He convulsed once, then lay still.

For a long moment, Will just stood there, the gun in his hand still pointing at Joe's fallen form. Then Mac stepped up beside him and said, "It's over, Will. He's dead."

"Better make sure of that," cautioned Will.

"All right." Mac moved toward the body, being careful not to get between Will and Joe. He knelt at Joe's side, rested a couple of fingers on his neck. After a moment he looked up at Will and nodded. "Dead, just like I said."

Still, Will didn't lower the gun. "Anybody else hurt?"

"Nope," Titus spoke from behind him. "The only shot Joe got off went into the floor."

"Yeah," Will said. "I sort of noticed that at the time. Not really, though. I was just looking at Joe."

Finally, he brought the revolver down. As Mac straightened and came back over to him, Will held out the gun. "This is yours. Much obliged."

Mac took it and put it back in his empty holster. Henry suggested, "You reckon we better make sure there aren't any other Fogartys around?"

Will gave a little shake of his head, not saying no, just trying to clear his brain. His head seemed to be full of powder smoke, just like the air here in the store. His lungs were burning again, and he needed to get outside and take a deep breath of fresh air.

"Good idea," he said to Henry. "Maybe you ought to be the sheriff, not me."

"No, sir," Henry replied without hesitation. "I got no desire to ever pin on a badge."

Will led the way outside. Titus offered, "I'll go fetch Van Zandt." He hurried off to the Dutchman's undertaking parlor.

"If the rest of the Fogartys are here in town, they'll be in one of the saloons," Will said. "Let's take a look."

"Maybe you'd better have this gun back," suggested Mac. "You'll do more good with it than I will, if it comes to that."

Will nodded and took it. "Yeah, maybe I'd better."

He wound up having no need for it, however. It took only a few minutes to check all the saloons and taverns in Culpeper. George and Ransom Fogarty weren't in any of them, nor were the Paynter boys or Israel Quinn. Plenty of people were already gathered on the porch of Davis's store, though, listening to the proprietor tell how Will had faced down Joe Fogarty and killed him in the exchange of shots. With Davis's natural tendency toward embellishment, it wouldn't be long before the story of the gunfight had become some sort of epic yarn.

"Van Zandt got the body yet?" Will asked the storekeeper.

Davis nodded. "Took it back over to his place. You know, Will, I'd have just as soon you hadn't killed Joe in my store."

"He didn't give me much choice."

"I just hope his brothers understand that," Davis said with a worried frown. "I don't want the Fogartys blaming me."

Will felt a flash of anger. Here he had put his own life on the line to bring a thief and a killer to justice, and Davis was worried about repercussions from Joe's brothers. But then Will realized that maybe Davis was right to be concerned. Ransom Fogarty wasn't the clearest thinker in the world; he might want revenge on anybody he saw as being involved in Joe's death, and Joe had certainly died inside the general store. George was smarter, though. George would rein in his remaining brother. He would want to take out his vengeance on Will.

Looking around at the crowd, Will raised his voice and announced, "I tried to arrest Joe Fogarty legally for the robbery of that wagon train and the killings of those two immigrants and my deputy. I called on him to come along peacefully. Davis's clerks can testify to that. If anybody has a problem with what happened here today, they need to come see me and nobody else."

The Fogartys probably had a few friends in this crowd, he thought. They would pass along what he had said to George and Ransom.

"All right," Will went on, "you all best break it up. Go on about your business."

That was what the townspeople did. Davis looked a little disappointed at losing his audience, but not much. He sighed and commented, "I reckon I'd better go see about getting that blood scrubbed up while it's fresh."

• • •

THE SUN was setting as the Brannon brothers rode up to the farm. Cordelia must have heard them coming, because she ran out onto the porch, her face set in anxious lines. Those lines cleared up and a big smile broke out as she saw four figures. Titus and Henry were riding double now, but Will and Mac each had a horse.

"Will!" she cried. "You're all right."

She was on him as soon as he swung down from the saddle, hugging him fiercely as his boots hit the ground. Will put his hands on her shoulders and tried to move her back a little, protesting, "Whoa, there. I'm too filthy for you to be grabbing me like that. You'll get your dress dirty."

"Oh, I don't care," she exclaimed as she hugged him again. "I'm just so glad to see that you're not hurt."

"Well, you're not huggin' us," Henry observed somewhat resentfully. "We're the ones who went to find him, after all."

"Yeah, but we got there too late to do much good," conceded Titus. "Luther was already dead, remember?"

Cordelia gasped and looked up at Will, and he wished Titus had just kept his mouth shut for the time being. "Luther?" Cordelia inquired. "Luther's dead?"

Will nodded. "I'm afraid so."

"That's not all," Henry said, ignoring a warning glance from Mac as he continued. "So's Joe Fogarty. Will shot it out with him in town."

"So." The voice came from the front door and belonged to Abigail. "You've killed another man."

Will looked up at the solemn face of his mother. "I didn't have much choice," he explained. "I tried to arrest him, but he pulled his gun. I had to shoot."

"That's right, Ma," Mac put in. "Will didn't have a choice."

"Yes, he did," maintained Abigail. "He never had to become sheriff in the first place." She looked at Will, and her voice softened a little. "Are you hurt?"

"No."

"Well, that's something to thank the Lord for, anyway. Go clean up, and come in to supper." She turned and went back into the house.

Will watched her go, then released a sigh between his teeth. Still in his arms, Cordelia smiled a little and said, "Don't mind her, Will. That's just her way. You know that. She doesn't hold with killing. But I'm just glad you're all right."

Will bent and planted a quick kiss on her forehead. "Run along. I'll be inside in a few minutes. Like Mama said, I've got to clean up."

Mac started up onto the porch. "I'll bring you some fresh clothes."

Will went around to the back of the house to the well. Henry fetched a bucket from the barn and pumped it full. In the dusk, Will stripped off his clothes that were coated with dried mud and pond scum, then stood shivering as Henry poured the bucket of water over his head. It took several buckets before Will had enough of the grime sluiced off to suit him.

He dried with rags that Titus brought from the house, then dressed in the clothes that Mac brought him. When he went in the house, he wouldn't have gone so far as to say he felt like a new man, but at least he was cleaner.

And his conscience was clean, too. He knew that killing Joe Fogarty had been the only thing he could have done under the circumstances.

Abigail and Cordelia had the table set for the whole family. They couldn't have known that Will and the other boys would be coming in at suppertime, though. Will frowned at the plates and the platters of food and said, "How did you know . . . ?"

"We had faith," Abigail stated quietly. "That's something you should try sometime."

Mac put a hand on his shoulder. "Sit down and eat, Will," he said.

Will looked around at the others. His mother didn't meet his gaze, but Cordelia wanted him to sit down, he could tell that. So did Mac and Henry. Titus's face was pretty much unreadable, as usual. After a moment, Will nodded. He pulled back his chair. "It all looks good," he said.

And in truth, it did. Roast beef, mashed potatoes and gravy, some of Cordelia's fluffy biscuits . . . Will suddenly became aware of how hungry he really was.

Everyone sat and joined hands. They bowed their heads, and Will prayed, "Thank You, Lord, for this food You've given us, and for all the blessings You've sent to this family. Amen."

The others all echoed, "Amen."

Will ate eagerly, but he found that he got full sooner than he thought he would. When he pushed back from the table, he gave a long, satisfied sigh. He might have some problems in his life, but it beat the hell out of being dead.

"Mama and I will clean up," Cordelia told him. "I know you must be wanting to smoke your pipe, so you go on, Will."

"We'll join you," Mac said as he pushed back his chair. "Come on, boys."

The brothers strolled out into the warm spring night. Will and Mac had brought their pipes with them, and as they stood on the porch, they filled the bowls and used lucifers to light them.

"You givin' up the pipe, Titus?" asked Will when he saw that Titus wasn't smoking.

"I've got a fondness for cigars," replied Titus.

"Because that's what his hero Duncan Ebersole smokes," Henry needled. "That's why Titus likes see-gars."

"Hush up," Titus snapped. He aimed an open-handed slap at Henry's head, a lazy move that Henry ducked easily. "You don't know anything about it."

"I sure do," Henry persisted. "I share a room with you, remember? I've heard you moanin' about Polly Ebersole in your sleep."

Titus turned on him sharply. "That's a da—! That's a lie!"

"No, it ain't. The way you carry on, I'd sure like to be able to see those dreams you been havin'."

"Blast it, Henry—"

"That's enough, you two," Mac cut in. "You can do your squabbling some other time. Will and I want some peace and quiet. Isn't that right, Will?"

Will didn't answer immediately. He had been enjoying the ruckus. Watching Titus and Henry pick at each other kept him from thinking too much about what had happened. When all was quiet and peaceful, a man sometimes had a tendency to brood.

But there were some things that needed to be said, and now was as good a time as any, Will supposed. "Listen," he began, "I want all of you to keep your eyes and ears open."

"What for, Will?" asked Henry.

Will took a deep breath. "I'm hoping that if George and Ransom Fogarty come after anybody for Joe's death, it'll be me. But you've got to remember, they don't like any of us, and they might decide to come after some of you to get back at me."

"But aren't you going to arrest George and Ranse?" Titus asked.

"If I can find them, I will. But now that they know I lived through that ambush of theirs, after they've sold my and Luther's horses, they'll probably be lying low. They'll probably sell them on the other side of the mountains. With everything that's happened, the community's going to be more stirred up against them than ever before. Likely they'll stay up in the mountains for a while. But sooner or later, they're going to come down, and when they do, they're going to want revenge for Joe's death."

"Well, they better not come around here," decreed Henry. "If they do, we'll make 'em wish they hadn't."

Those were bold words, and Will had no doubt that Henry meant them. But meaning something and being able to carry it out were sometimes two different things. "I'm just saying to be careful," he went on. "When you're working in the fields, maybe you'd better work in teams so that one man can always be standing guard."

"That'll slow everything down," Mac pointed out.

"I don't care," Will declared bluntly. "I'd rather some of the work not get done than to let the Fogartys ride in here and shoot some of you. There's something else to remember, too: we've got womenfolk here at home."

All three of Will's brothers tensed. "They wouldn't dare bother Ma or Cordelia," Titus argued.

"Not even the Fogartys could be that mean and crazy," Mac speculated.

"I wish I could believe that," said Will. "But until I've caught up with them and brought them in, I don't want any of you straying too far from the place. There'll be a loaded rifle close at hand, too. Cordelia can shoot if she has to."

"She's a good shot," Titus agreed. "But I don't know if she'd pull the trigger, Will. Not even on a Fogarty."

Will hoped Titus was wrong, but he shared the same concern. Cordelia had been hunting before, but shooting a squirrel was a whole lot different than pointing a gun at a man and pulling the trigger. That took an entirely different ability, and Will didn't know if Cordelia possessed it or not.

But with any luck, they would never have to find out. "I'm going to start right away trying to track down the Fogartys," Will said.

"Without a deputy?" asked Mac.

"Best let me be your deputy," suggested Titus.

Will considered the idea. It really wasn't a bad one; Titus was the best shot, the best tracker, the best all-around fighter in the bunch. But that was also the best reason for keeping him here, close to home.

"No, I'll get Luther's cousin. I reckon he'll be glad to help out, considering what happened to Luther."

"Jasper Strawn?" protested Titus. "You'd trust your back to Jasper Strawn?"

"Well, maybe not," Will admitted. "But he can handle the office, and in a pinch, I reckon he'd do for backing me up."

"In a pinch, you'd best fetch us," Mac warned. "The four of us together can handle the Fogartys."

"Shoot," Henry said with a grin. "Four Brannons together could lick just about anybody. If Cory was still around, I reckon we could take on a whole Yankee army!"

Will smiled back at him. He couldn't argue with Henry's boast. As long as the Brannons were together, no one was going to defeat them.

Chapter Eleven

WILL'S WORRIES that the two surviving Fogarty brothers might come after his family proved to be wrong, because the prediction he made about George and Ransom lying low turned out to be right. Several weeks passed, and neither Fogarty was spotted anywhere around Culpeper or the Brannon farm. Will heard rumors that they had been seen as far away as Shenandoah Valley, but most of the news went unconfirmed. That's probably where Will and Luther's horses ended up, because they were not to be found.

Just because everything was quiet where the Fogartys were concerned didn't mean that Will wasn't busy. He recruited Jasper Strawn—a bigger, slower-moving, and slower-thinking version of his cousin Luther—as deputy, then left Jasper in charge of the office while he spent several days trying to track the Fogartys from the site of the ambush that had taken Luther's life. The trail petered out in the rockier ground of the Blue Ridge, and Will was convinced that not even Titus could have followed it. George and Ransom might as well have dropped off the face of the earth.

In the meantime, tensions were growing in Virginia and everywhere else in the South. U.S. troops were still holed up in Fort Sumter, nearer starvation than ever. There was some talk of waiting them out, but Confederate forces and munitions in Charleston had swelled to a much higher level during the weeks Major Anderson and his men had been behind the walls of the harbor fort. Some two dozen cannon, howitzers, and mortars were now set up at Fort Moultrie, and their shells could easily reach Sumter if a bombardment was ordered. There were also six thousand Confederate troops on hand, ready, willing, and able to storm the fort the moment the command came. And with the voices of the fire-eaters growing stronger every day, it was almost inevitable that the command would come.

Will read about the situation in the newspapers and listened to talk about it all over town, as well as at home. When the month of April arrived, he didn't see how things could go on for much longer the way they were. Both presidents, Lincoln and Davis, were still making speeches about how neither one of them was going to be the aggressor in this conflict. Will didn't know if they honestly meant what they were saying, or if each man was just subtly daring the other to throw the first punch. Either way, Will had a sense of something huge and terrible looming over the entire nation. Folks were living through times that would one day be regarded as historic, he figured.

Then, as so often happens, for Will Brannon and his family real life got in the way of history.

• • •

MAC WAS restless. The night was warm, and the faint breeze that gently stirred the curtains in the room he shared with Will didn't do much to cool things off. Will was sleeping soundly. He didn't budge as Mac slid out of bed and walked softly to the window.

He pulled back the curtain that was trimmed with the Irish lace his mother loved so much. From the second floor of the Brannon farmhouse, Mac could see the horse barn opposite and also had a fairly good view of the fields and pastures beyond. He and his brothers had done a lot of work in those fields in the past few weeks, plowing and planting and cultivating. There was a lot of work yet to be done, all of it made harder by the need to stay on the alert for any trouble from the Fogartys. Mac feared that he was already growing accustomed to not worrying about the threat anymore. It would be easy to let his guard down. The same was true of Henry. Luckily, they had Titus around, and Titus was naturally suspicious of everybody . . . except Polly Ebersole and, by extension, her father.

Mac leaned forward, his hands resting on the window sill. The breeze blowing in around him freshened a little and grew stronger. He took a deep breath, relishing the coolness of the air against his face.

Somewhere in the distance, a horse whinnied.

There was nothing unusual about the sound other than the fact that it sounded like a challenge to someone. Mac stiffened when he heard it. The horses were all in the barn for the night, not running loose in the pasture. He turned his head slowly, narrowed his eyes, squinted into the darkness.

He couldn't see anything, but he heard the whinny again, almost as if it was calling to him. In his mind's eye, he saw the silver-gray stallion rearing up on its hind legs, hooves pawing at the air as it trumpeted another chorus into the night.

Mac's jaw clamped tight. That horse was out there somewhere. Damned if it wasn't.

He swung around toward the bed and thought about waking Will, then discarded the idea. It wasn't that he distrusted his older brother; he trusted Will more than any other man on earth. It was just that the stallion was calling to *him*.

And Mac was going to answer.

He pulled on a pair of pants over his long underwear and reached for his boots, carrying them with him as he slipped out of the room and headed downstairs. He stayed close to the edge of the steps so they wouldn't squeak. His mother was a light sleeper, and if she heard somebody walking around the house at this hour of the night, she would certainly raise a commotion. Once he was downstairs, Mac stepped out onto the porch, then sat down on the porch steps to put his boots on.

He listened hard while he was sitting there, listened for the stallion's whinny. He didn't hear it again, but that didn't matter. He knew the horse was out there. He had heard it, and the sound was unmistakable.

It had seemed that the stallion would never come back, but now it had, and Mac didn't intend for it to get away again. Somehow, he was going to lay hands on it this time.

He stood up and headed for the pasture, intending to skirt wide around the barn.

What made him pause again was not a sound this time but a smell instead. It was a sharp, biting scent, and it took Mac only a second to identify it as coal oil. A moment later he heard a faint murmur of voices. Frowning in puzzlement, he turned toward the barn, because that was where both the voices and the smell of coal oil seemed to be coming from.

Mac wasn't trying to move particularly quietly, and he was rounding the corner of the barn before it occurred to him that he ought to be careful. As that thought went through his head, he spotted movement at the rear corner of the barn. The smell of coal oil was stronger, and suddenly he realized what was going on and who was more than likely responsible for it.

The Fogartys were getting ready to burn down the barn.

Mac was about to back up out of sight and hurry to the house to raise the alarm. Before he could move, though, one of the shadowy figures at the rear of the barn exclaimed, "Hey! Look there!"

"Damn it!" snapped the other man.

Mac's instincts jerked him backward even as the second man hurriedly raised an arm. The gun in the man's hand roared as orange flame leaped from the muzzle. Mac was moving backward so fast that he stumbled and fell. At least, he hoped he had fallen. He hadn't felt the impact of a bullet, but he didn't know if that meant anything or not. Was it possible to be shot without knowing it?

The next moment, before the echo of the gunshot had a chance to fade away, a loud *whoosh!* sounded. Instantly, there was an orange glare in the sky above the rear of the barn. The two men had set the oil-soaked wood on fire, Mac realized as he pushed himself to his feet. His first impulse was to run to the back of the barn to see how bad the blaze was, but he knew if he did that, he would be running right into the gunsights of the two men. Instead he turned and dashed toward the front doors of the barn, yelling, "Fire! Fire!" in the direction of the house.

There were quite a few horses in the barn, and Mac didn't intend to let them perish in the conflagration. He unlatched the big double doors and threw them open, then ran down the broad center aisle, opening the gate on each stall as he passed it. The rear wall was fully ablaze, and tongues of flame were already darting hungrily toward the roof. The way the wall had been soaked in oil, there was no chance of extinguishing the fire. The barn was going to be lost.

But not the horses. Not if Mac had anything to say about it. He had completely forgotten about the Fogartys in his concern for the horses.

Thick, choking smoke rolled through the barn. The horses were frantic, and as Mac opened each stall, the occupants galloped out and headed for the open doors. As Mac threw back one of the stall gates, he remembered what had summoned him outside tonight: the call of the silver-gray stallion. With the mares loose, they might answer that call.

Better that the stallion steal every horse they had than that they should suffer the horrible fate of burning alive, Mac thought. He would gladly lose all of them if it meant saving their lives.

Two more stalls to go, one on each side of the aisle. They were the closest to the fire, and waves of heat slammed into Mac like giant fists. He could smell the stench of his own hair being singed off. Wracking coughs made him stumble. He wondered if it had been like this for Will during that fire in the brush thicket. It was appropriate that the Fogartys liked to fight their battles with fire, since in Mac's opinion they were no better than fiends from the pits of hell.

He grasped the latch on the next-to-last stall, pulled it back, threw the door open. As the horse inside bolted, Mac turned shakily toward the final stall. He was dizzy from the heat and smoke, and he had to hang on to the latch for a precious few seconds to keep from falling. Sparks fell around him like rain. The roof was burning above his head.

Somehow he fumbled the latch open and grabbed the top of the gate, letting his own weight swing it open as he sagged toward the ground. The last of the horses galloped frantically up the aisle and out of the barn to safety. Mac smiled a little as he watched it go, then another coughing fit made him lose his grip on the stall gate. He doubled over, vaguely aware that he was toppling off his feet. He landed on the hard-packed dirt of the barn floor and curled up there as he continued to cough. Smoke filled his lungs.

He wasn't going to make it out of the fire. He knew that, and though he was angry that the Fogartys had succeeded in killing him, he was glad that all the horses in the barn had escaped.

Abruptly, he felt himself grabbed and lifted by strong hands. "Wha—" he managed to gasp before another fit of coughing overwhelmed him. In that brief instant, however, he caught a glimpse of Will's face and knew that his brother was picking him up. He wanted to tell Will to leave him and get out of the barn before the roof collapsed, but the muscles of his throat wouldn't work. They were paralyzed by the smoke.

Mac was only half-conscious, but he was aware that Will had slung him over his shoulders and was carrying him out. A huge crashing filled the night as Will lunged forward. Titus and Henry told Mac later how the roof of the barn had come down just as Will staggered out into the night with Mac draped over his shoulders.

All Mac knew at the moment was that fresh air was suddenly flowing back into his lungs. In fact, it wasn't all that fresh since it still carried ashes and smoke, but compared to the choking clouds inside the barn, it tasted sweet to Mac. He drank in the air, still gasping and coughing but knowing now that he might not die tonight after all.

Titus and Henry caught him as he slid from Will's shoulders. They lowered him gently to the ground. Mac heard Will order, "Get some water."

Mac raised his head and rasped, "T-too late. Can't save . . . barn . . ."

"I know that," Will told him as he knelt beside him. "The water's for you, not the barn."

Mac reached up and clutched Will's arm. "F-Fogartys!" he hissed. "Started . . . fire . . ."

In the hellish red glow from the burning barn, Will's face hardened into grim lines. He asked, "The Fogartys started this?"

Mac nodded weakly.

"Where are they now?"

Mac could only shake his head. "Don't . . . know. They took a . . . shot at me . . . then I ran into . . . the barn. Had to . . . let the horses . . . loose . . ."

Henry came running up with a dipper full of water. Will turned to Titus, "Help him sit up." Titus moved in and took Will's place next to Mac, putting an arm around his shoulders and carefully lifting him. Henry held the dipper to Mac's mouth while he drank. The cool water soothed his throat.

While Titus and Henry were tending to Mac, Will hurried around the burning barn. Nearly the whole structure was aflame now. Will knew he needed to get his brothers formed into a bucket brigade so that they could wet down the area around the barn and keep the fire from spreading, but it was too dangerous for them to be out in the open like that if the Fogartys were still around. Will was unarmed, but as angry as he was, he was ready to take on George and Ransom with his bare hands if he came across them.

There was no sign of the Fogartys, and the burning barn lit up the area for almost a hundred yards all around it. Will found fresh horse droppings in a small clump of trees not far from the rear of the barn. That was where George and Ransom had left their mounts, he figured, and once the fire was burning strongly, they had come back here and ridden off.

That didn't mean they were gone, though. They might still be out there somewhere in the darkness. He might be filling their rifle sights right this very minute. But there hadn't been any shots after the first one. If the Fogartys wanted to kill all four of the Brannon brothers, they'd had their chance before Will and Titus and Henry knew that the fire was anything more than an accident.

The blaze was just the opening move in a chess game of revenge, Will sensed. He turned and ran back to the front of the barn to find that Titus and Henry had gotten Mac on his feet and half-carried him over to the house. Mac was sitting on the top porch step with his mother and sister fussing over him. Titus and Henry were already filling buckets at the well, and Will joined them.

The next few minutes were hectic as the three uninjured brothers raced back and forth between the well and the barn, flinging their buckets of water on the corrals and the hog pens and the open areas around the barn where grass grew. When Will was satisfied that they had the surroundings sufficiently doused, he and Titus and Henry switched to the barn itself, throwing bucket after bucket of water into the flames. Their efforts didn't accomplish much—the barn was beyond saving— but Will wanted the fire to burn itself out as soon as possible, just to stop the threat of its spreading.

Later, it was a wet, bedraggled, soot-covered bunch that sat on the porch of the farmhouse and watched the last of the smoldering embers collapse on themselves. Tendrils of smoke continued to rise from a dozen places in the ruin of the barn.

Mac was still coughing from time to time, but he was breathing easier now. In a hoarse voice, he asked, "What happened to all the horses? Where did they go?"

"They were mighty spooked when they ran out of there," said Will. "They probably didn't stop running for a while.

We'll have to get out in the morning and start rounding them up." He paused, then went on, "That's how we knew somebody was in there, the way those horses were running out. Somebody had to be letting them loose from their stalls, and since you were the only one who wasn't around, we figured it had to be you."

"So you came in to get me," Mac said.

Will shrugged his broad shoulders. "I wasn't going to stand around and let my brother burn up along with the barn."

"Thanks," Mac said, and Will nodded. Nothing more was said between the brothers, but nothing else needed to be.

"You still sure you don't want me to go after the Fogartys, Will?" asked Titus.

Before Will could answer, Abigail interrupted, "What do you mean by that, Titus?"

"I just figure it's time we put a stop to this."

"Not by breaking the law," Will warned. "It's my job to bring them in, not yours, Titus."

"Besides," Abigail protested, "having one person with blood on his hands in the family is enough."

Titus turned toward her and snapped, "Blast it, Ma, they burned down the barn! How much do you figure we have to let them get away with?"

"The Good Book says to turn the other cheek."

"It also says an eye for an eye and a tooth for a tooth," Titus retorted.

"'Vengeance is mine, sayeth the Lord.'"

"'If you wrong us, shall we not revenge?' *The Merchant of Venice*, act three, scene one." Henry smiled with pride at remembering the quote. His smile disappeared as Abigail frowned at him.

"Don't go quoting that man to me," she decreed. "I listened to your father do it for years, and I don't have to stand for it now."

Crestfallen, Henry nodded. "Sorry, Ma."

"The Fogartys will make a mistake sooner or later," Will predicted. "Then I'll bring them in and put them behind bars, where they belong. It'll be up to a judge and jury to say whether or not they hang."

"I'd bet on the gallows," Titus remarked dryly.

Mac coughed again. "Right now," he said when the spasm subsided, "I just want to get some sleep."

"That's what we all need," Abigail declared. "Come along. Up to bed, all of you."

"I'm staying down here to keep an eye on what's left of the barn," Will said. "I don't want that fire starting up again."

Abigail looked as if she wanted to argue, but after a moment she just nodded. "All right."

Will stayed where he was, sitting on the top step, while the others went inside. His forehead wrinkled in a frown as he stared across the big yard at what was left of the barn. Mac had come awfully close to dying in there tonight, and none of it would have happened if Will hadn't killed Joe Fogarty. Sure, the Fogartys and the Brannons had a deep and abiding mutual dislike, but it probably never would have come to barn-burning.

And there was no telling what George had in mind for the next step. Whatever it was, it wouldn't be good, Will knew that.

A half-hour after the others had gone inside, a footstep behind him made Will turn his head and look back. Mac stood there, hands tucked into the rear pockets of his trousers, and he too wore a bleak expression as he and Will contemplated the destroyed barn.

"Thought you wanted to sleep," Will said.

"I do, but I got to feeling restless." Mac's voice was scratchy, and Will knew it had to hurt for him to talk. Will remembered that feeling all too well from his own experience with eating a lot of smoke. Mac went on, "You know how I came to be out here so I could stumble over the Fogartys?"

Will shook his head. "No, not really. Come to think of it, what *were* you doing up and about?"

"I was on my way out to the pasture," Mac said. "The stallion was back, Will."

Will looked up at his brother. "The stallion?" he repeated. "You mean that horse we saw a couple of months ago? That big silver-gray brute?"

"That's the one," Mac replied with a nod. "I was awake, and I heard him calling out to me."

Will's frown deepened. "You're sure?"

"I'm certain. So we may not have any mares to round up. He may have run off with all of them."

"But you didn't actually *see* the horse?"

"Damn it, Will, I know what I heard!" Mac sat down beside his brother on the top step and stared out at the darkness. "No, I didn't see the stallion," he admitted after a moment. "That doesn't mean he wasn't there. I'm not imagining phantom horses."

"Of course not," Will agreed quickly. "It's just strange the way he turned up, tonight of all nights."

Mac nodded slowly. "Yeah, that's what I thought. But I got to wondering if maybe he was trying to . . . to warn us."

"About the Fogartys, you mean?"

"That's right." Mac gave a short, humorless laugh. "I know, that sounds more insane than ever. But maybe he sensed somehow that something was wrong. Maybe he smelled the coal oil and knew what the Fogartys were up to. Maybe it wasn't us he was trying to save at all, but those mares instead."

Will grunted and conceded, "Could be, I suppose."

Mac laughed again. "You think I've lost my mind."

"Nope. Just because what you're saying never would have occurred to me doesn't mean you're not right, Mac. I just don't know. You've always been the one to think about things like that more than I have."

"Well, I don't reckon we'll ever know who's right. I'm just glad nobody was hurt. We can always rebuild the barn."

"Damn right we'll rebuild the barn. I'm not going to let the Fogartys get the best of this family." Will put a hand on Mac's shoulder. "Now, you'd better go back up and try again to get some sleep. Tomorrow'll be a busy day."

"You're right." Mac got to his feet. "Good night, Will."

"Good night."

Mac went back in the house. Will stayed where he was, looking at the barn and thinking about what his brother had said. After a few minutes he muttered, "Next thing you know, Mac'll be saying that horse isn't even real, that it's some sort of ghost horse."

That thought kept him frowning for quite a while.

Chapter Twelve

FINALLY CONVINCED that the fire was out for good, Will went inside shortly before dawn and slept for a little while. He was up early, though, the inside of his eye sockets feeling as if they were coated with coarse sand. He intended to pitch in on the cleaning up with the rest of the family, no matter how tired he was.

Abigail took charge, parceling out the chores. "Titus, Henry, the two of you start clearing away that debris. Be careful, some of it may still be hot. Cordelia and I will help as much as we can. Will, you and Mac had better go see if you can find any of our horses."

"Yes, ma'am," Will said, feeling grateful that he wouldn't have to shovel ashes and haul away burned timbers and then feeling a brief twinge of guilt at the gratitude he felt.

"And when you have the horses," Abigail called after them, "one of you should ride into town and talk to Mr. Timmons at the sawmill. We'll need lumber to rebuild the barn."

"Can we afford to rebuild?" Mac asked as he and Will started walking down the lane.

Will nodded. "I reckon so. Our credit's good at the bank. We can get a loan to buy the lumber."

"We could always cut down some trees and use the logs to build," Mac pointed out. "That's the way folks did it when they first settled in these parts."

"Well, if it comes to that, that's what we'll do."

They kept a sharp eye out for the horses, watching on both sides of the path. The first movement they saw, however, was on the lane itself, and it didn't come from stray horses. Both Will and Mac spotted the wagon rolling toward them, pulled by a team of mules.

"That looks like Jacob Taylor's wagon," Will said.

"And that's Jacob driving, with those boys of his piled in the back."

Taylor was the closest neighbor to the Brannons, owning the adjacent farm. He had three sons, all of them in their teens. Taylor pulled the mules to a stop as he drove up to Will and Mac. He lifted a hand in greeting.

"Mornin', boys," he said. "I reckon you must've had some trouble last night."

"How'd you know?" asked Will.

"Saw the glow in the sky. A bad fire, was it?"

"Bad enough," Will confirmed with a nod. "It burned down our horse barn."

"Better that than your house. Anybody hurt?"

"Not too bad. Mac here breathed a lot of smoke and got his eyebrows singed off, but he got all the horses out. We're looking for them now, because they ran off."

Taylor nodded sagely. "Horses'll do that if they get a whiff of smoke. We saw some loose horses back up the road a ways but didn't know they were yours."

"Much obliged for the information."

"You go ahead," Taylor told them. "The boys an' me will give y'all a hand. I suspect your brothers have started cleanin' up the mess?"

"That's right, and I reckon they'll be mighty grateful for any help you can give them, Jacob."

Taylor lifted the reins, then added, "When you get ready to raise your new barn, just spread the word. There's plenty of folks around here who'll be glad to help out, Will. We all appreciate what you've done for us as sheriff." The farmer grinned. "And there hasn't been a good ol' fashioned barn-raisin' around here for too long a spell."

Will and Mac grinned and waved as Taylor drove on toward the Brannon farm. "A barn-raising sounds like a good idea," Mac said. "Folks could sure use something to get their minds off the trouble with the North for a while."

Will nodded. Ever since he'd heard Mac's shouts of alarm the night before, he hadn't even thought about the standoff at Fort Sumter. Now Mac's words were a reminder that life went on, both in large and in small events. Barn-burnings and impending wars were all just part of the picture.

"Come on," he said. "Let's go find those horses Taylor told us about."

• • •

THE NEXT few days were busy ones for all the Brannons. Will and Mac found several of the horses and drove them back to the farm. Then, riding bareback, Mac headed out to look for more horses while Will rode into Culpeper to see Timmons at the sawmill. Word spread quickly of the disaster that had befallen the Brannons, and people began showing up at the farm to lend a hand. Abigail and Cordelia spent most of their time cooking for the volunteers. Within a couple of days, all the burned debris had been cleared away. Mac had found all but three of the horses and herded them back. For the time being, they were kept in one of the corrals. The weather was pleasant, and there was no reason the horses couldn't stay outside until the new barn was built.

That project got underway with a minimum of delay. Wagons loaded with planks from Timmons's sawmill arrived early one morning, and the drivers began unloading the lumber. The next day was Saturday, and then would be the barn-raising. Work would start early in the morning and go on all day until the new structure was complete. That would be followed by a picnic and dancing and fiddle-playing. The settlers weren't going to pass up an opportunity to turn this into a social occasion. Hard work was nearly always followed by hard play.

Will had asked around, and no one had seen the Fogartys in the vicinity of the farm on the night of the fire. He was convinced they were to blame for it, anyway. No one else had any reason to want to hurt his family. As soon as the new horse barn was up, he had to return to the task of trying to root them out, but that wouldn't be easy. As long as they could retreat to their hideout in the Blue Ridge country, Will would have a hard time tracking them down.

The morning of the barn-raising dawned with high, thin clouds in the sky. The weather would be warm, Will could tell as soon as he stepped out on the porch. Behind him, the household was slowly coming awake. Abigail was already in the kitchen starting breakfast. Mac, Titus, Henry, and Cordelia were getting dressed before stumbling down the stairs.

Will stretched and started out to the remaining barn, the one where the cows were kept. Barn-raising or not, there was milking to be done. Will figured he could finish before breakfast was ready.

A short while later, as Will was coming out of the barn carrying a couple of buckets full of warm, foamy milk, Cordelia stepped out of the house with a basket in her hand. "Good morning," she called to him as she came down the steps and turned toward the chicken house. Abigail had sent her to gather the eggs, Will knew.

He said, "Good morning," and smiled at his little sister, and as he looked past her he saw the early morning sun reflect reddishly from something in a small clump of trees beside the lane, about halfway between the house and the road. Without even thinking about what he was doing, Will dropped the buckets of milk and threw himself forward, crossing the yard toward Cordelia as fast as he could. He launched himself into the air and tackled her, causing her to cry out sharply in surprise and alarm. The two of them hit the ground hard, Will being careful not to land on top of her so that the fall wouldn't hurt her any more than was necessary.

Breathless, Cordelia tried to push herself upright as she gasped, "Will . . . wha . . . what are you—"

He caught hold of her shoulder and held her down. "Don't get up," he hissed. "Stay as low as possible."

"Will, what's wrong? I'm scared—"

Heavy footsteps sounded on the porch. "What in the world?" Mac exclaimed. "We heard Cordelia yell—"

"Get back inside!" Will ordered.

He heard hoofbeats in the distance and raised his head enough to see two figures on horseback riding quickly away from the trees where he had spotted the reflection. They were moving too fast and were too far away for him to catch them, even if he had run to the corrals immediately and jumped on a horse. As the two riders turned onto the road and quickly vanished in the early morning haze, Will sat up and said, "It's all right now."

"Whatever possessed you to jump on me like that, Will Brannon?" Cordelia asked angrily. "You came at me like some sort of crazy man!"

Will ignored her for the moment and turned to call toward the house, "You and the others can come out now, Mac."

Mac stepped onto the porch again, followed by the rest of the family. With a puzzled frown on his face, Mac asked, "Why are you and Cordelia rolling around in the dirt, Will?"

"Because somebody was getting ready to take a shot at us," Will replied grimly.

"A shot!" exclaimed Titus. "How do you know?"

"Saw the sun glint off a gun barrel down yonder in that clump of trees beside the lane," Will said.

Without a word, Titus ducked back into the house. Will knew he was going to fetch the Sharps. Will stood up and gave Cordelia a hand, lifting her back onto her feet. She brushed herself off, still looking a little angry at him.

Abigail wasn't happy, either. "How do you know what you saw was a gun, Will?" she asked.

Will grunted. "I reckon I don't. The sun could have been shining on any piece of metal. But every time I've seen something like that in the past, it's been a gun. Besides, after I got Cordelia down out of the line of fire, whoever was hiding down there rode off in a hurry. I saw them."

"Could you tell who it was?" asked Mac.

Will shook his head, "No, but it was two men. I saw that much. You know as well as I do who they had to be."

"George and Ranse Fogarty," breathed Mac.

"Those Fogarty boys have always been heathens," Abigail snapped. "Their folks should have tanned their hides for them when they were young and given 'em a good dose of the Scriptures. Then maybe they wouldn't have turned out the way they did."

Will didn't agree with his mother about everything, but on the subject of the Fogartys, he figured she was probably right.

Titus came out of the house a moment later, carrying the Sharps just as Will had thought he would be. Looped over Titus's other arm, however, was Will's coiled shell belt, attached to the holster that held his Colt Navy.

"Here you go, Will," said Titus as he held out the gunbelt to his oldest brother. "We'd better go take a look."

"Breakfast is almost ready," Abigail stated with a warning stare at Will.

He hesitated, reflecting that only his mother would think breakfast was more important than a possible ambush attempt that had gone awry. He reached out and took the belt from Titus, buckled it on.

"It'll keep for a few minutes, but the rest of you go ahead," Will said. "Come on, Titus. Let's get some horses."

All the saddles had been in the tackroom in the horse barn, so they had burned up in the fire. But in the few days since, Mac had fashioned several bits and harnesses, so Will and Titus used those. They rode bareback out of the yard, and as they did, Will was well aware that their mother was still standing on the porch, arms folded in disapproval as she watched them go.

In the light of the rising sun, Titus easily spotted the tracks of horses under the trees. "Two of 'em, just like you said," he told Will. He pointed, "Look at how jumbled they are. Those horses were standing here for a good long while, I reckon since well before sunup."

"I don't much like the idea of George and Ransom watching the place like that," said Will.

"Neither do I." Titus jerked his chin toward the lane. "They rode off in a hurry. That's like you said, too. Did you hear any shots?"

Will shook his head. "Nope. I don't think they ever fired a gun at us. But they might have, if I hadn't spotted them."

"Could be," Titus said as he slowly nodded his head. "Or maybe they *wanted* you to see them. If I was tryin' to get back at somebody, I'd want them to know that I was around. I'd want them worried about me."

"Because worried folks sometimes make mistakes."

Titus nodded again. "That's right."

"Well, if it's a mistake to be worried about the Fogartys, I can't help it. I know that sooner or later they're going to come after us again."

"We've got to be ready."

"We will be," Will agreed.

And yet, how could a person stay on guard twenty-four hours a day? If somebody was bound and determined to try to kill somebody else, it was next to impossible to keep them from trying sooner or later.

There was no getting around it, Will thought. As long as the Fogartys wanted him dead, the whole family was in danger.

• • •

BREAKFAST WASN'T too cold by the time Will and Titus got back to the house. He and Titus ate hungrily, and before they finished, the first of the family's friends and neighbors began to arrive for the barn-raising.

The sounds of hammering filled the air as a couple of dozen men began framing the new barn. These men hadn't come by themselves; they had brought their families with them, so the house was full of women, all of them having brought covered baskets of food with them. Kids ran around playing, getting underfoot. Abigail placed Cordelia in charge of keeping up with the youngsters, so she had her hands full, perhaps more so than the men who were building the barn. As Will toted lumber and hammered boards into place, he was glad he didn't have the chore of riding herd on all those young'uns.

Tables brought from the house were set up in the yard, and bowls and platters of food were piled high on the gingham cloths that covered them. Ham hocks, steaks, fried chicken, black-eyed peas, greens, corn, potatoes, string beans, grits, gravy, biscuits, apple pies, peach pies, cherry pies, fritters, corn pone and johnnycake, pitchers of buttermilk and lemonade, pots of coffee . . . the tables practically groaned under their load.

By midday the frame was up and the walls were partially done. As Abigail used a spoon to bang on an empty pot, the men all put their hammers and saws aside and descended on the tables like a plague of locusts. As soon as the workers had loaded their plates with food, the children were turned loose on the feast, and finally the ladies who had prepared all of it served themselves. For a while, hardly anything was heard except the rattle of cutlery against plates and an occasional long sigh of contentment.

Will found himself sitting on the top porch step between Jacob Taylor and a man named Hindman. After sopping up the last of the gravy on his plate with a biscuit and popping it into his mouth, Hindman asked, "How long you think it'll be before we start shootin' at those damn Yankees on Sumter?"

"Can't be soon enough to suit me," observed Taylor. "It's past time we taught them meddlin' Yankees that they can't expect to run the whole blasted country. What kind of country would that be, anyway? What do you think, Will?"

"Well, my job as sheriff is stopping trouble, not starting it, so it'd be all right with me if those Federal troops would just go back where they came from," Will replied. "Then there wouldn't have to be any fighting."

Both Taylor and Hindman looked at him in surprise. "No fightin'?" Hindman questioned. He shook his head. "It's 'way too late for that, Will. There's been too many harsh words spoken, too many slaps in the face of the Confederacy." He pointed his fork at Will. "Mark my words, there's goin' to be bloodshed. Ain't no other way."

Will was afraid Hindman was right, though he would have preferred otherwise. The highhanded tactics of the northerners had ruffled too many feathers. The honor of the South demanded that all the insults not be forgiven too easily.

As soon as the meal was over, the work of the barn-raising got back underway. Men began hammering and sawing again, while the women cleaned up after the big dinner. Children, tired from a morning of play and stuffed full of food, found themselves too drowsy to stay awake and found places to curl up for a nap.

By the middle of the afternoon, the walls were substantially complete and the rafters were being lifted into place. The thick beams that formed the rafters were heavy, and it took several men, all grunting with effort, to hoist them into place. Will was one of the men holding the rafters steady while they were nailed down, and his muscles trembled slightly from the strain. When that part of the job was finally done, he heaved a sigh of relief.

Roofers got started on that chore, while other men began constructing the stalls inside the barn. The women were able to sit and talk for a few minutes, and youngsters woke up from their naps refreshed and ready for another round of roughhousing. All in all, it was a busy but pleasant day, and Will was glad he and his family had friends and neighbors who were willing to pitch in and help in time of need. Of course, he and his brothers and sister and mother would have done the same if it had been someone else who needed help.

By early evening the construction was still going on, but the end was in sight. Torches and lanterns were lit to give enough light to work by. No one paused for supper. There would be time to eat when the barn was finished. Not only to eat, but to kick up the heels, too. Men would lay down their hammers and saws and pick up fiddles and dulcimers and mouth harps. By the time the barn was done, people would be ready to celebrate.

Perched on top of the roof, Will nailed wooden shingles in place. Beside him, Mac worked on the same task. From time to time, they looked at each other and exchanged weary grins. Finally Mac noted, "Long day."

"Yep," Will agreed with a nod. "But worth it, I reckon."

"No doubt about it."

"Heard a lot of talk about the war."

It was Mac's turn to nod. "Everybody's convinced it's coming, and probably soon. Can't say that I disagree with them, either." He shrugged. "But it won't last long. We'll lick the Yankees in a fight or two, and that'll be the end of it. They'll see they can't push us around and decide to make peace."

"Maybe so." Will paused, then added, "What bothers me is knowing that there's probably a lot of folks up north saying the very same thing about us."

Mac just looked at him for a long moment, then started hammering shingle nails again.

About an hour after sunset, the last nail was pounded into place. The men climbed down the ladders from the roof of the new barn as cheers rose from the people on the ground. Will was the last one down, and he paused on the next-to-the-bottom rung of the ladder and turned so that he could look out over the big crowd assembled in the yard between the house and the barns.

"Everybody listen for a minute!" he called loudly, and gradually the hubbub died down. Will smiled and went on, "I just want to tell all you folks how much we appreciate what you've done here today. You're good friends, each and every one of you, and I want you to know that your kindness won't be forgotten."

"Aw, stop makin' speeches and come on down off of there, Will," Henry complained. "We want to get to the dancin'!"

Will laughed and waved at the crowd. "Thanks again!" he called, then descended the rest of the way down the ladder.

There was plenty of food left over from the midday picnic. It was brought out again, and once more the gathering fell to eating. Even before everyone had finished eating, though, several men had taken out their fiddles and started resining up their bows. The promise of music revitalized tired muscles, and people found themselves anxious to get up and start moving again.

When Will had cleaned his plate, he set it aside and went looking for his mother. He found Abigail talking to several other women and surprised her by reaching out and taking hold of her hand.

"You're going to dance the first dance with me," Will said.

"I most certainly will not," she replied without hesitation. "I won't deny these other folks their pleasure, but you know that us Baptists don't hold with dancing, Will Brannon."

"One dance won't send your immortal soul to hell, Mama," Will told her as he drew her toward the open area. "Come on."

Abigail protested, but Will stubbornly pulled her with him. As he passed Hindman and two other men holding fiddles, he called out to them, "You ready to strike up a tune, boys?"

"You bet, Will!" Hindman replied as he held up his bow in salute. He tucked the fiddle under his chin and started sawing on the strings with the bow. Will took both of his mother's hands and swung her into a reel.

"I don't know how to do this!" she protested.

"Don't worry," Will assured her. "I do!"

Laughter came from the crowd as they began clapping along with the music. Several more couples started dancing,

192 • *James Reasoner*

including a little boy who was dragged reluctantly into participating by a little girl with a mass of golden curls.

Abigail fell clumsily into the rhythm and seemed to become caught up in the exuberance of the moment. At least, she started smiling a little, Will noticed. He swung her around and around, placing his feet carefully to make up for her lack of knowledge about dancing. She was bound to wonder where he had learned to dance so well, but he would worry about that later. No need to ruin the moment and infuriate her by admitting that he'd been sneaking off to Methodist Church socials for years.

The fiddlers finished the first tune and immediately launched into another, this time a waltz. Will slowed down. Abigail pointed out, "You said the first dance. This is the second one!"

"But it's the first waltz," Will countered.

She rolled her eyes but kept dancing. A moment later, Will saw Cordelia sweep by in the arms of Jacob Taylor's oldest son. She was smiling brilliantly, and the boy was blushing until his face was about as red as the sunrise. Will looked around and saw that Mac and Henry were dancing with neighbor girls, but Titus was sitting on the porch with a frown on his face. Titus probably wasn't going to dance because Polly Ebersole wasn't here, and she was the only girl he was interested in these days. Well, he wasn't hurting anybody but himself by brooding, Will told himself. Titus shouldn't have expected a lady like Polly to come to a country barn-raising like this, even if her father would have allowed it, which was doubtful.

When the waltz was over, Abigail firmly disengaged her hands from Will's. "That's enough," she declared. "If you're bound and determined to keep up this heathen behavior, you go find somebody else to do it with. I'm going to sit down." A smile took any sting out of her words.

"All right, Mama. Thanks for dancing with me."

She sniffed. "I still don't hold with it."

Will turned to look for someone else to dance with. Before he could find anyone, the fiddlers started playing a jig, accompanied this time by a couple of men with mouth harps. Will gave up and stepped over to the side, content to sit this one out. He joined in the clapping with the other spectators as the music grew faster and more frenzied, and so did the actions of the dancers. Henry was in the center of the group, his feet flying as he danced with Hindman's oldest daughter, Rachel. Gradually, the dancers around them drew back to give them more room, then stopped dancing and started clapping, so that eventually Henry and Rachel were the only ones still moving to the music. Henry seemed to be aware that everyone was watching them, and he grinned with pleasure at all the attention.

That was his little brother, Will thought as he continued clapping in time with the music: a pure showoff. Every eye was on Henry, and he loved it, being the center of everyone's attention.

That was where Henry was a moment later when Will heard a faint crack that was almost drowned out by the music and the clapping. Will stiffened as Henry jerked back, then stumbled a couple of steps to the side. He let go of Rachel's hand and fell, a bright crimson flower blooming on his homespun shirt. Rachel stared down at him in horror, then began to scream.

"Get down!" Will bellowed as he threw himself forward toward Henry's fallen form. "Everybody down!"

The Fogartys, thought Will. He had let down his guard, and the Fogartys had finally struck. He should have known better.

He dropped to his knees next to Henry and prayed that the boy was still alive.

Chapter Thirteen

MAC PUSHED his way through the chaos that had suddenly broken out in the yard. Women were screaming, and men were shouting curses and angry questions. Mothers grabbed children and hustled them into the cover of the house and the new barn. Men tried to shield their wives. Mac thought he had heard a shot just before Henry fell, but he couldn't be certain. With all the commotion going on now, he figured a whole army could open fire without his being able to hear it.

Peering anxiously past the confusing jumble of people, Mac spotted Will kneeling next to Henry. Fear for his youngest brother's life burned like fire through Mac's brain. He caught a glimpse of blood on Henry's shirt, then someone got in front of Mac and he couldn't see anymore. Roughly, he shouldered the man aside, hospitality now the furthest thing from his mind.

A moment later, Mac reached Will and Henry. He dropped to his knees on the other side of Henry and lifted his voice over the racket to ask, "Is he alive?"

Will had torn Henry's shirt back, exposing part of Henry's chest. High on the right side, just below the shoulder, was a red-rimmed black hole surrounded by the blood that had poured from it.

"He's alive," said Will. Mac could see that for himself now. He saw Henry's chest rising and falling in a ragged rhythm. Henry was unconscious, and his face was pale from the shock of the bullet and from losing so much blood. But as Mac looked at the wound, he could see that despite being messy, it might not be too serious. If the slug had punched straight through Henry's body without hitting a bone or clipping the top of the right lung, then Henry stood a good chance of recovering.

197

"We've got to get him in the house," Mac said, and Will nodded.

Before either of them could do anything, Titus suddenly burst out of the crowd and cried, "Henry!" He looked frantically at Will and Mac and went on, "Is he all right?"

That was a mighty foolish question under the circumstances, thought Mac, but Titus was too upset to be thinking straight. Mac said, "He's hit, but he's still alive. We're going to take him in the house."

Titus nodded, and Will said, "You get his feet. Mac and I will get his shoulders."

They bent to their task, getting good grips on Henry and lifting him as gently as possible. He let out a groan of pain despite their caution, even though he was still unconscious. Several men, seeing what they were doing, got in front of them and cleared a path to the house.

Abigail and Cordelia were standing on the steps, Cordelia urging her mother to go inside the house in case there was more trouble, but Abigail wouldn't budge. When she saw her sons coming, three of them carrying the fourth one, she cried out, "Henry! Oh, dear God, Henry!"

"He's all right, Mama, at least for now," Mac assured her, but he couldn't tell if his words penetrated her shocked brain. "He's been shot, but he's alive. We're taking him inside."

Henry's arms were hanging limply. Abigail reached down and caught hold of one of his hands, bringing it up and clasping it to her. "Oh, my baby," she wailed. "My poor baby."

Will said quietly, "Cordelia, help Mama inside so we can tend to Henry."

Cordelia was almost as pale as Henry, making the few freckles that were scattered across her face stand out boldly. She took hold of her mother's shoulders and turned her gently but firmly toward the door. "Come on, Mama," she prodded in a low, urgent voice. "We have to let the boys carry Henry inside now so we can take care of him."

Abigail nodded jerkily. "Yes," she agreed. "Take him inside. We have to pray."

Prayer was all well and good, thought Mac, but it was also important that they take a look at that wound and make sure the bullet wasn't still somewhere inside Henry. Once that was done, the wound would have to be cleaned.

Someone else had already thought of the same thing. Jacob Taylor and Bob Hindman both came hurrying up, each of them carrying a jug. Hindman held his up and said, "I know your ma doesn't like whiskey, boys, but it's the best thing in the world for cleanin' out a bullet hole."

"Yeah," added Taylor. "And if you have to dig out that bullet, you'd better give young Henry there a few drinks of it beforehand, too."

Will, Mac, and Titus carried Henry up the steps and across the porch. Will looked back at the two neighbors and said, "Much obliged. Bring those jugs along."

Abigail and Cordelia were waiting inside. Abigail seemed to have composed herself a bit. She directed, "Take him to my bed."

Will headed for the parlor instead. "I don't want to carry him all the way upstairs. Cordelia, get a blanket, and we'll put him on the divan."

"Wait," Mac said. "The table would be better."

Will considered for a second, then nodded and changed directions, heading for the dining room instead. "Get the table cleaned off," he called over his shoulder. "Cordelia, we still need that blanket."

Henry hadn't groaned anymore, but Mac didn't know if that was a good sign or not. Along with his brothers, he carried Henry into the dining room. Some of the neighbor ladies were taking everything off the table, and Cordelia came running downstairs with a folded blanket. She shook it out and draped it over the table, and Will and Mac and Titus gingerly deposited Henry's still unconscious form on it.

"Roll him onto his left side," Will ordered. He stepped back a little as Mac and Titus shifted Henry's position. To his relief, Mac saw a bloodstain on the back of Henry's shirt that matched the one on the front. That meant the bullet had gone all the way through. That was a good thing, he told himself. The bullet had probably done less damage by leaving Henry's body than if it had stayed inside and someone had had to dig it out.

Will took a Barlow knife from his pocket and cut away most of Henry's shirt. Abigail caught her breath as the hole on Henry's back was exposed. It was larger than the one on his chest. She took a deep breath to calm herself and said, "Somebody heat some water. We've got to get all that blood off him."

The blood on the outside wasn't as important as what was inside, Mac thought. He turned to Taylor and Hindman, who had followed them into the dining room. "Give me one of those jugs," he said.

Abigail started to say, "I don't hold with—"

Will interrupted her. "That whiskey is just what he needs right now. Go ahead, Mac."

Mac took the jug from Hindman and poured the fiery stuff over the wounds on Henry's chest and back. Henry stirred a little, indicating the searing pain that the whiskey was inflicting on raw flesh. The liquor puddled under Henry's body, soaking the blanket on which he lay. Abigail stood by and watched, her expression a mixture of disapproval and outright fear for her youngest son's life. After a moment, fear won the battle and disapproval vanished.

Old habits died hard, Mac thought, especially old Baptist habits.

"You ever doctored a gunshot, Mac?" Will asked quietly.

"Nope. I've tended to plenty of horses that've hurt themselves, though."

"I've patched up a few bullet holes, and I reckon we're going about this the right way. I'll still want the doctor from Culpeper to come out here and take a look at him, though."

Mac nodded. "I'll send Titus." He looked around for him and then frowned. Titus was gone.

• • •

WITH THE Sharps held ready across his chest, Titus ran through the night. In addition to the heavy rifle, he carried a pistol tucked behind his belt. He wasn't much good with a handgun, especially compared to somebody like Will, but if he caught up with whoever had shot Henry, he might need more than one shot. Titus could fire the Sharps, reload, and fire it again just about as fast or faster than anybody else in these parts, but cocking the hammer of a revolver and pulling the trigger were even faster.

It had taken him only a moment to look at Henry's body and calculate the direction from which the shot had been fired. The bushwhacker had been hidden somewhere along the lane, probably in the same clump of trees where the Fogartys had been lurking early that morning.

They should have posted someone there, he thought bitterly. He and Will could have taken turns. Hell, it had been only a little over twelve hours since Will had seen the Fogartys in those trees.

And yet, after a long day of hard work, followed by plenty of food and music and dancing, folks had let their guard down, him included. He had never dreamed that the Fogartys would try anything with so many people around.

That had been one hell of a shot, too, to hit Henry like that with all those people around him. The gunman had had to aim by the flickering, uncertain light of lanterns and torches. True, Henry and Rachel had been out in the open to a certain extent, but the spectators had formed a large ring around them.

Maybe the gunman hadn't cared *who* he hit. If he had killed one of the Brannons' guests, that would have been just as bad as hitting one of the family. Maybe, in a way, even worse.

But regardless of who the real target had been, or if there had even been a target, Henry was wounded, and Titus meant to see that the man or men responsible paid for what they had done. That was why, as soon as Henry was safely in the house, Titus had grabbed his rifle and started off down the lane.

He should have gotten himself a horse, he thought as he approached the trees. If the Fogartys had taken off as soon as the shot was fired, they were long gone by now.

Or maybe they were still there, and Titus was running right into their sights. He veered off the path and bellied down on the ground, aiming the Sharps at the looming patch of darkness that was the clump of trees.

"Fogarty!" Titus yelled. "George and Ransom Fogarty! I know you're in there! Show yourselves, damn it!"

He didn't really expect any response and didn't get one. The grove was dark and quiet.

The same couldn't be said for the area around the house and the barns. It was still ablaze with light, and Titus could hear folks clamoring loudly. As the noise abruptly got louder, he twisted his head and looked back over his shoulder to see two wagons coming down the lane toward him. They were packed with men, several of them holding torches aloft. Titus also saw quite a few shotguns and rifles in evidence.

His brother Will was at the reins of the lead wagon. Titus pushed himself to his feet and stepped out into the lane as Will brought the wagon to a halt. "Blast it, Titus, what are you doing out here alone?" Will demanded.

"I was looking for whoever shot Henry," replied Titus. "Don't know if I would have found them or not, but I damn sure won't now that you've brought this parade out here, Will."

"You had no business coming after them by yourself." Will handed the reins to another man and then jumped down from the wagon. "See or hear anything?"

Titus shook his head. "Nothing. I reckon they must've taken off as soon as one of 'em fired that shot."

"Were they hidden in the trees again?"

"That's what I figure. Get one of those torches, and we'll go take a look."

Will did as Titus suggested and took one of the torches from a man in the wagon. Followed by several other men, they walked into the grove of trees, and Titus studied the ground in the light cast by the torch Will carried.

"Fresh tracks," he grunted, pointing at the ground. "And I reckon it was the same two men as were out here this morning. Look at that nick in one of the shoes. You can see it in the older tracks, too."

One of the men who had followed them into the trees, a blacksmith named Olson, said excitedly, "I know that shoe. I put that shoe on Ranse Fogarty's horse not six weeks ago!"

Will looked intently at the burly man. "You sure about that?"

Olson nodded. "Dang right I'm sure. I got a good memory for things like that."

Will and Titus exchanged a glance. "I reckon that's more proof than we've ever had up to now," Will observed. "It was the Fogartys, all right."

"We knew that," Titus said scornfully. "You keep goin' on about proof, Will, but everybody here knows what sort the Fogartys are."

"We sure do, Will," echoed Jacob Taylor. "They got to be hunted down and shot like mad dogs, or else you and your family will never be safe."

"They've been a thorn in the side of this county for a long time," added Hindman.

Will sighed. "You're right, all of you."

Titus hefted his Sharps and declared, "I'll start tracking them soon as it's light, whether you deputize me or not, Will. Might as well make it legal."

"Might as well. Let's go back to the house, and I'll swear you in."

"How's Henry?" Titus asked as he climbed up into the first wagon with Will.

"I left him with Mac and Cordelia. I think he's going to be all right. But he'll be laid up and sore as blazes for a while."

"Time he's on his feet again I intend to have both Fogarty boys under the ground," Titus vowed grimly.

Will nodded. He believed his brother, and if anyone was capable of carrying through on such a promise, it was Titus.

But after George and Ransom were dead, what about the Paynter boys? What about Israel Quinn, and all the other kin the Fogartys had around here? If they came after the Brannons, then he and Titus would just have to kill them, too, Will supposed bleakly.

Or else he and Titus would be killed, in which case it would be up to Mac and Henry to even the score and kill some more of the Fogartys' relatives.

And around and around it would go, with more blood being spilled on every turn . . .

Will and Titus came into the dining room just as Cordelia finished tying the last bandage around Henry's chest. The upper part of his torso was almost completely swathed in bandages. His left shoulder was bare, but that was all.

"He's still out?" asked Will.

"He woke up for a minute," said Mac. "Just long enough to ask what happened, and to tell us it hurt like the devil."

"That's not what he said," Abigail commented from the foot of the table. "But I'm sure the Lord will forgive him for his profanity. Henry was out of his head from the pain."

"We can take him upstairs now," Will said. "He'll need plenty of rest."

This time, Taylor, Hindman, and Olson moved in to help Will, Mac, and Titus carry Henry, and with that many willing hands, Henry was hardly jolted at all as he was taken upstairs to his own bed. Mac tucked him in, and Titus suggested "I can sleep in the barn tonight."

"Might be a good idea," Will agreed. "I may join you. We can keep an eye on the place better from that hayloft."

Titus nodded, and the men filed out of the room, leaving Cordelia behind. She moved a ladderback chair over by the bed and said, "I'll sit with him for a while, just in case he wakes up and needs anything."

Will was the last one out. He gave his sister a weary smile of gratitude, then followed the other men downstairs. Mac was telling Abigail, "He's resting comfortably, Mama. We've done all we can for him now. I'll ride into Culpeper first thing in the morning and fetch Doc Tate out here to have a look at him and make sure we did everything all right."

"I suppose that's all we can do except pray." Abigail looked around at her sons. "I expect you all will be doing that shortly."

"Soon as we see everybody off," Will assured her.

He and Mac and Titus stepped out onto the porch with Taylor, Hindman, and Olson. The big blacksmith commented, "I reckon the partyin' is over."

That was true enough, Will saw. People were loading up in their wagons and heading home. As they passed the porch, they called out their farewells to the Brannon brothers and their hopes that Henry would be all right. Will smiled solemnly, nodded, and waved to them as they left.

Olson trudged back to his wagon, followed by Taylor, who gathered up his sons as he went. Hindman was left on the porch with Will, Mac, and Titus, and he sighed and said, "You know, my girl Rachel was just a couple of feet from Henry when he was hit. That bullet could have got her just as easy."

"I'm sorry, Bob," Will said. "I'm sure glad Rachel's all right."

"She will be, I reckon," replied Hindman. "She was still shakin' and cryin' a little while ago. My missus was tryin' to make her feel better." He looked over at Will. "Understand, I ain't blamin' you for anything that happened, Will, but—"

"But if I hadn't killed Joe Fogarty, George and Ransom wouldn't be after me, and nobody would have gotten hurt tonight." Will's face was etched in tight, grim lines. "That's what you mean, isn't it, Bob?"

Hindman looked embarrassed and defiant at the same time. "There's some truth to that," he agreed. "But you were only doin' your job when you tried to arrest Joe Fogarty. You gave him a chance to come along peaceably, too. I heard the story a dozen times from Davis."

"You and Taylor both said the Fogartys need to be hunted down," Will pointed out.

"I know, but . . . ," Hindman scrubbed a hand over his face. "But my girl was right there, Will. Right there next to Henry."

Will nodded. He understood why Hindman felt as he did. It was one thing to recognize that the Fogartys were thieves and killers and all-around troublemakers and ought to be dealt with. It was another thing when a loved one was caught, or even nearly caught, in the resulting violence.

Will put a hand on Hindman's shoulder and said, "Thanks for all your help, Bob. You collect your family and go on home now. Sorry about the way things turned out."

"I reckon we all are, Will. I reckon we all are." Hindman tried to smile as he started down the steps from the porch. "But you got a nice new barn, anyway."

"Yep, we sure did," agreed Will.

But at what price?

• • •

WILL DIDN'T sleep much that night. He and Titus took turns sitting up and keeping an eye on the place from the small door in the new barn's hayloft. There was no hay up there yet, of course, so they brought blankets with them to make bedrolls. Even while Titus was standing guard, though, Will was restless, tossing and turning in his blankets and dozing only sporadically.

The farm was quiet and dark, except for a light burning in the window of the room where Henry lay. Will wondered if

Cordelia was still sitting up with him, or if their mother had taken over that task. Every time Will looked, the light was burning. It stayed lit all night.

There was no more trouble. If the Fogartys were out there somewhere nearby in the darkness, they were content to just watch the farm, biding their time until they were ready to strike again. It made Will's insides tighten with anger every time he thought about George and Ransom. Wherever they were, they were probably laughing about how they had shot Henry. For all they knew, he was dead now.

By the time morning dawned, Will was exhausted, yet his anger easily kept him going. The same seemed to be true for Titus. They climbed down from the loft and entered the house, carrying their rifles with them.

As soon as Will stepped in the door, he smelled the aroma of bacon cooking. He took a deep breath, drawing strength just from the smell. Despite all he had eaten at supper the night before, he was hungry this morning.

He and Titus walked into the dining room just as Cordelia entered the room from the kitchen. She was carrying a plate stacked high with biscuits. A crock of honey was already on the table, just waiting to be slathered on the hot fluffy biscuits. She stopped short at the sight of Will and Titus.

"Didn't mean to scare you," Will said. "How's Henry?"

"He slept peacefully all night," Cordelia reported. "A little while ago, he woke up and said he was hungry. Mama thinks that's a good sign."

"Means he's gettin' back to normal, anyway," said Titus.

Cordelia's eyes were red rimmed, Will noticed. "Did you stay up all night with him?" he asked. "I saw that the lamp was burning all night."

Cordelia shook her head. "No, I . . . I stayed with him for a while, then Mama came in and insisted I go get some sleep. She said she'd sit up with Henry." She smiled weakly and shrugged. "You know what Mama's like."

Will knew, all right. There was no arguing with her when she had her mind made up about something. But then he saw a tear roll down Cordelia's cheek and knew more than that was wrong.

"What is it?" he asked. "Something else bothering you, Cordelia?"

She started to speak, then more tears joined the first one. Without answering Will's question, she hurriedly put the plate of biscuits on the table, then turned and rushed out of the dining room.

Will and Titus looked at each other in surprise. "What was that all about?" wondered Titus.

"I don't know," said Will. "But I aim to find out." He started toward the kitchen door.

Before he could reach it, it swung open again and Abigail stood there. She folded her arms and regarded Will sternly.

He stopped short and frowned. "Mama?" he asked. "What's wrong? Cordelia said that Henry was doing all right—"

"For someone who's been shot, I suppose he is," Abigail snapped.

"Will . . . ," Titus's voice was tentative. "There's only four places set at the table."

Will looked around at him. "I don't reckon Henry feels like coming down to eat, so he'll get a plate taken up to him . . ."

Will's voice trailed off as he realized that still didn't account for the other missing place.

His mother didn't leave him in confusion for long. Abigail announced, "We only need four places at the table because you won't be eating with us, Will."

"Why not?" he asked, his frown deepening.

Abigail's face hardened even more. "Because I want you to get your things and get out. You're no longer welcome in this house, Will Brannon. You're no longer a part of this family."

Chapter Fourteen

FOR A long moment Will stared at his mother, unable to believe that he had heard her correctly. He was searching for something to say when Titus beat him to it.

"What are you talkin' about, Ma?" Titus demanded. "Will's one of us. Always has been, always will be."

Abigail shook her head. "He may still be a Brannon, but he's no longer my son or your brother." She looked at Will. "I'm sorry, but my mind is made up. The Lord has spoken to me, and He says that I have to cast you out for the good of the rest of my children."

Will finally found his voice. "You're turning me out? You're really turning me out?"

"I have no choice."

"Because of what happened to Henry?"

Abigail began to tremble. "I sat at the bedside of my youngest son for hours last night, and I prayed and prayed, asking the Lord for guidance. Then this morning, not long before dawn, God spoke to me and gave me the answer. You never should have become sheriff, Will. You never should have given in to that violent nature of yours. You've brought this trouble down on our heads. Now you have to . . . you have to go . . ." Her shuddering grew stronger.

Will stepped forward, reaching out to her. "Mama—"

Abigail jerked back and cried, "No! Don't touch me! There's blood on your hands, Will Brannon. The blood of an innocent boy!"

"You don't mean Joe Fogarty?" exclaimed Titus.

"I mean your brother Henry!" Abigail shrieked. "He's lying up there on death's doorstep—"

"Henry's not going to die," Will broke into the tirade. "He's going to be all right, Mama."

"You don't know that! You don't know how close he came to being taken home by the Lord!"

Titus turned to Will and directed, "Don't pay any attention to her. She's gone crazy—"

"Hush up," snapped Will. "That's our mother you're talking about, Titus, and I won't stand for it."

Titus gaped at him. "But . . . but she's blaming you for everything, Will! She's saying it's your fault the Fogartys shot Henry and burned down our old barn—"

Footsteps clattered on the stairs, and a second later Mac hurried into the dining room. "What's all the commotion about?" he asked as he rubbed his eyes. His shirt was only half tucked in. "I heard shouting."

"Ma says that she's turning Will out," Titus explained.

Mac's eyes widened in shock. "What?"

"Mama wants me to leave," Will said hollowly, without looking at Mac. His gaze was still fastened on his mother. "She's thinks I'm to blame for everything that's happened."

Mac began, "But that's—"

"Don't say crazy," Titus interrupted. "Will don't like that."

Mac stepped over to Abigail. "Mama, you can't mean it," he protested. "Will hasn't done anything but what he thought was right—"

"He spends his days with robbers and drunkards," Abigail interrupted, as if that explained everything.

Titus threw his hands in the air. "Yeah, I reckon he does," he said bitterly. "Will spends his time arrestin' folks like that!"

"A man is known by the company he keeps."

Will ran his fingers through his dark tousled hair. After a moment he asked, "Does Cordelia know about this?"

"I told the girl what I'd decided. We prayed about it."

Likely that meant his mother had done the praying and Cordelia had listened and cried. Well, that explained why she had been upset when he and Titus first came in, Will thought.

"What about Henry?"

"He's too weak to burden with such a thing."

Mac argued, "Henry wouldn't want Will to leave, Mama."

Abigail shook her head. "It doesn't matter. The Lord has spoken to me, and I intend to do His will."

Will looked at her for a moment longer, then turned abruptly and stalked out of the dining room without saying anything. Mac and Titus hurried after him and caught up to him just as he was pushing out through the front door of the house onto the porch.

"Hold on, Will," Mac said as he caught the sleeve of his older brother's shirt. "She doesn't mean it. She's just upset."

Will stopped and looked around at Mac. "She means it, all right. She never has liked the idea of me being sheriff."

"But you were just doing your job . . . ," Titus began.

"Doesn't matter," Will responded with a shake of his head. "Not to Mama. The Bible says 'Thou shalt not kill,' and I've broken that commandment twice now."

"But—"

"It doesn't matter what you say, Titus." Will looked at Mac. "It doesn't matter what either of you say. Mama's right about one thing: I have to leave."

Titus tried again. "Damn it, Will—"

"Don't make it worse. The best thing is to go along with what she wants. I'm going to resign as sheriff."

"That won't stop the Fogartys," Mac pointed out grimly. "Joe's still dead, whether you're sheriff or not."

Will nodded. "I know. That's why I'm going to do the rest of what Mama wants. I'm leaving the farm, leaving this whole part of the country."

"What you mean is, you're runnin' out on us, just like Cory did!" Titus barked.

Anger flared up inside Will. He grabbed Titus's shoulders tightly and said, "George and Ransom know that *I* killed Joe. If I'm gone, they won't come after the rest of you."

"Can you be sure of that?" Mac asked quietly.

214 • James Reasoner

Will looked over at him, frowning uncertainly. "I . . . I don't know," he said as he relaxed his grip on Titus and stepped back, looking slightly ashamed. Then his resolve grew visibly stronger, and he nodded. "I'll make sure of it. Mac, go inside and tell Mama to get ready to ride into town. The three of us are going to Culpeper. Titus, you and Cordelia will stay here and look after Henry."

Mac's expression grew worried. "Will, what are you up to?" he asked.

"Just giving Mama what she wants, and the Fogartys, too."

• • •

ABIGAIL DIDN'T want to go anywhere with Will. "I won't do it," she insisted a few minutes later when he came in to see if she was ready to leave. "I refuse to go to town with you."

"I'm your first-born son, whether you want to admit it or not," Will told her, not letting his mother see how much the whole situation hurt him. "Do this one last thing for me, and for the good of the family."

"I don't see how it can help anything . . ."

"It will," he promised.

In the end, she was persuaded to go, but only because it was Sunday morning. "It's the Sabbath," she said before she went upstairs to change her clothes. "I'll be going to church in a little while anyway. Might as well go a bit early."

Breakfast was forgotten. None of the Brannons had any appetite except Henry, and Cordelia took a plate up to him and sat with him, helping him eat.

Will didn't put on his Sunday suit. He didn't intend to do any worshiping, even though the Baptist Church in Culpeper was his destination. At Abigail's insistence, Mac dressed in his go-to-meetin' clothes, and she was wearing her usual Sunday attire, a severe black dress and bonnet, when she came back downstairs. Will and Mac were waiting for her.

"I looked in on Henry," she told Mac without looking at Will. "He ate good, and he's resting again."

"That's good," Mac said. "I reckon we should still have Doc Tate ride out and take a look at him, but I'm sure he's going to be all right."

"Yes. The Lord is healing him."

Will wasn't going to argue with that, even though he knew that the way they had cleaned Henry's wound so thoroughly so soon after it happened was responsible in large part for the recovery that had begun. Will was no Bible-thumper, but he believed a person's intelligence and abilities came from God, so it was only right that God got the credit most of the time.

Only thing was, if that was true, then Will's ability with a gun had come from God, too, along with his sense of right and wrong. He never would have said that becoming sheriff was his way of following God's calling, but that was certainly one way of looking at it.

He gave a little shake of his head to clear his mind of those thoughts as he climbed up to the seat of the wagon. Mac started to help Abigail up beside him, but she balked and stayed on the ground.

"You drive, Mac," she asked. "I'll feel better if you're handling the reins."

Mac started to argue, but Will shook his head and stood up to step over the back of the seat into the wagon bed. If that was the way his mother wanted it, that was fine. He could ride in the back, and she could pretend he wasn't even there.

Mac helped Abigail up, then settled down on the seat beside her. He untied the reins and called out to the mules. They strained against their harness, and the wagon began to roll toward Culpeper.

The ride was a silent, strained one. None of the three people in the wagon said anything. Will sat with his back against one of the sideboards and watched the Virginia countryside move past. It was certainly lovely this time of year. This

216 • *James Reasoner*

early morning, with a little mist hanging over the fields, was even more beautiful than ever. If he really left, as he intended to do, he would miss this land.

But where would he go? That question gnawed at his brain.

Reaching the decision to leave had been fairly easy. He realized now that a similar thought had been in the back of his mind ever since he'd been forced to kill Joe Fogarty. As sheriff, he was sworn to protect the citizens of Culpeper County, but protecting his own flesh and blood was even more important. The one sure way to do that was to give George and Ransom Fogarty a target a long way from the rest of the Brannons.

As soon as his mother had told him that she was turning him out, those nebulous thoughts had all come together in his brain, and he knew she was right, though his reasons were different from hers. Ultimately, however, they had the same goal, which was the safety of Mac and Titus and Henry and Cordelia. That was all that mattered.

But until today, he had never given any serious thought to where he would go if he left his home. He had to get far away from Culpeper County. He could go to Norfolk, maybe ship out on one of the boats that sailed from there. The problem with that was that he had never been on a boat in his life and didn't know a blasted thing about being a sailor. He could head south, to the Carolinas or Georgia, and try to find himself a piece of ground where he could farm. That wasn't likely to make him happy, either. He had never been fond of farming, and without his brothers and sister around to make the place a home, he wouldn't have any interest in plowing and planting and cultivating. Going north was out of the question. He didn't want to have anything to do with the Yankees and their big, dirty, noisy cities and factories.

That left the west, where his brother Cory had gone. Kentucky, Tennessee, Missouri, Arkansas, and beyond. Texas. He'd heard a lot about Texas. Maybe he'd find Cory and they'd go take a look at the place . . .

Will leaned forward a little, feeling a tingle of anticipation go through him for the first time in a long while. The idea of heading for the frontier with one of his brothers held some appeal for him. More than just a little appeal, in fact. John Brannon's wanderlust had led him from Ireland all the way to America. It was only natural that more than one of his sons would share some of the same inclination to roam . . .

That would be another failing he had inherited from his father, at least in the eyes of his mother, thought Will. But he wasn't sure it was a failing at all.

• • •

Even though it was early, quite a few people were up and about when the wagon rolled into Culpeper. There were several churches in the county seat, and all of them were well attended. The townspeople were on the streets, heading for the houses of worship, and quite a few wagons and buggies belonging to people from the surrounding countryside were in evidence, too.

"Head for the Baptist Church, Mac," Will instructed. He saw how his mother's back stiffened at the sound of his voice.

Mac turned to look over his shoulder. "It's too early for services, Will," he said.

"Some folks will already be there, though." Will wanted plenty of witnesses for what was going to happen.

Mac glanced over at Abigail. "Mama . . . ?"

"Do as he says," she told him.

Mac guided the mules to the church and pulled the team to a stop under one of the big trees next to the sanctuary. The whitewashed sides of the building gleamed in the morning sunlight. Its steeple stabbed into the bright blue sky. Several wagons and buggies were parked under the trees, and quite a few people had gathered in front of the building and were talking before it was time to go in and begin the service.

Will vaulted over the side of the wagon, landing lightly on the ground beside it. Mac jumped down from the seat and turned back to offer a hand to Abigail. Will looked past his mother and brother at the other members of the congregation who were already on hand and suddenly wished he had washed up and changed his clothes. He was grimy from the work of the barn-raising the day before, and his homespun shirt and whipcord pants looked out of place among the sober black suits worn by the rest of the men. Well, he told himself, this was the last time he would have to worry about such things.

Mac took his mother's arm and walked her to the front of the church. Will trailed along behind. Several of the ladies present greeted Abigail with concerned questions about Henry's well-being, and she assured them all that he was recuperating nicely at home. "The Lord watched over him," she said. "He could have been killed, but the hand of God spared my boy."

Some of the men looked at Will and frowned. He saw Taylor, Hindman, and Olson among them, and standing with the three men was Pastor Crosley. Crosley was a far cry from the fierce Obadiah Vickery, the preacher who had spoken at the rally in Richmond during the winter fair. Stocky and pleasant-featured, he was a peacemaker rather than a firebrand. But at the moment, as he looked at Will, he didn't seem very happy.

"Good morning, Brother Brannon," he said as Will came up to join the small group. "I'm sure you realize this, but folks generally dress a bit nicer on Sunday mornings to show their respect for the Lord."

"I know, Pastor," Will replied. "But I reckon you've heard that there was some trouble out at our place last night."

Crosley glanced at Taylor, Hindman, and Olson. "Our brethren have told me all about it. I'm sorry to hear about the injury that has befallen poor Henry, but praise the Lord that he wasn't hurt worse."

"Amen, Pastor. After all that, I didn't sleep much last night, and I just came on like I was this morning. You don't reckon the Lord minds a little dirt too much, do you?"

"Ah . . . of course not. God cares what's in our hearts more than anything else."

Will nodded toward Abigail. "Well, my mother's got something in her heart that ought to be shared with the congregation." He raised his voice. "Isn't that right, Mama?"

Abigail looked at him in surprise. "Will, what are you doing?"

Will moved toward her and waved a hand at the crowd growing around them. "I want you to share what you told me earlier this morning. I want you to tell all these people what the good Lord wants you to do."

Mac caught hold of his arm and hissed, "Will, for God's sake, don't—"

Will glanced over at him. "Too late, Mac. It's too late for anything else." He turned his attention back to Abigail. "The Lord answered your prayers, Mama. Tell them what He said."

"All right," she said, her face as gray as stone. She looked around at the congregation gathered in front of the church. "I've told this man that he's not my son anymore. God has told me to banish him from my family and my house."

That brought murmurs of surprise from the crowd. Crosley put a hand on Abigail's arm and asked compassionately, "Sister Brannon, are you sure about this?"

"God spoke to me," Abigail declared. "I heard His voice as plain as day. This man has brought shame to my family with his violent ways, and now he has placed us all in danger. I won't tolerate it anymore."

Will noticed a few sympathetic glances being cast in his direction, but most of the members of the congregation were glaring at him. They knew what had happened with Joe Fogarty, of course; almost everybody in the county knew about that. And many of them knew about how Henry had been shot the night before. It was clear from their expressions that some of them agreed with Abigail about his being the cause of all the trouble.

He returned the stares defiantly and addressed the crowd, "You all heard my mother. She says I'm not one of the family anymore, and that's fine with me."

That brought more surprised mutters. Will ignored them and continued, "She's right that I never should have taken the job of sheriff. That's why I'm resigning it right now."

He wasn't wearing his badge, but it was in his pocket. He took it out, turned, and placed it in the hand of the shocked Pastor Crosley, who stared down at the tin star and opened and closed his mouth wordlessly.

"Will, you can't do this," Mac protested urgently. "It's not right."

"It's done," said Will. He raised his voice. "Spread the word, folks. I'm not the sheriff of Culpeper County any longer. Find somebody else for the job. And I'm no longer a member of the Brannon family, either. I'll be moving on as soon as Mac goes back to the farm and gets my gear. I don't intend to ever set foot on the place again."

Mac looked horrified as he shook his head in disbelief. Even Abigail seemed surprised.

Crosley thrust the badge back at Will, who didn't take it. "I . . . I can't have this," the preacher confessed. "I'm a man of God—"

"I don't expect you to pin it on yourself, Brother Crosley," Will said. "Just hang on to it until folks figure out what to do. Maybe Jasper Strawn will want the job."

Jasper Strawn was no sheriff, and everybody knew it. He was barely competent to handle being a deputy. But surely there was someone else in Culpeper County who would want the job.

Either way, it wasn't really any of his concern anymore, Will reminded himself. Before the sun set today, he intended to be out of Culpeper County.

Mac took hold of Will's arm, his fingers digging in firmly. "I want to talk to you," he insisted quietly. The shock on his face had faded, to be replaced by taut lines of anger.

"I don't know what else there is to say," Will began as he let Mac tug him away from the others.

"There's plenty to say! You can't do this, Will."

"It's done."

Mac shook his head. "You mean to tell me that you're going to just ride away from here, from your home and your family, and never look back? What about Titus and Henry? You haven't said goodbye to them. What about Cordelia? How do you think she's going to feel when she finds out you ran away without a word to her?"

Will frowned. Mac was saying things he didn't want to hear, things he hadn't really thought of in his determination to do the right thing. "I reckon the others will be mad at me," he said slowly. "But that's better than them being dead, and that's what's liable to happen if the Fogartys keep coming after us."

"You really think they'll leave the rest of us alone if you're gone?"

"That's right," Will nodded. "They've got no reason to bear a grudge against anybody but me."

"And what are you planning to use to ride away?"

"You're going to bring me a horse, of course."

"No, I'm not," Mac retorted. "If you're bound and determined to go through with this, Will, you're going to have to go back out to the farm and get a horse for yourself. That way you'll have a chance to say some proper farewells."

Will stiffened. Having to say goodbye to Titus and Henry and Cordelia was the last thing he wanted. Cordelia would cry, and Titus and Henry would be upset with him, and if they all carried on enough, they would make it mighty difficult for him to actually go through with his plan. Cordelia's tears alone might be enough to make him stay.

"My mind's made up—" he began.

222 • *James Reasoner*

"I don't care. I won't help you with this, Will. Breaking up the family is the wrong thing to do. It was bad enough when Cory left, but at least he was just fiddlefooted, not angry."

Why couldn't he see? Will thought. Why couldn't Mac understand that he was just trying to make certain the rest of the family was safe?

Before either of them could continue the argument, however, a commotion broke out down the street. Hoofbeats and shouts made Will turn his head and look, and he saw a couple of men riding hurriedly along the street toward the church. People were trailing after them, breaking into a run and yelling questions. Several men began firing pistols into the air, and Will saw that a pair of Confederate flags had been found somewhere and were now being waved over the heads of the growing crowd.

Mac was staring at the uproar in confusion. "What in the world—" he began.

"It's started," Will said hollowly. He wasn't sure how he knew, but he knew.

That certainty was borne out a moment later when the two riders reached the church and reined in. Will recognized them as the ticket agent and the freight clerk from the Orange and Alexandria Railroad depot. The ticket agent shouted, "The word just came over the wire! We've captured Fort Sumter! It's war, boys, war!"

"'Cry havoc,'" Will muttered, quoting his namesake, "'and let slip the dogs of war . . . ,'" as people cheered and shot off guns.

Those dogs were sure barking now.

Part Three

Chapter Fifteen

A T 4:30 ON the morning of April 12, 1861, on Morris Island in Charleston Harbor, Captain George S. James gave the order to fire the signal shell that would begin the Confederate bombardment of Fort Sumter. A young lieutenant named Henry S. Farley stood at the gun awaiting that order, and he carried it out immediately, sending the shot with its trailing arc of sparks high into the black sky. That was all it took. The combined batteries of Morris Island, James Island, and Fort Moultrie illuminated the sky with their fire. The war that everyone had demanded was finally a reality.

Up until just an hour before the bombardment began, negotiations had been going on between Major Anderson, the U.S. commander, and envoys from the Confederate leaders in Charleston. Anderson had, in fact, offered to surrender the fort and evacuate his troops on April 15 . . . providing that he had not received reinforcements or more supplies in the meantime. Both of those possibilities were highly unlikely, considering that the Confederate batteries controlled access to Charleston Harbor, but Anderson's proposal was short of the outright and immediate surrender sought by the Confederate officers. As soon as they returned from Sumter under flag of truce, the orders were given and firing commenced.

The first volleys were too high, screaming over Sumter's tall stone walls to land harmlessly in the waters of the harbor. It didn't take the Confederate gunners long to get the range, however, and soon cannonballs were slamming into the walls of the fort, blasting bricks and mortar high into the air. Fortunately for the troops inside, the walls were thick and stood up well under the bombardment. They were even able to eat their breakfast at the usual time, although their supplies had dwindled to the point that the fare was nothing more than gamy salt pork. The Federals didn't get around to returning the Confederate fire until seven o'clock, when Capt. Abner Doubleday touched off the first shot at the Cummings Point battery on Morris Island—a clean miss.

That set the pattern for the Federal gunners. None of them were very accurate in their aim. Working in four-hour shifts, the soldiers manned the guns and sent ball after ball screaming toward the Confederate positions, only to see them fall short, or pass overhead, or sail wide of their targets. Those that did manage to actually strike the heavily reinforced Confederate positions did little damage.

The biggest of Sumter's guns were on the top level of the fort, the barbette. These cannon, known as Columbiads, were capable of doing significant damage to Charleston if they were brought to bear on the Confederates, but they were also the most exposed. Knowing this, Anderson ordered his men to remain below and that the big guns not be fired. Midmorning, however, three of his men disobeyed the order and fired a volley from the already-loaded guns. Aside from the men's bravery, their deed elicited the response Anderson most feared: the Confederates concentrated their fire on the barbette. The Southern projectiles chewed great hunks out of Sumter's upper level and rendered the Columbiads useless.

Anderson was outgunned and knew it. He was also facing a shortage of ammunition and ordered that only token resistance fire be directed toward the Confederates in order to preserve the remaining charges as long as possible. Throughout the long afternoon of April 12, only a handful of Federal guns answered the heavy barrage of the Confederates.

Tantalizingly, several relief ships lay just outside Charleston Harbor, and Anderson knew it. On those ships were the supplies and the ammunition he needed to maintain the defense of the fort for an indefinite period of time. Without warships to protect them, however, the relief ships could not run the gauntlet of fire from the Confederate batteries. More

U.S. ships were on the way, if Anderson could hold out long enough in Fort Sumter.

That was growing less and less likely. Confederate gunners had begun firing "hot shot" at the fort. These cannonballs were heated until they were red-hot before they were fired, and when they smashed through the brick walls of the fort and penetrated into the wood beneath, their smoldering heat soon started several fires. Anderson's troops, unable to put up much of an actual defense, were kept busy extinguishing these small fires. If one of the blazes got out of control and began to spread throughout the fort, that would be the beginning of the end, and everyone on Sumter knew it.

As the long day wound to a close and night began to fall, the Federals received their first lucky break since the battle began. A squall blew up, and a heavy rain shower pelted the fort. That put out the scattered fires, and it also diminished the Confederate bombardment, as many of the gunners sought shelter from the rain. Major Anderson ordered his batteries to cease fire altogether, and the Confederates kept up only a token show of force, occasionally lobbing a mortar shell toward the Federal fort.

Despite the relative calm, no one on either side got much sleep that night. By morning, the rainstorm was long since over, and the Confederate guns opened up again, pounding at the beleaguered fort. With his ammunition so low, Anderson had his gunners direct their fire only at Fort Moultrie, since they had done little or no damage to all the other Confederate positions. And the Federals' fire was now so sporadic as to be practically useless.

Meanwhile, as the morning went along, the Confederates began using more and more of the hot shot, and by noon a thick cloud of smoke hung over Sumter from the fires started by the heated cannonballs. The barracks and the officers' quarters were ablaze, and the fires were too widespread for the Federals to contain them. All they could do was move as much of their remaining gunpowder as possible from the magazine and hope that what was left wouldn't explode.

The fort's flagpole, where the Stars and Stripes was flying, was struck by a cannonball and toppled. The flag itself was retrieved and carried up to one of the gun batteries, where it was tied on so that it would still be flying in plain view of the Confederates. Its earlier fall, however, encouraged the Southerners to once again send envoys to the fort to determine if Anderson was ready to surrender. These negotiations, complicated by the interference of a self-appointed Confederate negotiator who also rowed out to Sumter, took all afternoon, but by early that evening, a deal had been struck: all firing would cease on both sides, and the next day Anderson and his men would leave Fort Sumter after first being allowed to fire a final salute to their flag. General P. G. T. Beauregard, in charge of the Confederate forces, agreed to these terms.

The first battle of the war was over, and the South had emerged victorious. The news set off wild celebrations in Charleston, and as it was spread throughout the rest of the South by telegraph and riders, so too did the festivities of triumph spread.

All the way to the Piedmont, in fact, and the community of Culpeper, where Will Brannon and the other members of his family knew nothing of the details of the battle, only that the Confederacy had won and that the great war against Northern aggression was underway.

• • •

MAC CAUGHT hold of his brother's arm again. "Will, this changes everything," he said.

Will shook his head, "It doesn't change anything."

"But we're at war now."

"You reckon that'll stop the Fogartys?" Will asked sharply. "They don't have any slaves, and they don't give a damn about anybody or anything except getting their revenge on me because I killed Joe. What do you think they're going to do, run off and join the army?"

Even as he spoke those words, Will stiffened. That wasn't a bad idea, he thought. Heading for Texas would have meant a long arduous journey. And he was enough of a patriot to feel that he would be deserting his country in its time of need if he started west right now. He resented the North's bullying, domineering, holier-than-thou attitude as much as anybody else in the South, and he had to admit that he felt a stirring of emotion inside as he looked at the Confederate flags waving in the morning sun. Someone in the crowd had gotten a makeshift band together, and the strains of "Dixie" suddenly filled the air. A thrill tingled through Will's body.

"I'm going to join up," he announced.

"What?" asked Mac, who was still working on what Will had said about the Fogartys. "What did you say, Will?"

"I said I'm going to enlist. The South's going to need soldiers, and since I was leaving the farm anyway . . ."

One of the men who had been standing nearby overheard Will and rushed over to clap a hand on his shoulder. "Will Brannon's enlisting!" he shouted. "And so am I!"

Another man pumped a fist in the air and called out, "Let's go kill us some Yankees!"

"Where do we sign up?" shouted yet a third man.

No one knew the answer to that, but it didn't really matter. Yankee-killing fever was sweeping through the crowd, and these men weren't going to let a little thing like not knowing where to enlist stop them.

A middle-aged man in a brown tweed suit and a beaver hat pushed his way through the growing mob and stepped up into one of the wagons parked beside the church. He was rather portly, and the effort of climbing into the wagon left him puffing for breath. He recovered quickly, however, and when he raised his hands above his head and called out for quiet, his voice boomed out so that everyone paid attention. Will recognized the man as Cyrus Trafford, the mayor of Culpeper.

"Hush up, all of you!" Trafford bellowed. "I reckon the Army of Virginia will be sendin' out recruitin' officers soon enough, so that all of you who want to can enlist. In the meantime, startin' tomorrow, why don't any of you men who want to sign up come by my bank, and we'll make a list of you."

"Why not today?" asked one of the men.

"I don't intend to do the army's work for 'em on the Sabbath," replied Trafford. "Tomorrow mornin' is time enough. The war ain't goin' to be over by then."

"Might be by tomorrow afternoon!"

Trafford grinned at the shouted comment from the crowd. "Well, sir, you may be right," he began. "Once those Yankees get a taste of fightin' and realize that it'll only take one good Southern boy to whip a dozen of them, I reckon this war will be over in a hurry!"

That prompted another round of cheering. Once again, Mayor Trafford held up his hands for quiet, and when the crowd finally settled down, he took off his hat and held it over his heart. "In the meantime," he said, "I reckon we'd better all go on to our churches and do some prayin' that this war will be both short and victorious!"

That sounded good to the people assembled in front of the Baptist Church. Some of them streamed into the whitewashed building, while others who didn't belong to this particular church headed for one of the other steeple-topped structures in town.

Will didn't plan to go inside. The service could proceed without him. Followed by Mac, he went over to his mother and said, "You ought to be happy now, Mama. The war's finally here, and I'm going to fight in it."

She stared at him for a moment and then reminded him curtly, "I told you, you're not my son anymore."

Mac exclaimed, "Mama, for God's sake—!"

Will held up a hand to stop him. "No, if that's the way it has to be, that's the way it has to be. You just keep telling that to anybody who'll listen, Mama."

He wanted the word of his impending enlistment to get back to the Fogartys as quickly as possible. He hoped the recruiting officers showed up in Culpeper soon, too. The sooner he was out of the county and a member of the Army of Virginia, the safer the rest of his family would be.

Will wondered if the Fogartys would still come after him, army or no army, war or no war. He decided that it was possible. George and Ransom had never been ones to let anything stand in the way of whatever they wanted, and their ultimate goal was to see him dead. Burning down the barn and shooting Henry had just been gestures on their part to remind him of what was going to happen to him.

Abigail went inside the church with some of her friends, while Will remained outside with Mac. Taylor and Hindman stood nearby. Taylor broke the silence and asked, "So you're going to join up, Will?"

"That's right, Jacob. I was on my way out of town anyway." Will smiled grimly. "I hadn't thought about going north, but it looks like that's where I'll be headed after all."

Taylor stuck out his hand. "Good luck to you. I'd enlist myself, but I've got those boys to look after." He chuckled humorlessly as he shook hands with Will. "The way they like a good scrap, I reckon I'll have my hands full just keeping *them* from signing up."

Hindman said, "You can't stop them if they really want to go, Jacob. Not the older one, anyway."

"I know," Taylor acknowledged with a nod. His lean face was a study in emotions. He was as caught up in the patriotic Southern fervor as anyone else, but he was also the father of at least one boy who might go off to war and be killed.

Might have been nice to see some of that concern on the face of his mother, Will mused before banishing the thought.

Hindman looked at Mac and asked, "What about you? You goin' to enlist, Mac?"

"No, he's not," Will answered before Mac could reply.

Mac looked sharply at him. "What do you mean by that?" he demanded. "Since when do you go around making up my mind for me, Will Brannon?"

"Since I figured out that I have to leave home, which means you have to stay," Will replied heavily. "You're the next oldest, Mac. It's your duty to take care of the farm and keep things going. You'll be looking after Mama and Cordelia and the other boys."

"I can fight Yankees just as good as you," Mac declared.

Will doubted that seriously, but he chose not to argue that point. Instead, he repeated, "Somebody's got to take care of things." Mac was the most responsible one in the family, except when it came to horses and other animals. Appealing to his sense of duty was the surest way to make him see reason.

Mac glared for a moment, opened and closed his mouth as if he was about to protest some more, but he didn't say anything and finally heaved a long sigh. Will knew he had just won the argument.

"All right," Mac conceded. "But I don't think you should go, either."

Will shrugged. "Too late for that."

It was too late for a lot of things, he thought.

• • •

"No need to say anything to the others about what I was planning to do," Will told Mac as they rode back out to the Brannon farm after church. Abigail was sitting on a folded blanket in the back of the wagon now. She wasn't any friendlier toward Will, but she had at least spoken to him as she left the church, telling him to sit with Mac so that they could discuss how the farm would be managed. There were plenty of things about his mother that he would never understand, thought Will, but he knew she was a practical woman. Now that she'd had time to think about it, she wouldn't want the anger she felt toward him to keep the farm from being run as efficiently as possible.

"You mean about how you were going to run away?" asked Mac.

"That's not what I was going to do, and you know it."

Mac shook his head. "Looked that way to me. You thought it was better to leave than to stay and let your family help you with your troubles."

Will glanced back over his shoulder toward Abigail and said in a low voice, "I don't have a family, remember?"

"That's not the way I see it. And neither will Titus and Henry and Cordelia." Mac sighed, something he had done a lot this morning. "But I reckon it's all different now. You've got a good reason to leave. The Confederacy has to be protected."

Will nodded. He had wandered around town and heard plenty of war talk while Mac and Abigail were in church that morning. More than half of the able-bodied men in Culpeper and the surrounding vicinity were already planning to enlist. That number would doubtless swell as the news of the Confederacy's capture of Fort Sumter spread.

"We're going to have our hands full keeping Titus and Henry from signing up, you know," Mac said.

"They're too young," Will replied, but even as the words left his mouth, he knew they weren't true. Both Titus and Henry were of legal age. If they wanted to enlist in the army, he couldn't stop them. He could sure try to talk them out of it, though, and he expected Mac to do the same. "They need to stay on the farm."

"Especially Henry, with that gunshot wound," agreed Mac. "We don't know yet how he's going to recover from that."

Earlier in the morning, Will had spoken to the local sawbones, a man named Tate, who had told him that they had done just about everything for Henry that a medical doctor could have. Still, Tate had agreed to ride out to the farm later in the afternoon and take a look at Henry, just to make certain he was healing properly.

When the wagon rolled up to the house, Titus stepped out onto the porch to greet them. He looked at Will and said, "Didn't know if I'd be seein' you again or not."

Will shrugged. "Things have changed."

Mac stepped down from the seat and went around to help Abigail out of the wagon bed. He turned to Titus, "The Confederates have taken Fort Sumter."

Titus's eyes widened, and his habitually gloomy expression disappeared. He let out an exuberant whoop and then asked, "Do you mean it? Are we really at war with the Yankees?"

"It sure sounds like it," Mac replied.

Cordelia hurried out onto the porch, drawn by Titus's shout. "What's going on?" she demanded. "Titus, you woke up Henry. He was dozing again."

"He needs to be woke up," Titus responded excitedly. "There's big news, Cordelia. We're at war with the North."

Cordelia lifted a hand to her mouth. "Really?"

Mac nodded. "We've captured Fort Sumter, in Charleston Harbor."

It was time for him to speak up, Will decided. "I'm going back to Culpeper tomorrow to enlist," he said as soon as he had stepped down from the wagon.

Abigail was going up the steps with Mac at her side, his hand under her left elbow. She didn't look back at him as he spoke. Instead, she fastened her gaze on Titus, and before he could even say anything, she was declaring, "You're not going to enlist. You're going to stay right here on this farm where you belong."

"But . . . but, Ma . . . ," Titus whined, looking flabbergasted. "I thought you hated the Yankees!"

"I think they're a heathen bunch of bullies," Abigail snapped. "But that doesn't mean I want my sons going off to fight them."

Titus was so shocked all he could do was stare at her. You would think that by now he would have realized what a bundle of contradictions their mother was, Will thought.

"Don't argue," Will quietly directed Titus as Mac and Abigail went on inside the house with Cordelia. "You and Henry and Mac are all staying here on the farm. I'm all the contribution the Brannon family is going to make to the war."

"But that's not fair!" Titus protested.

Will shrugged. "Still the way it's going to be."

"I'm a better shot with a rifle than you are."

"You won't get any argument from me about that."

"And I can track better."

"Don't know that the army will need trackers. I reckon they'll have plenty of scouts."

Titus stepped closer to Will. "And I don't mind killing as much as you do. It bothers you, even when you know you're right. It won't bother me."

Will returned his brother's defiant stare and said, "You've never killed anything but animals, Titus. Looking at a man over the barrel of a gun is a whole different thing, and I hope you never get to know that."

For a moment, Titus didn't say anything. Then, "I'm wasting my breath, aren't I?"

"Yep."

"It's still not fair."

Will just nodded solemnly. "There's a whole heap of things in life that aren't."

• • •

IT WAS amazing that, considering the number of shots fired by both sides during the bombardment of Fort Sumter, no one on either side was killed or even seriously wounded. The only fatalities connected with the battle, in fact, occurred the next day after it was over, during the one-hundred-gun salute to the

Stars and Stripes that had been one of the conditions of Major Anderson's surrender. A Federal gunner attempted to reload his cannon too soon after firing a shot, and the resulting explosion set off by a lingering spark killed not only the unfortunate gunner but a nearby comrade as well. The lengthy salute being fired as the American flag was lowered had to be cut short, and the final evacuation of Fort Sumter began. Charleston Harbor was crowded with sightseeing boats packed by citizens of the town, who cheered and waved Confederate flags and the state flag of South Carolina as the Federal troops were taken off the fort on the steamer *Isabel*.

Two hours after the last of the Federals had departed, a group of Confederate officers led by General Beauregard landed and took possession of the hard-won fort, claiming it in the name of the Confederate States of America. The Stars and Stripes was replaced by the seven-starred Stars and Bars, one star for each of the states that had officially seceded.

The damage to the brick-and-stone walls of the fort was impressive. They were marked with deep craters, and entire chunks of the walls around the upper level had been blasted away. Inside the fort the destruction caused by fires and explosions was even greater. Many of Sumter's cannon were still workable, however, and no one doubted that sooner or later they would be put to good use. It was inevitable that the Northerners would eventually attempt to reclaim the fort.

But that was a worry for another day. For now, the Confederates had engaged the hated enemy—and won.

Already, all across the South, people were looking forward to the next battle, the next victory.

Chapter Sixteen

MAYOR TRAFFORD had said that preliminary enlistment would take place at his bank, but by the time Will got to Culpeper the next morning, there was no need for that. Officers from the Army of Virginia had arrived on the train and then set up shop on the lawn of the county courthouse. The line of men waiting to enlist stretched across the lawn and around the stone building.

Will was alone, having insisted that none of his family accompany him this morning. That decision had been fine with Abigail, of course, but it hadn't gone over well with the others. Mac had looked pained as he shook hands with Will on the front porch, and Titus was downright sullen. Earlier, Will had gone upstairs to bid farewell to Henry, who was envious but still subdued from the wound he had suffered.

The worst moment had come when Cordelia had flung her arms around his neck and hung on for dear life as the tears falling from her eyes dampened the front of Will's homespun shirt. "I wish you didn't have to go," she had sputtered between sobs. She had said the same thing when Cory rode away from the farm, but he had laughed it off and assured her he would be back in a year or so as a rich man.

Today all Will could do was reply honestly, "I wish I didn't, too." He had never meant anything more in his life. But he knew this was the only thing he could do, the right thing to do. He would be defending his homeland and protecting his family from the vengeance of the Fogartys at the same time.

Releasing himself from Cordelia's embrace as gently as he could, he turned to go down the steps and mount the horse that Mac had saddled for him. He was taking one of the best horses on the place, the rangy lineback dun he had often ridden while tracking down lawbreakers. The horse was

241

242 • *James Reasoner*

accustomed to gunfire, and where Will was going, that would probably come in handy.

He was traveling light: his Colt Navy, his rifle, and a bag containing a clean shirt, a clean pair of socks, and extra ammunition. Anything else, he figured, would be furnished by the army.

When he reached Culpeper and saw the line around the courthouse, he found a place to hitch the dun in front of Davis's store and went to take his place. He found himself standing behind a farmer from the southern part of the county, a man he knew slightly. Will couldn't recall his name, but the man recognized him and called out, "Howdy, Sheriff. What are you doin' here?"

"I'm not the sheriff anymore," Will replied with a shake of his head. "I resigned yesterday. I'm here to enlist, just like you, I reckon."

The farmer nodded. "Yes sir, that's what I'm goin' to do, all right. Gonna go give them Yankees a little what for."

"Who's going to look after your place and your family while you're gone?"

"Oh, I ain't worried none about that. My missus an' the young'uns can get by all right for a few weeks. I'm only signin' up for three months. Figure that's all it'll take."

"I hope you're right," said Will.

The line moved slowly. By midday, it stretched a long way behind Will, but he was finally nearing the table the army officers had set up underneath one of the big shade trees on the courthouse lawn. When he got a better look at the two men, he saw that they looked more like businessmen than officers. They were wearing tweed suits instead of uniforms, but their hats were decorated with army insignia.

One of them slapped a paper down on the table in front of Will when he finally reached the front of the line. "Name?" he barked curtly.

"William Shakespeare Brannon."

The man glanced up. He was in his forties, a burly man with a scruffy salt-and-pepper beard. "Named after the immortal Bard of Avon, I take it?"

"Yes sir. My father read all of Mr. Shakespeare's plays."

"So have I," the enlistment officer said. "Until two weeks ago, I was a professor of literature at the University of Virginia." He dipped his pen into a pot of ink and scrawled Will's name on the list in front of him, then indicated another paper. "Sign that. You're agreeing to serve for three months. You'll be released earlier if there's no longer any need for your service."

Meaning if the war was already over, Will thought. He nodded, picked up a pen lying on the table, dipped it in the ink, and signed the paper.

"Welcome to the Army of Virginia, Mr. William Shakespeare Brannon." The man looked past him. "Next?"

"Wait a minute," said Will. "What do I do now?"

"This unit is mustering on the edge of town, by the train station. Go along and join them."

Will looked and saw men streaming toward the eastern edge of Culpeper. There were several large open patches of ground there, near the railroad depot, so that was likely where the newly enlisted troops were gathering, he decided. He nodded to the officer, "Much obliged."

"Don't thank me, son," the man replied. Then, more briskly, "All right, who's next? Name?"

Will moved along, following the other enlistees and wondering what the officer had meant about not thanking him. He supposed he would find out soon enough.

When he reached the depot, he saw that his guess about the troops assembling in the large field on the far side of the tracks was correct. Most of the men were sitting around on the ground, smoking pipes or playing cards. They had all sorts of weapons with them, ranging from scatterguns to squirrel rifles to a couple of old muskets that looked as if they might have been used in the Revolution against the British, eighty-five years earlier. Will's guns were better than most of the ones he saw, and he found himself thinking that it was a good thing most Southerners were such good shots, since they certainly weren't equipped like a regular army.

He was leading the dun, and as he crossed the railroad tracks and entered the field, a stout figure bustled toward him. The man was wearing a blue jacket with a red sash across the front of it, and his pearl-gray hat had a feather sticking up from the band. It took Will a second to recognize the mayor of Culpeper, Cyrus Trafford.

"Good mornin', Will," Trafford said as he caught hold of his hand and pumped it enthusiastically. He looked at the dun. "That your horse?"

Will nodded and retrieved his hand from the mayor's clammy grip. "Yep."

"Good. You're an officer in the Culpeper Catamounts. We're an infantry unit, but the officers will ride horses."

Will stared at Trafford for a second, then said, "I never figured to start out as an officer."

"Well, it's not a problem." Trafford looked around at the men nearby and raised his voice to ask, "Any of you boys mind if Will Brannon here is a captain?"

The new recruits shook their heads, and a couple of men called out, "Nope."

Trafford turned back to Will. "Congratulations, Captain Brannon. Would've made you a major or a colonel, but those jobs are already filled."

"Captain's all right with me," replied Will, who was still taken aback by the unexpected promotion. "What did you say we're called? The Culpeper Catamounts?"

"That's right. The other officers held a vote on the name, and that won over the Culpeper Yankee-Skinners. Reckon I'd better ask you, though, since you're an officer, too, now. Is the name all right with you?"

Will nodded. "It's fine, Mayor."

"Colonel."

"Sorry, Colonel."

Trafford waved a hand. "Oh, hell, don't worry about it. That professor fella who's signin' us up said we wouldn't have to worry with military discipline until the train gets here."

"The train?" repeated Will.

"Yep. We're goin' to Richmond. Word is, the Virginia legislature will vote to secede in a day or two, and once it's official, President Davis and the capital are goin' to move up to Richmond from Montgomery, down in Alabama. The capital of the whole dang Confederacy is goin' to be right here in the Old Dominion. If you ask me, that's where it ought to be."

"I figured we'd be going north from here to fight."

"Nope. That Illinois ape has sent out a call for troops to mass in Washington, so we're goin' to gather up in Richmond." Trafford shook his head. "Lincoln says he wants peace, even after we took back Fort Sumter—which was rightfully ours in the first place, mind you—but then he goes and starts buildin' up an army. He plans on invadin' us, Will. You mark my words. Those damn Yankees are goin' to march on Richmond before the month's out. Well, they'll have a surprise waitin' for 'em, won't they?"

"I reckon," Will agreed, and then the talkative Trafford—Colonel Trafford now, Will reminded himself—moved on to greet more of the new enlistees.

One of the men sitting nearby jerked a thumb over his shoulder and said to Will, "The officers are over yonder, under them trees."

"Thanks," Will nodded. He hadn't planned on being an officer, at least not right away, but since things had turned out that way, he supposed he might as well go along and see what happened. He led the dun toward the clump of trees on the edge of the field.

He wondered if this was the way it was happening all across the South: local units forming up and electing their own officers

246 • *James Reasoner*

or having officers foisted on them by local dignitaries such as Trafford. Will didn't know much about military matters, but it seemed to him that the people in charge ought to have at least a little training in leading men into battle. Everybody was expecting the next fight against the Yankees to come soon. Might be better if it took awhile, thought Will. Surely going to war took some practice.

He heard laughter as he approached the group of his fellow officers. They were passing around a jug, he saw. Must have been some of that going on when they came up with the name Culpeper Catamounts, he decided. But at least that was better than Yankee-Skinners.

Several faces turned toward him as he came up to the group, and Will was surprised to see that one of them belonged to Duncan Ebersole. The wealthy planter wore a gray uniform jacket and black uniform trousers. His hat was adorned with a rakish feather, just as Trafford's had been. Will wondered where Ebersole had gotten the outfit, wondered as well what the man was doing here.

"Brannon!" Ebersole called out to him curtly. "Ye lookin' fer somethin'?"

"I believe it's *Captain* Brannon," Will said, and he found that he enjoyed saying the words to Ebersole. "Reckon I'm one of the officers now."

As he spoke, he looked around at the group and realized that they were all well-to-do businessmen or plantation owners like Ebersole. That was how they had gotten to be officers, he thought: power and money moved smoothly from the civilian world to the military one.

Ebersole blinked owlishly at him. The planter had clearly been drinking quite a bit. "Who made you an officer?" he demanded.

"Colonel Trafford."

"Well, I'll just have to have a word with th' colonel," Ebersole said with a sneer, "since I myself am a general and I dinna recall tellin' the colonel he had the right to pick more officers without consultin' me."

This could be trouble, Will realized, and for a moment he considered backing off and telling "General" Ebersole that he didn't care if he was an officer or not. But then Will's stubborn streak asserted itself, so he shrugged and said, "All I know is that the men agreed I should be a captain." He patted the dun on the shoulder. "And I've got a horse."

"A mighty ugly one, too." Ebersole clasped his hands together behind his back and started strolling around Will and the dun. "But the animal appears t' have some sand. Might make a good mount for a general."

Will's hand tightened on the reins. He was damned if he was going to let Ebersole or anybody else take his horse.

Before the budding confrontation could escalate any further, one of the other officers reached out and laid a hand on Ebersole's arm. "I wouldn't push it, Duncan," the man said. "Brannon was sheriff, remember? He also killed Joe Fogarty."

That wasn't necessarily a good thing to be remembered for, Will thought. But Ebersole paused in his assessment of the dun and after a moment nodded in agreement. "All right," he said. "I suppose ye can be a captain, Brannon. Ye'll be in charge of a company o' eighty men. Think you can handle it?"

"I reckon we'll find out."

"You'd better be sure before ye go leadin' 'em into battle. I expect ye'll be in the front rank?"

"I expect," Will said. Right up front where he would be one of the first ones killed, which was probably what Ebersole had in mind. "By the way, I'm not sheriff anymore. I resigned yesterday and turned in my badge."

Ebersole cocked an eyebrow. "That so? Overcome wi' patriotism, were you? Just couldn't wait t' sign up?"

"Something like that," said Will.

"What about tha' brother o' yours?"

"Which one?"

"Titus." Ebersole spat out the name as if it left a bad taste in his mouth.

Will knew quite well why Ebersole was asking and took some satisfaction in reporting, "Titus isn't signing up. And the rest of my brothers are staying on the farm, too."

Ebersole sneered. "They dinna care enough about their homeland to defend it?"

"They'll defend it, all right . . . starting with our farm."

"Well, I suppose if that's all they're willin' t' do . . . ," Ebersole waved a hand dismissively.

Will wondered briefly what the punishment would be for assaulting a make-believe general. Then he controlled his anger and asked the group at large, "What time's that train to Richmond supposed to get here?"

"Sometime this afternoon," replied one of the other officers, extending his hand to Will. "I'm Yancy Lattimer. Captain Yancy Lattimer, I suppose."

The two shook hands. "From Tanglewood?" Will asked, recalling that a Lattimer family owned a plantation in the area.

"That's right," Lattimer said with a grin. "I've followed your exploits as sheriff with great interest, Captain Brannon."

"I wouldn't call them exploits," Will said.

"You're too modest." Lattimer's voice was a soft drawl. He was about Will's age, in his late twenties or early thirties. He wore dark brown whipcord pants, a riding jacket of the same color over a silk shirt and an elegantly draped cravat. His broad-brimmed planter's hat was cream colored. He was a bit of a dandy, Will supposed, but his broad shoulders and the strength of his handclasp were proof that he was no weakling.

"That's right," Ebersole chimed in. "Brannon here is famous as a shootist now."

"It's not a reputation I want," said Will. "My job was to keep trouble from happening."

"But you dealt with it decisively when it did," Lattimer noted. "Just as we'll have to do when we confront the enemy."

Ebersole grunted. "Can't be soon enough to suit me." He took the jug from one of the other officers and enjoyed a lengthy swallow.

Will turned away to hide the look of disgust on his face. If Duncan Ebersole was an example of the sort of generals the Confederate army had, then God help the South, he thought.

Trafford suddenly came bustling up to the group. "That professor fella says we ought to get the men formed up into companies and start drillin' 'em while we wait," he reported excitedly. "What do you think, General?"

Ebersole gave another languid wave. "Whatever ye want to do, Trafford."

It was clear that the planter wanted no part of any organizational work. Trafford looked around at the officers and pointed to several of them, including Will and Yancy. "Come along with me," he ordered.

Will wasn't sure what to do with his horse. He looked around for some place to tie its reins, but Ebersole noticed and snapped his fingers. "Oh, hell, let one o' the niggers tend to it," he said.

A young slave came hurrying up in response to Ebersole's summons. "I'll take that hoss for you, Massa," he said quietly as he held out his hand for the reins. "I'll put it right with the other gen'lemans' hosses."

"Thanks," Will replied as he handed over the reins. He wondered who the slave belonged to, Ebersole or one of the other officers.

That question was answered as he, Yancy, and the others trailed after Trafford. "That's one of my boys," Yancy said. "Name's Roman. He's a good lad, and I intend to take him with us."

Will nodded. He didn't have any slaves to take with him and didn't want any. But he wasn't a plantation owner, either.

Quietly, Lattimer continued, "I saw the look you hid from our esteemed general."

"Which one?" If Yancy was trying to trick him into admitting that he didn't like Ebersole, that wasn't going to take much work, Will thought.

Yancy laughed. "You were wondering how in God's name a man like that became a general so quickly, weren't you?"

"It occurred to me."

"Ebersole is the richest man in the county, and the good colonel up there is afraid of him." Yancy nodded toward Trafford. "They appointed themselves. You won't find much of that in the Union army, unfortunately. It would be easier to defeat them if they had a few Ebersoles on their side."

That struck Will as pretty bold talk about a commanding officer. But Yancy Lattimer's family was wealthy, too, so he didn't have any real reason to fear Ebersole.

"Luckily, we have our own share of trained officers," Yancy went on. "I'm hoping that President Davis will put General Lee in charge of the army, because I know he'll appoint good men as his commanders."

"You sound like you know him," Will commented.

Lattimer nodded. "Met him when I was at the Point several years ago, but I wasn't fortunate enough to serve under him."

"The Point?"

"West Point. I attended the academy, then served three years in the regular army before resigning my commission."

Will looked at him with some surprise. "You were a Yankee officer?"

"There weren't any Yankees or Rebels then," Lattimer noted with a smile. "We were all on the same side."

Will shrugged and said, "I reckon. Why'd you resign your commission?"

"Because I knew this day was coming," Yancy replied softly. "I resigned the week after Lincoln was elected."

"You figured war was inevitable?"

"I hoped I was wrong." Lattimer looked around at the field full of brand-new recruits to the Confederate army. "Unfortunately, my instincts were correct."

Trafford began splitting up the large group of recruits into companies of eighty men each, counting them off at random and sending them with the captains. Each officer marched his men to a different part of the field. The so-called marching was decidedly ragged, and the ranks were uneven. Will looked at the group assigned to him and wondered what he was supposed to do. Whatever had possessed him to think that he had the makings of an officer?

"Stand up straight," he told them. "Get into rows of ten."

The men shuffled around, gradually forming into more regular ranks. It was more by accident than intent that they were properly aligned. Will took a deep breath and surveyed the faces of his charges. Most of them were farmers; he could tell that by their clothes. A few townies were mixed in with the bunch. They all looked at him with eager expressions, waiting for him to tell them what to do next.

He glanced over at another part of the field, where Yancy was walking along the ranks of his company, inspecting their weapons. That seemed like a good idea, so Will started doing the same thing. He began with the soldiers in the front rank.

"Let's see those muskets, boys," he called, knowing that he ought to be phrasing the commands differently but unsure of what words he was supposed to use. He walked along the row, and as he came to each man inspected whatever weapon he happened to be carrying. Most of the guns seemed to be in good repair.

Will spent quite awhile looking at the weapons. Recruits were still streaming into the field, and as they arrived they were split up among the companies. Will added a few of these stragglers to his group, then checked again to see what Yancy was doing. By now, Lattimer had his company marching up and down the field and executing relatively crisp turns. Will waved a hand at them and said to his own men, "Let's give that a try."

They got started marching fairly well, but when Will shouted out a command he had overheard Yancy using—"Left face!"—his men practically fell over each other. Some of them

252 • *James Reasoner*

turned left, some turned right, and some kept going straight ahead. Will yelled, "Hold it! Hold it!" and tried not to sound too disgusted.

He was saved from having to explain the command and straighten out the mess by the whistle of a locomotive in the distance. A moment later the train came rolling into sight, smoke billowing from the stack. Will formed his company into ranks again and waited to see what was going to happen.

The locomotive was pulling about a dozen boxcars and flatcars. A couple of the flatcars were covered with men, and several boxcars were packed with recruits, visible through the open doors. There were cheers and shouts and whoops from the men already on the train, and their exuberance was met with answering yells from the men in the field.

When the train had come to a stop, Ebersole climbed up onto one of the empty flatcars. He had gotten a saber from somewhere and waved it above his head as he called for silence. Gradually, the soldiers settled down, and Ebersole shouted hoarsely, "Culpeper Catamounts! Are ye ready t' go kill some Yankees?"

The answering roar was deafening. Every man in the field shook his rifle or shotgun or musket over his head and shouted at the top of his lungs. Will found himself whooping madly right along with them. It was impossible not to.

When the cheering died down again, Ebersole said, "I expect each an' every one o' ye to send them Northern sons o' bitches runnin' back home to that pitiful excuse for a president wi' their tails tucked 'tween their legs! Fight for th' South, boys! For Dixie! For your wives and sweethearts!"

Even though he disliked Ebersole, Will felt chills running through him as the sounds of cheering men filled the air. Flags waved and a band piped up as Ebersole shouted, "All aboard! All aboard for glory and honor!"

The recruits swarmed onto the train. There was no holding them back, no chance of loading them onto the flatcars and boxcars in an orderly fashion. Will didn't even try. He could reassemble his company later, when the train got to Richmond, and if he didn't get all of them, that didn't really matter. Someone else would take the place of anybody he missed.

In the confusion, Will heard his name called and looked up to see Yancy standing on one of the flatcars. He was holding a hand down toward Will and helped him onto the car.

"Pretty hectic, isn't it?" Lattimer yelled over the hubbub.

Will nodded. "I'll bet this isn't the way they do things in the regular army."

"It's a bit more chaotic, all right," Lattimer admitted with a grin. "Still, all this enthusiasm is a good thing, if the men can maintain it and direct it toward the enemy. That'll be our job."

"I don't know if I'm up to it," Will said, shaking his head. "I never commanded anybody before except a deputy or two."

Lattimer clapped him on the shoulder. "Don't worry, you'll make a fine officer, Brannon. Any time I can give you a hand, just let me know." He looked past Will and suddenly frowned. "Who's that?"

Will turned and looked in the same direction, and he stiffened as he saw two men climbing up into one of the boxcars. Both of them were looking straight at Will. One of the men was short and a little stocky, with lank brown hair under a pushed-back hat. The other was taller and heavier, with freckles all across his broad face and a thatch of ginger-colored hair. Despite the differences in their appearance, there was a family resemblance between them. The other thing they had in common was the look of hatred each of them directed toward Will.

Will met their stares for only a second, then they were gone, vanishing into the boxcar with dozens of the other recruits. But that second had been plenty long enough for him to recognize them.

George and Ransom Fogarty.

Chapter Seventeen

THOSE FELLAS looked as if they didn't much like you."
Yancy Lattimer's words broke into Will's tense reverie. He turned, looked at his fellow officer, and shrugged. "I reckon they don't."

"Seems like I ought to know them. I've been away from here for a while, though—"

"They're brothers. George and Ransom Fogarty," said Will. "The little one's George; the big one's Ransom."

"Of course," Yancy nodded. "I remember them. Trouble-makers of some sort, aren't they?"

"You could say that," Will noted dryly.

"Well, now they've signed up to make trouble for the Yankees. I don't suppose their background matters as long as they're fighting on our side."

Will nodded, but he wasn't necessarily agreeing with Yancy. He didn't believe for a second that the Fogartys had joined the army to fight Yankees. They had heard that he had resigned as sheriff and decided to enlist, so there was nothing they could do except sign up, too. Otherwise, they would have had to let him get away, far out of the reach of their vengeance.

He wanted to heave a sigh of relief. His plan had worked. Once this train pulled out, with every click of the wheels on the rails, George and Ransom would be getting farther away from the rest of the Brannon family. Will had been halfway afraid that they would decide to let him go and save their revenge on him until after he came back from the war. In the meantime, they could have wreaked havoc on the rest of the family.

But that would have meant trusting to luck that Will would even return to Culpeper County. He was going off to war, after all. He might not survive to come home. And George and Ransom hadn't been able to stand the thought of somebody

257

else getting to kill him. They wouldn't allow themselves to be cheated by some nameless, unknown Yankee soldier.

"What are you grinning about?" asked Yancy.

"Just looking forward to getting to Richmond," said Will. He didn't think Yancy would understand if he explained what had really provoked the grin.

Loading all the troops took awhile, but eventually the train was ready to pull out. The officers' horses had been led up a ramp into one of the boxcars. Will had watched as Roman, Yancy's young slave, led the dun into the car. The boy had a sure touch with horses and reminded Will of his brother Mac. The two of them would get along well, Will suspected.

Not all the officers had climbed onto the train, however. To his surprise, Will saw Duncan Ebersole and Cyrus Trafford sitting on horses next to the tracks, watching as the train lurched into motion. Both men saluted as the loaded cars rolled past them.

Will caught hold of Yancy's arm and used his other hand to point to Ebersole and Trafford. "Looks like the general and the colonel aren't coming with us. Reckon they'll be along later?"

Yancy chuckled. "Not very likely. I heard them say earlier that they would stay here to command the local militia unit. They were just pitching in to help get things organized today. They're not actually in the army, you know."

"They're not? I thought Ebersole was a general."

"He calls himself one. He lacks one vital ingredient for a man who aspires to lead troops into battle, though."

"What's that?"

Yancy looked at Will and announced bluntly, "Courage."

"He figures the war won't ever get this far, so he won't see any real fighting?"

Yancy nodded. "And for the sake of the citizens of Culpeper County, we'd better all hope he's right."

• • •

THE TRAIN full of recruits rolled south from Culpeper some twenty-five miles to a junction with the Virginia Central Railroad. There it pulled onto a siding, and the new soldiers were all unloaded. The Virginia Central used a different gauge track from the Orange and Alexandria, so the men had to change trains for the rest of the journey to Richmond.

Unfortunately, there was no train at the junction, so they were forced to wait there for several hours until one arrived.

While everyone was waiting, Will looked for George and Ransom Fogarty. He didn't see them, but with well over a thousand men gathered here, that was no surprise. If the Fogartys wanted to blend into the background, they were in the right place for it. Most of the men here were dressed similarly. There was nothing to make anyone stand out.

Finally, just as night was falling, a Virginia Central locomotive pulling a train of boxcars rumbled into the junction. All the cars were empty, and the recruits piled into them eagerly, though without quite as much frenzied excitement as they had displayed earlier in Culpeper. No one whipped them into a frenzy with a speech, as Ebersole had done, and they had spent several tiring hours sitting around waiting, so that dampened their enthusiasm, too. But the loading was accomplished fairly quickly anyway.

Will found himself climbing into a boxcar with most of the men who had been in his company earlier. One of them looked up at him in the fading light and asked, "Hey, Cap'n, when are we goin' to eat?"

Will had to remind himself that the man was talking to him; he wasn't used to being called by his rank yet. And he hesitated, too, because he didn't have the answer to the man's question. Not the slightest notion, in fact.

"I reckon they're bound to feed us when we get to Richmond," he said. A groan of disappointment went up from many of the men. Will held his hands up and went on, "If any of you have any food with you, how about sharing it?"

"I got some pone," announced one of the recruits, adding hurriedly, "but I brung it for myself, not to feed ever'body in the whole damned company."

Will wished they hadn't started talking about food. He realized he hadn't eaten since breakfast that morning, and his stomach was all too aware of that fact. He said, "Once we start fighting the Yankees, you boys are going to be trusting the fella next to you to help keep you alive. Seems to me like sharing a little grub isn't too much to ask when the gent you share it with might save your life in a few days."

There was still some grumbling, but his logic convinced most of the men. The ones who had brought biscuits and corn pone and dried beef and salt pork dug the rations out of their gear and began splitting it up. It wasn't going to go far, but something was better than nothing, Will supposed. He was reminded of the miracle of the loaves and fishes in the Bible. These boys could have used something similar right about now.

He took half of a biscuit and a small piece of salt pork from one of the recruits who offered him more. "This is plenty," Will assured the man. He hunkered next to the wall of the boxcar and gnawed slowly on the tough fare.

The car rocked back and forth gently, and the clicking of its wheels on the rails was hypnotic. When he finished his meager meal, Will leaned his head back against the wall of the car and closed his eyes. It wasn't but a moment until he felt himself starting to drift off into sleep.

His eyes snapped open. The shadows inside the car had been thick when he climbed in, and he hadn't gotten a good look at all of his fellow passengers. It was possible that George and Ransom Fogarty could have been back in one of the corners, unseen. Now, with the only light in the car coming from the faint glow of moon and stars that seeped in through the open sliding doors on the sides, the Fogartys could crawl over to him and slip a knife between his ribs without him ever seeing them, especially if he was asleep. He had to stay awake and alert and listen intently for the sounds of anyone trying to sneak up on him.

It was asking too much of his tired body and mind. Sometime during the dark night journey to Richmond, Will dozed off into a deep sleep.

• • •

HE WOKE up with a jerk, sitting up straight and letting his hand fall to the butt of the pistol holstered at his hip. Instantly, his eyes were open wide, and he peered around him in the darkness, wondering what had roused him from sleep.

A moment later, he knew. The locomotive's whistle sounded again, and Will realized that the train was slowing down.

All around him, men stirred and sat up groggily. There was more light in the car now, and when Will looked outside, he saw that the sky was gray with the approach of dawn. The trip had taken all night.

He took his hand away from his gun, feeling a little foolish that he had almost yanked it out of the holster. None of the other men seemed to have noticed, though. He pushed himself to his feet, feeling several twinges of pain from stiff muscles that had spent the night in unaccustomed positions. Sitting on the floor of a boxcar was a far cry from being in his own bed. He figured that before the war was over, he would have to sleep in a lot of uncomfortable places, some of them no doubt worse than this boxcar.

"Everybody up," Will called to his troops. "We're coming into Richmond. Best be ready to get off the train."

He braced himself with a hand against the wall as the train slowed even more. Through the open doors of the boxcar, he could see the city spread out on both sides of the James River. Railroad trestles were visible up ahead as the rails curved, appearing skeletal in the predawn mist. The depot was on the other side of the river. A few minutes later, the cars clattered over one of the trestles.

When the train finally came to a stop, Will was the first to jump down from the boxcar in which he had been riding. He looked up and down the tracks and saw that the locomotive had halted in the middle of a vast trainyard. Other locomotives were sitting on other sets of tracks, their stacks belching steam and smoke. Will was trying to figure out what to do next when a man in a gray uniform came along on a horse.

"Are you an officer?" the man asked. He was a lean, well set up figure in his early forties, with a brown mustache and a tiny patch of beard underneath his lower lip. His speech had a slight, exotic accent that Will couldn't identify.

"Yes sir," replied Will, unsure of what the insignia on the man's uniform and cap meant but recognizing the aura of command about him. "Captain Will Brannon, Culpeper County."

"Captain Brannon, form up your men and march them out of the trainyard and across the street to the open area next to the river." A faint smile tugged at the man's mouth. "By the way, I take it you're not regular army?"

"No sir. I was the county sheriff before I enlisted."

"Well, I'm sure you'll make a fine officer, but you should learn to salute your superiors. Like this." The man lifted his right hand to the brim of his cap, then snapped it down sharply.

Will tried to imitate the salute, then nodded and said, "Thanks. I'll work on it."

"Very good. Now, get these men moving." The man turned his horse and rode on alongside the train.

Will was getting his men into ranks a few minutes later when Yancy hurried over to him. Yancy's company was already in formation. He grinned at Will and told him, "The general must have been impressed with you. He mentioned that he'd met you."

"That man on the horse? He was a general?"

"General P. G. T. Beauregard," said Yancy. "He directed the bombardment of Fort Sumter."

Will didn't feel all that impressed with the hero of Fort Sumter. "Really? Seemed like a nice fella for a general," he said.

Yancy just looked at him for a second and then shook his head, unable to comprehend Will's attitude. "We'd better get the men moving," he finally said. Will nodded his agreement.

The two companies marched out of the trainyard and across the cobblestone street that fronted the depot. On the other side of the street, next to this stretch of the James River, was a long grassy area dotted with trees. Farther to both the north and the south, the river was lined with warehouses, but this section was parklike. It was rapidly filling up with men, however, as they disembarked from the train that had brought Will and his companions to Richmond, as well as from other trains that had converged on the city from other parts of the Old Dominion.

Will kept an eye out for George and Ransom but didn't see them anywhere. Could they have deserted already, after being in the army less than twenty-four hours? That didn't seem likely, especially in light of the fact that Will was convinced the only reason they had enlisted was to settle their score with him. There were thousands of new recruits here in Richmond, however, and it was impossible for him to look at each and every one of them.

When trouble came, it was from an unexpected source. Will had marched his men into the park and had them all sitting down cross-legged on the ground, waiting for further orders, when he heard his name called from somewhere behind him. "Brannon! Is that you, Will Brannon?"

Will started to turn around to see who the voice belonged to, and as he did, he saw from the corner of his eye that someone was rushing at him. He didn't have time to set his feet and brace himself before the man crashed into him, tackling him around the waist and knocking him over backward. Will landed hard, with the weight of his attacker on top of him driving all the breath from his body. He gasped for air as he tried to throw the man off.

He couldn't get the leverage he needed. Instead, the man slammed a fist down into Will's face, bouncing his head off the ground. Blackness tried to close in from the sides of his vision, but Will fought off unconsciousness and managed to reach up and throw a wild punch of his own. It grazed his attacker's ear and only seemed to make the man more angry. He bellowed a curse and wrapped his hands around Will's throat.

Caught without any air in his lungs, Will felt the life being choked out of him. His eyesight was blurry, like a red haze had fallen in front of his face, but as he thrashed around on the ground, he finally got a good enough look at the man's face to recognize him: Darcy Bennett, a farmer from back in Culpeper County whom Will had arrested several times for drunkenness and disturbing the peace. Darcy had spent quite a few nights in the old stone jail, sleeping off his binges, but when he was sober, he wasn't that bad a sort. Right now, his face above his beard was flushed and bloated, and Will figured he was drunk. That was the only time Darcy was a troublemaker.

It didn't matter what had prompted this attack. What was important was that in another few moments, Will was going to black out and probably die . . . unless he got loose from the crushing force of Darcy's fingers.

He arched his back and brought his right leg up as high as it would go. He was able to get it in front of Darcy's face and hook his ankle under Darcy's bearded chin. Will straightened his leg, putting all his remaining strength in the maneuver. Darcy had no choice but to let go of Will's throat as Will's leg drove him backward.

Darcy sprawled on the ground. Will rolled over on his belly and dragged deep, ragged breaths into his body, filling his starved lungs. He knew he had only a moment before Darcy recovered, so as he tried to catch his breath, he scrambled to his feet and turned around. He was dizzy from lack of air, and the world spun crazily around him. He thought about reaching for the Colt Navy on his hip, but he didn't want to kill Darcy.

Besides, he was so dizzy that he probably couldn't shoot straight, and he sure didn't want to send any stray slugs into the mob of soldiers.

Will didn't have to worry about that. As his vision cleared a little, he saw that several men from his company had leaped forward to grab Darcy's arms and hold him back. Darcy was strong like a mule, but he was outnumbered. As Will watched, the men who had hold of Darcy forced him facefirst to the ground. It was a little like a tree falling.

During the fight, Will had been vaguely aware of shouts that sounded as if they were coming from a million miles away. Now, as he saw the recruits crowding around, he realized that they had been eager spectators to the battle. Some of them had probably been cheering him on, but he couldn't speak to that. He had been too busy with Darcy to be sure of what was going on around him.

The crowd suddenly parted as a couple of men on horse-back rode through the ring of recruits. One of them was the officer Will had met earlier—General Beauregard, Yancy Lattimer had called him—and the other man was undoubtedly an officer, too, probably the general's aide. Beauregard said sharply, "What's going on here?" Then his angry gaze fell on Will. "Captain Brannon?"

Will lifted his right hand and saluted like Beauregard had shown him earlier, despite the fact that his hat had been knocked off in the brawl. "General, sir," he answered, still a bit breathless. "Just a little scuffle."

"It sounded like a full-scale battle," Beauregard observed. "I would advise you and your men to save your strength and your passion for the Yankees."

One of the men from Will's company nudged Darcy in the side with a booted foot. "This here jackass jumped on the cap'n and tried to choke him to death," the soldier explained.

Beauregard frowned. "Attacking a superior officer? That could warrant a firing squad."

Will stepped forward and lifted a hand. "Begging your pardon, General, but until today I wasn't anybody's superior. And Darcy here, well, he's likely been drinking some, and he saw me and remembered that I've thrown him in jail several times. I reckon he just lost his head."

Beauregard leaned forward in his saddle and looked intently at Will. "Are you trying to defend this man's actions, Captain, even though he almost killed you?"

"I don't reckon he came *that* close to killing me."

"So you don't wish any disciplinary action to be taken against him?"

"Once he sobers up, he'll be all right," said Will. "He just needs a chance to sleep it off."

Beauregard nodded as he came to a decision. "Very well. But I'm holding you responsible for his future behavior, Captain Brannon. To that end, I'm placing him in your company."

Will tried not to frown. He didn't particularly want to have to ride herd on Darcy Bennett, but he supposed if that was what General Beauregard wanted, that was what would happen. Where they were going, Darcy wouldn't have much chance to get drunk, so maybe Will could keep him under control.

"Yes sir," Will said.

Beauregard saluted, Will returned it, and then the general and his companion turned their horses and rode back toward the railroad depot. Will looked at the men who were still holding Darcy on the ground and ordered, "Let him up."

"You right sure about that, Cap'n?" one of them asked.

Will nodded. "I'm sure."

The men let go of Darcy, stood up, and backed off. Slowly, Darcy pushed himself to his feet and shook himself like a bear. As shaggy as he was, he sort of looked like a bear, Will thought.

"You going to behave yourself now, Darcy?" he asked.

"I reckon." Darcy's face above the beard was taking on a greenish tinge in the early morning light. "Did I hear that fella on the horse say I was in your bunch now?"

"That's right. I'm your commanding officer. Can you live with that, Darcy . . . or do you reckon I'd better go ahead and shoot you and get it over with?"

Darcy looked like he was going to be sick. He managed to say, "Hell, I don't mind. You and me get along fine, Will, long as you ain't tryin' to put me in jail."

"As long as you're not drunk, you mean."

Darcy rubbed his forehead. "I'm gettin' sober, I think. I'm gettin' a mite sick, too—"

With that, he turned and dashed for a nearby clump of trees.

Will let him go. Darcy might have the makings of a good soldier; Will didn't know about that. Will didn't even know what sort of soldier *he* was going to make. But for the time being, as long as Darcy didn't try again to kill him, that was about all Will could expect.

"Well, that was some ruckus."

The familiar voice spoke from behind Will. He turned, fighting down the instincts that had warning bells clanging in his head, and found himself looking into the smiling face of George Fogarty.

• • •

IT WAS amazing, thought Mac, how empty the place seemed just because another member of the family was no longer there. He had better get used to Will being gone, he told himself, because there was no telling when the war would be over and Will would get to come home. There was even the chance that —

Mac stopped himself from allowing that thought into his head. He went into the dining room, nodded, and said to Cordelia, "Good morning."

She looked up with a wan smile. "Good morning." She was setting the table, and Mac could smell breakfast cooking out in the kitchen.

"Get much sleep last night?" he asked.

"Oh . . . some. You?"

"Not much."

Cordelia nodded. Will was on both of their minds, especially now on this first morning after he had left home.

"I looked in on Henry," Mac went on. "He's still asleep. He's going to turn into a regular layabout while he's getting over that bullet wound."

"Where's Titus?"

"He'll be down in a minute."

It was less than a minute before Titus's bootheels rang on the steps of the staircase. He came into the dining room and said to Cordelia, "I just want a cup of coffee this morning."

"And good morning to you, too," Cordelia replied tartly.

Titus shrugged and said, "Mornin'. Now, how about that cup of coffee?"

"Why are you in such a big hurry?" asked Mac.

"I've got things to do today."

"Such as what?"

Titus hesitated, then said, "Such as riding into Culpeper and seeing if Mayor Trafford will appoint me to finish out Will's term as sheriff."

A crash from the doorway made Titus, Mac, and Cordelia spin around. Abigail had stepped through the door from the kitchen just in time to hear Titus's statement, and the bowl of grits in her hands had fallen to the floor to shatter in a thousand pieces. She ignored the mess at her feet and stared at Titus in horror.

Mac started toward her. "Mama . . ."

"No," she spoke quietly, then her voice rose as she repeated, "No! I won't have it!"

"Somebody has to take the job," Titus shot back at her, "since Will ran out on it."

"Stop it!" cried Cordelia. "Will didn't run out on anything, Titus. How dare you—"

Mac held his hands up, "Why don't we all just calm down—"

He didn't get to finish his plea, because a new voice came from the front door of the house, which stood open to let in the morning breeze. "Hello? Is anyone home?"

All four of the Brannons turned to look down the hall from the dining room that led into the foyer. They saw the figure in the long dress and bonnet step into the house, saw as well the horse and buggy stopped outside, which none of them had heard drive up.

Polly Ebersole stepped through the foyer and into the dining room, a bright smile on her face as she said, "Good morning. My, I do hope it's not too early to come callin'."

Chapter Eighteen

TITUS COULDN'T believe his eyes. Polly was right here in the dining room of his own house, as beautiful as ever, turning her radiant smile on him. If she noticed the broken bowl and the pile of spilled grits in the floor, she was too polite to acknowledge their existence. Titus tried not to gape at her.

Mac regained the use of his tongue first. He said, "Good morning, Miss Polly. Come in and sit down. We were just about to have breakfast, and it would be an honor if you'd join us."

Damn it, thought Titus, he should have been the one saying that, not Mac. Instead he was standing here staring at her like a fool.

"Oh, I can't stay," Polly said, still smiling, "but I certainly do thank you anyway. I just came by to deliver an invitation."

Mac started to say something, but Titus beat him to it. "What sort of invitation?" Then he winced because of the abruptness of the question.

"To a ball at Mountain Laurel," said Polly. "A grand ball to celebrate the beginning of the fight for liberty and honor and the impending defeat of the Northern aggressors."

"I don't hold with dancing," Abigail declared.

"Oh, there'll be more than just dancing," Polly replied. "There'll be music, and a grand feast. It should be a glorious, enjoyable evening."

Titus took a step toward her. "It sounds wonderful. When, uh, when will it be?"

"Next Saturday night." He was close enough to her that she was able to reach out and lay a hand gently on his arm. Her touch sent a ripple of longing up his arm and through his entire body. "You will be there, won't you?"

273

Titus managed to nod, but he couldn't find his voice to say anything.

Mac stepped up and spoke for his brother. "Thank you, Miss Polly. We'd be pleased to attend."

"Oh, good." Polly squeezed Titus's arm. "See you then."

Titus felt an incredible pang of loss as she took her hand off his arm and turned away. He watched her as she walked back through the foyer, pausing at the door to wave at them, and then she was gone, being helped into the buggy by the dark-suited slave who had brought her over from Mountain Laurel. The slave hopped onto the driver's seat of the buggy, turned the vehicle, and sent the horse trotting briskly away.

Titus still stood where he was, his mouth hanging open, all thoughts of going to Culpeper and trying to get the sheriff's job gone for the moment from his head.

"That . . . that hussy!" Cordelia fumed.

His sister's words shocked Titus out of his stunned state. He turned on her and cautioned, "Shut your mouth! Don't talk that way about Miss Polly!"

Mac pointed out, "She *did* invite us to a party, Cordelia."

"But don't you see?" Cordelia implored. "She doesn't really want us there. She . . . she just wants to stir up trouble for some reason."

"You're crazy," snapped Titus. "Polly's the sweetest girl I've ever known."

"You're the one who's crazy," Cordelia observed. "Crazy, and blind in love!"

"You hush up! I swear—"

Mac interrupted by turning to Abigail and asking, "What about you, Mama? Will you go to the Ebersoles' ball?"

"I suppose it would be the neighborly thing to do, since Polly asked us," Abigail said slowly. "But I don't think Henry will be up to traveling by then. I'll stay here with him, so the three of you can go."

"But I don't want to go," Cordelia declared.

Titus grabbed her arm. "You're goin'," he said. "You're not goin' to be rude to Polly by not showin' up."

"I don't care what Polly thinks!"

"Titus is right," Mac observed. "Mama has a good reason for not attending, and so does Henry, but I think the rest of us ought to make an appearance."

Cordelia looked back and forth between her brothers. "You don't know that girl like I do. She's up to something, mark my words, but I suppose I'd better go along, just to keep somebody else . . ."—she looked meaningfully at Titus—". . . from getting into more trouble than he can handle."

"You just tend to your own business," he told her. "I'll tend to mine." He remembered what he planned to do today. "And right now, my business is with Mayor Trafford."

"Titus! I've lost two sons already," Abigail pleaded. "Don't make me lose another."

Something in her voice made all three of them look at her. They saw the single tear that trickled from her left eye and slid down her cheek.

Titus swallowed hard, "I'm sorry, Ma. This is something I've got to do."

Then he turned and walked out of the house without looking back.

• • •

SHAKEN UP as he was by the encounter with Darcy Bennett, there was nothing wrong with Will's reactions. His hand dropped to the butt of the Colt Navy, his fingers curling around the smooth wooden grips.

"Hold on there," George Fogarty said quickly, taking a step back and holding up both hands, palms out. "I ain't lookin' for trouble, Will."

Will's eyes darted around, searching for Ransom. He didn't see the other Fogarty brother. That meant Ransom was probably hidden somewhere nearby, drawing a bead on Will with a rifle while George kept him occupied.

"You better hope Ranse kills me with the first shot, George," Will grated, "because if he doesn't I'll put a bullet through your head before I go."

"Hell, Will, you got me all wrong," George protested. "Didn't you hear me? I ain't lookin' for trouble."

"Where's your brother?"

George waved a hand negligently. "Off over yonder somewheres. I heard a commotion and decided to come see what was goin' on, but Ranse figured he'd stay where he was. He didn't sleep much in that boxcar last night, so I reckon he's tired."

George's voice was calm, even friendly. Will didn't trust him for a minute. "What are the two of you doing here?"

"In Richmond, you mean? That's where the army fellers said we had to come."

"I mean, why did the two of you enlist?" Will knew the answer to that already, but some perverse part of him wanted to hear George admit it.

"To kill damn Yankees, of course," George replied, sounding surprised.

One of the men in Will's company, seeing the captain's tense attitude, stepped up and jerked a thumb at George Fogarty, asking, "Are you havin' more trouble, Cap'n?"

"No, that's all right," Will assured him. "Just talking to an old acquaintance."

The recruit was from Culpeper County, too, so he recognized George and knew the history of the Fogartys. "But this is—"

"I know who it is," snapped Will. To George, he went on, "Whatever you've got to say to me, Fogarty, spit it out."

George's eyes hardened a bit, but he still sounded jovial as he said, "All right. I just thought I ought to tell you that Ranse and me don't bear no grudge against you, Will. There's been bad blood 'twixt your family and our'n in the past, but that's all behind us now. We got us a whole bunch o' Yankees to worry about now."

"You mean to say you're giving up the feud?"

George nodded solemnly. "That's right."

"Even though I shot your brother?" Will said, trying to goad the man into breaking down and revealing what he and his brother were planning.

George took a deep breath and confessed, "Joe never should've drawed on a lawman, even though he was innocent o' what you accused him of."

"You're saying you and your brothers didn't rob that wagon train, didn't bushwhack me and Luther Strawn, didn't kill Luther and do your damnedest to kill me?"

"That's what I'm sayin'," George answered emphatically.

"You didn't burn down our barn and shoot my brother Henry?"

"Heard about your bad luck." George pushed his lips in and out then clucked sympathetically. "Sure was sorry to hear about it."

Will trembled with anger. He knew the Fogartys were to blame for everything that had happened, knew it as sure as he knew his own name. With an effort, he controlled himself and pointed out, "The blacksmith recognized the print of one of the shoes he put on your horse not long ago."

"Really? Where'd you find this hoofprint, Will?"

"In the grove of trees next to the lane that leads to our farm. Where you and Ranse hid when you shot Henry."

"We might've rode by your place a time or two on our way here or there," said George with a shrug. "That don't prove nothin'. Nobody claims to have *seen* us shootin' at you or your kin, do they?"

Will's mouth twisted bitterly. "Nobody saw you. You're too slippery for that. Like a pair of snakes."

"Call all the names you want, Will. All I really wanted to say once I saw it was you in the middle of that ruckus was that you don't have to worry 'bout me and Ranse. We're here to kill Yankees and defend the Confederacy, and that's all." George turned and started to walk away.

It would be easy, so damned easy, to pull his gun and put a bullet in the middle of George's back, thought Will. But he knew he couldn't do that. As much as he hated the Fogartys, he couldn't shoot anybody in the back. That would just bring him down to their level.

Yancy came over a moment later and inclined his head toward the area of the park where George had disappeared among the teeming recruits. "What was that all about?"

"Just an old enemy with a few words to say to me."

"You looked like you wanted to kill him."

"I did," Will admitted. "I surely did."

Yancy frowned. "That was one of the Fogartys, wasn't it? The ones you told me about?"

"Yep. George, the oldest one."

"I thought he looked familiar. You've had a few run-ins with him before, you said."

"He and his brothers have tried to kill me several times."

Yancy looked worried. "You'd better be careful, then," he advised. "I hate to think that any good Southerner would do something so dishonorable, but if he wants to kill you, the middle of a battle would be a good place to do it."

"I know," said Will. "I reckon whenever we do go into battle, I'd better have eyes in the back of my head."

• • •

BREAKFAST IN the Brannon farmhouse had been a grim affair after Titus left. Cordelia cleaned up the spilled grits and retrieved the pieces of the broken bowl. She and Abigail and Mac ate in near silence, then Abigail took a plate of food up to Henry. Left alone in the dining room, Mac and Cordelia remained quiet for a moment, then Cordelia said, "I wish this family didn't have to argue all the time."

"We come by it honest, I reckon," Mac observed. "Mama and Papa went 'round and 'round sometimes. Or rather, Mama did." Mac smiled faintly at the memory, but it wasn't a particularly happy smile. "Papa tried to laugh it all off, no matter what the fuss was about, but then he'd quote Shakespeare and that would set Mama off all over again."

Cordelia sighed. "I miss Papa. If he was here, he'd know what to do."

Mac didn't say anything. He didn't want to disabuse Cordelia of any notions she held about their father, but Mac was old enough, just like Will, to know that most of the time John Brannon hadn't had any idea what to do to make things right. All he had really wanted was to slide through life with the least amount of effort and the most amount of pleasantries as possible.

"Well, I'd better get to work," Mac announced as he pushed his chair back from the table. "Looks like I'm going to be holding down the fort by myself until Titus gets back."

That turned out to be midmorning. Mac was in the barn when he heard the horse outside. He had been in the fields already, doing some plowing in an unplanted area, but he had brought the plow back to sharpen it. He set the whetstone aside and left the plow where it was as he stepped outside.

Titus was just swinging down from the saddle, his shoulders slumping dispiritedly. "What's wrong?" Mac asked.

"They already got a sheriff," Titus said without looking at him.

"Not Jasper Strawn?" Mac exclaimed.

Titus shook his head. "Nope. Mayor Trafford gave the job to Marcus Gilworth."

"Gilworth? He's a hundred years old! He claims he went over the old Wilderness Road to Kentucky with Daniel Boone."

Titus scratched his jaw. "I don't reckon he's really that old. Anyway, he's the sheriff now, and Jasper's stayin' on as deputy. So I guess I won't be a lawman after all."

"Just as well," Mac answered. "Mama's going to be glad to hear it."

Titus grimaced, then summoned up a smile. "Well, at least I've got that party at the Ebersole plantation to look forward to." He looked at Mac. "I know what Cordelia thinks, but why do you reckon she invited us?"

Mac shrugged. "Maybe because she wants us to come? I don't know, Titus." He started to turn toward the barn door, intending to get back to sharpening that plow again.

Titus stopped him with a hand on the arm. "Hold on, Mac. What do you think about . . . about me and Polly?"

Mac pursed his lips. He didn't particularly want to answer that question, and he didn't figure that Titus really wanted an honest answer. That was the only kind Mac knew how to give, though, so he finally said, "I think you're setting your sights a mite high."

Titus stiffened. "You mean she's too good for me."

"I mean she's liable to *think* she is, anyway. And I know her daddy would feel that way. Duncan Ebersole doesn't have much use for anybody who has less money and land and slaves than he does, and that includes just about the whole county."

"Polly likes me," insisted Titus. "I can tell. I know she does."

"Maybe so. But does she like you because she really likes you, or because she's trying to get her father's goat?"

Titus stared at Mac for a long moment, his face flushing. Finally, he said, "I can't believe you said that. Damn it, Mac—"

"You asked," Mac replied, pulling his arm loose from Titus's grip. "It's not like I wanted to tell you such things."

This time when he turned away, Titus let him go. When Mac was in the barn, he glanced over his shoulder and saw Titus still standing there, silhouetted in the doorway, his stance stiff and taut with anger.

• • •

IT WAS late in the afternoon before orders came for the men waiting beside the James River in Richmond to move out. They were marched through the streets of the city and across a bridge to more open ground on the northern outskirts of town. Will rode the dun, which he had reclaimed from the herd of officers' horses, at the head of his approximately eighty-man company. He figured there were actually closer to ninety men in the company, and he had appointed two of them as lieutenants, men from back home whom he knew to be fairly reliable. On a whim, he had found Darcy Bennett and made him a sergeant, assigning him to bring up the rear of the column. Darcy had still looked a little queasy from his hangover, but he had perked up at being promoted from private straight to sergeant.

Of course, that wasn't as big a promotion as Will had gotten the day before. He had gone from civilian to captain in the space of a few minutes.

Word had filtered through the huge group of men that they were on their way to a temporary camp where they would be given rations and issued uniforms. Will hoped that was right. His men were hungry. Morale was still high, but food and some uniforms would make it even higher.

The landscape was familiar, and Will wasn't surprised when the troops wound up marching into the open fields along Shockoe Creek, near the racetrack where Mac had lost to Edward Symington back during the winter. Usually, by this time in the spring, plans would be underway for another race, but this year was different. Everyone was occupied with the war against the North and had no time for such things as races.

This would make a good campground, Will thought as he watched his men spread out across the field. They would need tents in case of rain, but the creek was handy for water and there was open space for drilling and marching. The men would also need plenty of practice, he figured, before they were ready to go into battle against any troops from the North.

They might not get that chance, however. With the Union massing their forces in Washington City, there was no telling how long it would be before Lincoln and his generals decided to invade Virginia.

Will swung down from the saddle, and one of his new lieutenants came up to him.

"What do we do now, Captain?"

"Wait and see what happens, I reckon," said Will.

They didn't have to wait long. A lengthy train of mule-drawn wagons arrived at the campground, and soldiers clad in light blue uniforms and black caps began unloading tents and long wooden crates full of supplies from the wagons. Some of the new recruits pitched in eagerly to help with the unloading, while others began setting up the tents.

It quickly became obvious, even to Will's untrained eye, that there weren't enough tents to go around. Some of the men would have to sleep outside, even with more men crowded into the tents than they were meant to hold. Nor were there enough uniforms. Everyone got a belt with a Virginia Volunteers buckle and a shot pouch with the same insignia on its flap, but some men got the light blue shirts while others received trousers. The decision of who got what seemed pretty random to Will. Rifles were issued only to those who didn't have long arms of their own.

Will stood in line with the other men as they waited to receive their gear, and when he reached the spot where Confederate sergeants were unloading uniforms from open crates, he said to one of them, "I'm Captain Brannon."

"Officer, eh?" the man grunted. "You get a full uniform, then." He picked up a shirt and trousers and added a short jacket to the pile before thrusting it into Will's arms. "See the regimental commander for your insignia," the man went on. "Got your own pistol and rifle? Good. Wait just a minute." He turned to another crate and brought out a curved saber in a brass scabbard. "This is yours, too," he said as he balanced the sheathed saber on top of the folded uniform Will was holding.

"I never used one of these pigstickers," Will protested.

"Get used to it," the sergeant advised him with a gap-toothed grin. "You'll be wavin' it over your head when you lead your boys in a charge against them damn Yanks."

Will supposed the man was probably right. He turned away and went in search of a tent.

Yancy spotted him and walked toward him. "The officers' tents are this way," he said. "Come on, I'll show you."

"Much obliged," said Will. "I'm afraid this is new to me."

"You'll get used to it," Yancy assured him. "Before long, it'll be second nature and you'll feel like you've always been in command of your company."

Will didn't think he would ever get that accustomed to being in charge of such a large group of men, but he kept that thought to himself. He followed Yancy to a cluster of somewhat larger tents than those being issued to the recruits.

"The lap of luxury," Yancy told him with a grin as he waved toward one of the tents.

"I figured I'd be staying with the rest of the company."

"They're close by, don't worry. We'll all be pretty close together for a while."

"That supply sergeant said something about getting an insignia from the regimental commander . . ."

"Change into your uniform, and then we'll go see Colonel Newcomb."

"He's the man in charge?"

"That's right."

Will stepped into the tent and quickly pulled on the uniform. He buckled his gunbelt around his hips and attached the scabbarded saber to his other belt so that it hung on his left hip. Settling his broad-brimmed hat back on his head, he stepped out and found Yancy waiting for him.

284 • *James Reasoner*

"You're the picture of a dashing young Confederate offi-cer," Yancy observed, grinning again.

"I don't feel too dashing," Will admitted.

"That'll change. Just wait till you've led your first charge."

People keep talking about that, thought Will. It would probably be quite an experience, all right . . . provided he survived it.

Yancy led the way to an even larger tent. Several men were seated on three-legged stools in front, metal plates balanced on their laps as they ate corn bread, beans, and salted beef. One of the men, wearing a cap much too small on a wild thatch of graying hair, looked up when Yancy came to attention in front of him and saluted. Will followed Yancy's example.

The officer set his empty plate aside and returned the salute, then stood up, revealing himself to be a tall, heavyset man. Juice from the beans had run into his thick beard, which was as tangled as his hair. He looked to Will more like a ridge-runner from the Blue Ridge than an army officer, but the gold braid on the shoulders of his jacket and the stars on his collar told a different story.

"Colonel Newcomb, this is Captain Will Brannon from Culpeper County," Yancy said.

"Ethan Newcomb," the colonel rumbled as he extended his hand and shook Will's in a bone-crushing grip. "Welcome to the Thirty-third Virginia. We don't stand much on ceremony around here, Captain. The way I see it, we're here to kill Yan-kees, not to put on a show."

"Yes sir," Will said with a nod.

"You'll be after your captain's bars." Colonel Newcomb turned his head and bellowed, "Lieutenant Kirby!"

A young officer with a short, neat beard hurried up. "Yes sir, Colonel?"

"A set of captain's bars for Captain Brannon here," New-comb ordered.

"Yes sir." Lieutenant Kirby ducked into the tent and returned a moment later with a pair of gold-plated brass bars.

He attached them to the collar of Will's jacket by means of pins on the back. Handing Will three yellow cloth patches, he said, "Have one of the seamstresses sew one of these on each shoulder of your jacket, sir. There's one for your hat as well."

"Thanks, Lieutenant."

Kirby snapped a salute. "Sir!"

Will returned the salute, then turned back to Colonel Newcomb, who asked, "Any questions, Captain?"

"Well . . . how long do you reckon we'll be here, sir?"

Newcomb threw back his head, and a huge laugh boomed out of him. "I'd say that depends on Mr. Lincoln and General McDowell. They'll decide when and if they want to continue with the insane aggression that's led us all to war."

"Yes sir, I understand. I was just hoping there would be time for the men to sort of get used to being in the army and fighting together."

Newcomb nodded. "Indeed. We shall all be living together, fighting together, and I daresay, dying together in defense of our homeland and our glorious cause."

The colonel clapped a hamlike hand on Will's shoulder. "Go on back to your company, son, and teach 'em everything you know about fighting." Newcomb heaved a sigh and added, "They're going to need it."

Chapter Nineteen

MOUNTAIN LAUREL was within sight of the mountains—the Blue Ridge rising in the distance to the northwest—but there were no real peaks on Duncan Ebersole's sprawling plantation. Instead there were gently rolling fields planted with tobacco, wheat, oats, and other grains, along with orchards full of apple trees. Tobacco was the plantation's main cash crop, and Ebersole was proud of the blend that he grew. He was proud, as well, of the whiskey made in his own distillery. It was as fine, he had been known to declare, as any from the Highlands of his native land.

The plantation house itself was at the end of a half-mile-long drive lined on both sides with the trees that gave the estate its name. Several slaves were charged with the care of the trees, and that was their only job on the plantation. On Saturday evening, as the wagon carrying Mac, Titus, and Cordelia rolled along the drive with Mac at the reins, Cordelia looked at the pink-and-white flowers with purple markings that covered the trees and thought they were beautiful. Titus paid no attention to his surroundings; all his interest was centered on the huge house up ahead, where the woman he loved was waiting. Mac just hoped the evening went smoothly, with no trouble.

The house rose three stories tall and was made of brick and granite. Pillars of whitewashed masonry supported a massive portico that extended over the front entrance. The drive circled up to the portico. Mac looked at the multitude of carriages with their shining, intricate brasswork that were parked near the entrance and was acutely aware that he and his brother and sister were in a plain old farm wagon with no frills about it.

Nor were the three of them dressed as elegantly as the guests who were being ushered into the plantation house by an elderly white-haired slave in a cutaway coat, brocade vest, and silk cravat. That slave was rigged up a whole lot fancier than any of them were, thought Mac.

But they were wearing their Sunday best, and no one could ask any more of them. Mac and Titus were clad in dark suits, white shirts, and black bow ties. Cordelia looked better than either of her brothers, in Mac's opinion. She wore a dark green gown that went well with her red hair, which she had arranged into a mass of curls that fell freely around her shoulders. She was downright beautiful, Mac told himself, and of the three of them, she had the best chance of fitting in here with the rest of Ebersole's guests.

Mac brought the wagon to a stop near the portico and hopped down from the seat, turning back to help Cordelia. Titus had already jumped down on the other side of the wagon and was hurrying around it toward the front door. "Hold on a minute," Mac called to him. "We should all go in together."

Titus scowled as if he didn't care for that idea, but he stopped and waited for Mac and Cordelia to join him. Mac linked his left arm with Cordelia's right and motioned for Titus to take her other arm. With the two of them flanking her, they started toward the entrance.

The elderly servant's lined face pinched into a pained expression as the Brannons approached.

"Beggin' your pardon, Massa Brannon," he said, "but what are y'all doin' here?" Music drifted out into the dusk from inside the house.

Mac frowned and halted abruptly, bringing Titus and Cordelia to a stop with him. "Why, we were invited," he said.

"I doesn't recollect Massa Duncan sayin' anythin' about the three o' you comin' tonight. He done gimme a list o' all the guests." A proud smile curved the old man's lips. "I can read, you know."

Mac hadn't known, and he didn't care. "I'm sure there must have been some sort of mistake," he said. "Miss Polly invited us personally."

"Really?" The servant's white, bushy eyebrows arched in surprise. "I can go ask Miss Polly—"

"Ask Miss Polly what?" came a voice from behind the old man. "Is there some sort o' trouble here?"

Duncan Ebersole stepped into the doorway, and it was his turn to look surprised as he saw Mac and Titus and Cordelia standing there. "Brannon?" he questioned, looking at Mac.

"We were invited," Mac stated tightly, in answer to the unasked question. "Your daughter, Polly, delivered the invitation herself. But if we're no longer welcome . . ." Beside him, Cordelia stood stiffly, while on her other side, Titus had begun to flush with anger.

Ebersole's eyes swept coldly over them. "Just a moment," he commanded. "We can easily clear this up." He turned and called for his daughter.

Polly must have been nearby because she appeared only a moment later. "Yes, Father, what—" She broke off her question and smiled at the new arrivals. "I'm so glad to see you!" she greeted them, holding out her hands. "Come in, come in."

"You invited these people?" demanded Ebersole.

"Why, of course," said Polly, looking up at him innocently. "They're our neighbors, after all, and they have always attended our parties."

"So they are," Ebersole acknowledged. He stopped just short of gritting his teeth together as the words came out. "Well, then, I certainly apologize for the misunderstanding. Welcome to Mountain Laurel, all of you. Please, come in."

Mac exchanged a glance with Cordelia and Titus. Cordelia's green eyes sparkled with anger, and Mac knew that she would just as soon leave as go inside the plantation house. But Titus was eager to attend the party and was willing to forget about Ebersole's snobbery if it meant being able to be near Polly. Mac could tell that from the anxious expression on his brother's face.

"Thank you," Mac said to Ebersole. He tightened his grip on Cordelia's arm. "Come along."

She didn't hang back as he led her inside; he gave her credit for that much. They would give this a try, for Titus's sake, and see how it worked out.

Mac had been to Mountain Laurel before, but as always, he was impressed by the luxuriousness of the house as he and Titus and Cordelia moved through the foyer into the main ballroom with its high, vaulted ceiling. The polished hardwood floor shone brilliantly in the light from scores of candles burning in crystal chandeliers. The walls were covered with gold-filigreed paper and hung with paintings, a mixture of hunting scenes set in the Scottish Highlands and portraits of dour Ebersole ancestors.

Tables covered with fine linen cloths were set up around two sides of the big room. The musicians were seated on the third side, and the far end of the room was dominated by several sets of French doors that opened upon the gardens behind the house. The open area in the center was filled with guests sweeping around in carelessly elegant circles as they danced to the waltz being played.

Mac turned to Cordelia and smiled. "I know I'm only your brother," he said, "but will you dance with me?"

She returned the smile and took the hand he held out to her. "I'd be honored, kind sir."

Titus looked toward Polly as Mac and Cordelia swirled away on the dance floor. He didn't know if he dared hope that she would dance with him or not.

But before he could even ask, she had his hand clasped in hers and was saying, "You must dance with me, Titus."

He struggled to make his mouth work, knowing that he must look like a fool, hating himself for it, but unable to do anything about it. "I . . . I'd be glad to," he finally said, then immediately felt as if such a simple response was much, much less than the magnificence of this moment deserved.

He hesitated as he started to put his other arm around Polly's waist, and she asked, "Is anything wrong, Titus?"

"No, I . . . I just can't quite believe I'm here and actually about to dance with you." He managed a smile. "I'm afraid you're just a dream, and I'm going to wake up any minute."

"What a sweet thing to say! But I assure you, Titus, I'm very real."

He knew that. The warm softness of her hand clasped in his sent tremors all the way through him, and when he slipped his arm around her waist, the heat of her body seemed to sear his flesh right through the sleeves of his coat and shirt. They moved into the steps of the dance, Titus awkward at first but soon falling into a rhythm inspired by Polly's natural grace.

Elsewhere on the floor, Mac caught a glimpse of his brother with Polly Ebersole in his arms, and Mac didn't know whether to feel happy for Titus or sorry for him.

Mac was not the only one watching. On the far side of the room, near one of the French doors, Duncan Ebersole stood with a snifter of brandy in his hand. His face was flushed almost as red as his hair had once been, and even though he spoke politely to every one of the guests who greeted him, it was clear that he was distracted. After several minutes, he turned and opened the door, slipping out into the darkened garden, carrying his drink with him.

A quarter of an hour passed before Ebersole entered the house again, and when he did, he wore a self-satisfied smile.

By this time, Mac was sitting at one of the tables, watching Cordelia dance with a series of young men, all of them sons of the wealthy planters who were Ebersole's neighbors. Her gown might not have been as expensive or as fancy as those worn by the other young women in attendance, but Cordelia was easily the prettiest girl here, thought Mac. Her beauty more than made up for any perceived lack of social standing. Before the night was over, there might even be a fight or two between some of the young men vying for Cordelia's attention, Mac decided. He didn't like trouble, but he found that prospect amusing. His baby sister was growing up.

294 • James Reasoner

Titus, on the other hand, would be a surly little boy forever, Mac feared. At first, Titus had obviously been overjoyed to be dancing with Polly, but then someone had cut in on them, and Titus had yielded her grudgingly. Each time when he cut back in to reclaim her, after only a few minutes someone else would tap him on the shoulder. Though Titus stepped aside each time, as custom demanded, his face grew darker and darker. Polly had to be able to see that, but she was smiling and laughing, clearly enjoying the attention.

Cordelia had been right about Polly, Mac mused. She wasn't really interested in Titus. The belle of Mountain Laurel obviously knew that Titus was infatuated with her, and it was equally obvious that she was using him to infuriate her other would-be suitors. It was like a game to her, thought Mac. Maybe he was wrong about Polly; he hoped he was. But he was afraid he was right.

Growing more impatient and angry with each passing moment, Titus glowered at the young man currently dancing with Polly. He waited what he felt was a reasonable amount of time, then he stepped onto the dance floor and tapped sharply on the man's shoulder. Maybe a little more sharply than he had intended, because the man turned toward him with an angry expression on his face.

"See here," the man began, "I just started dancin' with Miss Polly, and I don't intend to—"

"Oh, that's all right, Rawley," Polly remarked sweetly as she moved past him toward Titus. "I promise I'll dance with you again later."

"Do I have your word on that, Miss Polly?" the disappointed suitor asked as Polly stepped into Titus's embrace.

She laughed and threw an "Of course," over her shoulder as she danced away with Titus. A moment later, the musicians began playing a Virginia reel, and their movements in time to the quick tempo of the music carried Titus and Polly toward the French windows.

"I have a wonderful idea," she said as she leaned close to him. "Let's go out into the garden."

Titus gulped in surprise. "Are you sure we should?" he asked.

"I'm sure we shouldn't, but let's do it anyway."

Polly turned gracefully toward the door, holding Titus's hand as she did so. She opened the door and moved out into the night, and he had no choice but to go with her. They left the door open behind them, so the music followed them outside into the garden.

"Dance with me here," said Polly. Titus put his arm around her again, and they began dancing along the flagstone walk that led between the flower beds dotting the lawn. Titus stumbled a little as their steps carried them off the path and into the grass, but he quickly regained his balance. Polly was so light on her feet that the change didn't seem to affect her at all. The two of them kept turning and turning to the music until Titus was dizzy. Either that, or just holding Polly in his arms was what was making his head spin.

Suddenly he leaned forward, taking himself by surprise as much as her, and kissed her. He pressed his lips to hers for only an instant, but that was long enough to experience the sweet warmth of her mouth. The sensation made him even dizzier.

Titus was so distracted he didn't feel the hard grip on his shoulder right away, didn't even realize he was falling until he slammed into the ground. Polly cried out, but the cry was quickly stifled.

A booted foot crashed into Titus's side, then another and another, the kicks thudding against his ribs as he tried to curl himself into a ball to avoid them. Instinct told him to fight back, but he was already hurt too badly. Flight was all he could manage, so he rolled again and tried to come to his feet. A glance upward told him that he was surrounded by dark, bulky shapes. A rough voice grated, "Get back down there, you son of a bitch," and then one of the men kicked him in the head.

Titus almost blacked out as he slumped to the ground. He was vaguely aware that he was not being kicked anymore, and he was glad of that. It seemed to him as if he ought to do *something*, but he couldn't figure out what.

"That's enough," a familiar voice said. "Ye can leave him alone now."

Ebersole.

"Yes sir, boss." That was the man who had called him a son of a bitch, Titus thought woozily. He sounded like a white man, not a slave, probably one of Ebersole's overseers.

Titus heard sobs. "How . . . how could you do that to him?" protested Polly.

"Ach, don't carry on so! Ye dinna love him, ye know that. Ye dinna give a damn. Ye're just usin' him t' annoy me."

"That's not true! I do like Titus."

He should have taken a little pleasure from hearing Polly say that, thought Titus. But under the circumstances . . .

"Go on inside, and dinna say anything to the others. I'll have the brother come out here an' get him. Not a word to anyone, do ye hear?"

Titus hoped that Polly would argue, that she would try to defend him and would see that Mac heard the truth of what had really happened out here in the garden. But after a moment, in a voice so soft Titus could barely make out the words, Polly said, "All right."

That hurt more than any of the kicks, even the one to the head.

• • •

MAC STOOD up to take a snifter of brandy from a tray being carried by a passing servant. His mother would have had some strong words to say about that if she had been here. But Abigail was back home with Henry, and right now Mac didn't really care whether she held with drinking or not.

But before Mac could lift the brandy to his lips, Duncan Ebersole came up to him and said solemnly, "Ye'd better come wi' me, Brannon."

"Why?" asked Mac. "Are you throwing us out of here?"

"'Tis that brother o' yers. He's out in the garden. Must've fallen down and hurt himself."

Mac put the snifter on the table so quickly that some of the brandy sloshed out. He ignored it and said, "Titus? He's hurt?" Then, without waiting for Ebersole to answer, he grated, "What have you done to him?"

Ebersole was unruffled. He returned Mac's angry stare and replied, "I told ye—he must've fallen. Come wi' me and see for yerself."

The plantation owner turned and started toward the French doors. Mac wanted to grab Ebersole's shoulder and jerk him back around to demand some more answers, but he realized that wouldn't solve anything. Instead, he hurried after the Scotsman, knowing that he had to find out what had happened to Titus.

A figure was kneeling on hands and knees on the lawn, shaking his head slowly back and forth as if trying to clear it. When Mac saw the man, he rushed past Ebersole and caught hold of the figure under the arms. "Titus!" he exclaimed.

"Mac . . . ," Titus groaned as Mac helped him to his feet. "Wh . . . where's Polly?"

"Don't worry about Polly. What happened to you?"

"Some bas . . . bastards jumped me. Stomped me. Ebersole's men . . ."

Mac turned toward Ebersole, still supporting Titus as he did so. "I thought you said you didn't have anything to do with this," he flung at the plantation owner.

Ebersole shrugged lazily. "I didn't. My men found yer brother like this. Could be he just had too much t' drink."

"N-no," Titus mumbled. "Didn't drink. Was dancin' . . . with Polly . . ."

298 • *James Reasoner*

"My daughter isn't here," Ebersole said coldly. "She's inside, where she's supposed t' be. And I suggest ye take this whiskey-sodden brother o' yers home, Brannon. Go the long way around the house, instead of through the inside. I dinna want my other guests disturbed by th' sight of him."

"I'll take him home, " Mac blazed. "But I don't believe your story, Ebersole, and I won't forget what happened here."

"It's of no matter to me what ye believe, or what ye forget, just as long as ye get yer brother out o' here."

"We're going. Come on, Titus." Awkwardly, with Mac's arm around his waist to steady him, Titus began limping around the side of the house.

"I'll tell yer sister to meet ye out front," Ebersole called after them.

As mad as he was at Ebersole, Mac felt some anger directed toward Titus as well. When they were out of earshot of Ebersole, he growled, "Maybe tonight will teach you a lesson."

"Polly . . . ," muttered Titus.

No, thought Mac, Titus would never learn.

But Ebersole would. He would learn that when you hurt one Brannon, you hurt them all.

And they all had long memories.

• • •

RUMORS RAN wild in the Confederate camp near Richmond over the next few weeks, traveling faster than anything Will had ever seen. Every day a new story made the rounds: the Union army was advancing from Washington; the Union army was pulling back; a secret peace treaty had been worked out; French and British troops were on their way to reinforce the Confederacy. Will didn't know what was true or false. He got up every morning and spent every day the same way—drilling his troops in the manner he had quickly picked up from watching Yancy Lattimer.

During a meeting with the other officers, Will had been issued a copy of the standard drill manual, *Hardee's Tactics*. He knew from talking to Yancy Lattimer that the Union army used the same manual, or at least it had while Yancy was at West Point. That meant both sides would be starting from the same place, thought Will. What would separate them was their ability as fighting men, and he was convinced, as was every other man in the camp, that that was where the Confederacy held a definite advantage.

The company began by learning to march together. For hours each day under an increasingly warm sun, the men tramped up and down the drill field that had been marked off. At first, it was as hard for Will to keep in step as it was for any of the others. He supposed that as the man in charge, he didn't have to learn how to march, but he wasn't going to ask his troops to do anything that he wasn't capable of doing himself. Gradually, the men developed a rhythm that enabled them to step lively without falling all over each other.

April turned to May, and May began slipping away toward June. Though the solstice was still several weeks away, summer came down with a vengeance, bringing blisteringly hot days under a brassy, cloudless sky. Dust hung in the air, kicked up from the roads and the drill field.

There was also the matter of shooting. More rifles had arrived, Enfield rifled muskets that had been imported from England before the Union had slapped a blockade around Southern ports. Will tried one of them and immediately saw that it was a good weapon, though he preferred his own rifle.

The .577 caliber Enfields were muzzleloaders, like most of the other Confederate long arms. All of Will's troops had used similar guns before, so they were familiar with the process of loading. The first step was to tear open a paper cartridge taken from the pouch at each soldier's waist and pour the powder from the cartridge down the barrel of the rifle. The conical bullet called a Minié ball was inserted into the barrel next, then shoved home with the ramrod that was carried in a groove in the wooden body of the rifle underneath the barrel. When the ramrod was back in place, the weapon was half-cocked and a percussion cap was placed on the nipple under the hammer. Once that was done, all the trooper had to do was to finish pulling back the hammer to full cock, aim the rifle, and pull the trigger. If the percussion cap worked properly, and if the charge of powder in the barrel ignited, then the rifle fired and the whole process could be started over.

And of course, all the while the enemy would be doing its damnedest to load and fire first.

Will watched his men as they practiced loading and firing while they were also advancing in regular ranks up and down the drill field. He rested his hands on the pommel of his saddle and leaned forward, eyes narrowing. If this was the way they were supposed to fight their battles, then every time his men advanced toward the Yankees, they would be sitting ducks whenever they stopped running to reload. A defender would have a natural advantage. It seemed to Will that it would be better to fight from a defensive position than from an offensive one. He supposed it would depend on the circumstances, and he would do whatever his superior officers and *Hardee's Tactics* told him to do.

By the middle of June, after more than six weeks of drilling, Will's company looked like a different group. They marched crisply and efficiently, and many of them could load and fire their rifles as many as three times a minute, even while they were advancing. Yancy's company was also in excellent shape, as were the other companies in the regiment. The Thirty-third Virginia was turning into a crack outfit, and that fact had not escaped the notice of other officers.

One evening, Will was summoned to Colonel Newcomb's tent. He found the colonel talking to another officer with a long curling beard, deepset eyes, and a high forehead. Newcomb and the other officer returned Will's salute, then Newcomb said, "General Jackson, this is Captain Will Brannon. Will, Brigadier General Thomas Jackson is the commanding officer of the Thirty-third Virginia."

The general was standing with his left arm raised to the level of his head for some reason, but he extended his right and shook hands with Will. "I'm pleased to meet you, Captain Brannon," he said.

"It's an honor, sir," replied Will. He had heard that Jackson had been in charge of the Confederate forces that had occupied the armory at Harpers Ferry after the Union troops had withdrawn from it. Jackson had a reputation as a dashing commander, but he didn't really look the part, Will decided. Jackson's uniform was unkempt, and like Newcomb, he looked as if his beard hadn't been combed in a week. When he turned from Will back toward Newcomb, he lowered his left arm and raised his right, as if trying to keep himself in balance.

"I was just telling General Jackson about the fine job you've done whipping those boys of yours into shape, Captain," said Newcomb.

"There wasn't any whipping involved, Colonel," Will said. "Just a lot of hard work by the men."

Jackson laughed. "Well said, son. It's a good officer who gives credit to his men whenever he can."

"General Jackson has brought us new orders," Newcomb went on. "We're moving out. You curious as to where, Captain?"

"Yes sir," Will answered honestly.

Jackson told him. "The Thirty-third Virginia will be crossing the Blue Ridge into the Shenandoah Valley to help guard the Old Dominion in case those godless Yankees launch an invasion from the northwest. We and the other regiments shall be under the command of General Joseph E. Johnston."

Will frowned a little and asked, "Begging the general's pardon, but how likely is it the Yankees will attack from that direction? I thought most of their troops are in Washington."

"True enough," Jackson acknowledged. "But it's feared that they'll try to swing wide around our left and hit us from behind. If they managed to get past the Shenandoah and the Blue Ridge, there would be nothing to impede them in their advance across the Piedmont toward Richmond."

What General Jackson said made sense, and Will decided it was worth sending some of the troops to the Shenandoah to guard against just such a possibility. He nodded and asked, "We'll be traveling by railroad, sir?"

"That's right. We'll leave for Manassas Junction first thing in the morning, and from there the Manassas Gap Railroad will carry us over the Blue Ridge."

Will nodded. "Yes sir. My men will be ready."

"See that they are," Newcomb ordered. "The general and I are explaining our orders to all of the captains, since it's you lads who'll have to make sure the companies are ready to travel." Newcomb saluted. "Dismissed."

Will returned the salute, then returned one from General Jackson. His heart was pounding as he left the tent.

He and his men weren't going into battle . . . not yet. But this journey to Manassas and then the Shenandoah Valley might well bring them one step closer to that fateful day.

Part Four

Chapter Twenty

To LOOK at the Shenandoah Valley, a fella wouldn't know there was a war on, Will thought as he did just that, standing in front of his tent in the Confederate camp near the town of Winchester. The fields and orchards of the valley were quiet and peaceful in the middle of what was, to all appearances, a normal growing season.

Will knew how wrong that impression was. So far, none of the regiments gathered here in the Shenandoah Valley had seen any fighting, but there had been skirmishes between Confederate troops and Union soldiers farther to the west in the Alleghenies, as well as all the way to the east, down in the Tidewater.

And a short distance to the northeast, in the town of Harpers Ferry, where the regiments under the command of General Johnston had first been quartered, there were quite a few signs of war. The destruction had not been the result of a battle, however. Johnston had decided that Winchester was a more defensible position, so he had withdrawn his forces from Harpers Ferry. Before they left, the arsenal and the munitions factories located in the village had been stripped of anything usable, and the railroad bridge over the Potomac River had been blown up.

Will had never heard anything louder than the charges of powder that had sent chunks of the stone bridge flying high in the air when they were detonated. The bridge was in ruins now. No Federal troops would ever march over it again.

The Confederates might not have been fighting during the weeks since their journey to the Shenandoah Valley, but they had been putting their time to good use. Will had continued drilling his men with the able assistance of Sergeant Darcy Bennett, who had stayed sober the entire time and turned into the best assistant Will could have hoped for. The lieutenants were still green, of course—nearly everybody in the company was, including Will—but they were learning all the time. Will had found the tactical sessions with General Jackson particularly helpful. Jackson was an odd bird, with that habit of his of always holding up one arm or the other because he thought it kept him in balance, but he was also one of the smartest men Will had ever run across, especially when it came to military tactics. Before the war Jackson had been a professor of physics and artillery at the Virginia Military Institute, down in Lexington. The coming hostilities would be a good chance for him to test his theories of warfare.

The hot weather continued as June became July. Almost three months had passed since Will and hundreds of other men from Culpeper County had enlisted in the army. Their enlistment papers, Will recalled, had been good for three months. It was unlikely, though, that they would be allowed to go home when that time was up. Regardless of that technicality, most of the men were still itching for a fight. They weren't about to call it quits until they'd had a chance to kill a Yankee or two.

Will was dozing in his tent on the afternoon of July 18. This was the hottest part of the day, and most of the officers chose to let the men take it easy during this time. Suddenly, though, a commotion broke out in the camp, and Will sat up sharply on his cot. He swung his legs to the side and stood up, pulling the suspenders he had loosened back up over the shoulders of his light blue uniform shirt. He pushed the canvas flap aside and stepped out to see what the ruckus was.

General Johnston's adjutant was hurrying through the camp. "Moving out in two hours!" he called as he passed each tent. "Moving out in two hours!" Behind him, officers and enlisted men popped out of the tents to shout questions after him, but the adjutant ignored them and continued making his rounds.

Will didn't give him the chance to keep going. As the adjutant passed him, Will's hand shot out and closed over the man's arm. "What in blazes is going on?" Will demanded.

The adjutant, a lieutenant, reacted tensely, "Beggin' the captain's pardon, but you'd better let me get on my way, sir. We're moving out in two hours."

"I heard that part. Why? Where are we headed?"

The adjutant hesitated, then apparently decided it would be quicker just to tell Will what he wanted to know. "Word has reached General Johnston by telegraph that the Yankees have attacked at a place called Blackburn's Ford. They're trying to get to Manassas. We're being sent to reinforce General Beauregard."

Will let go of the man's arm and stepped back with a nod of gratitude. The adjutant hurried on.

Several officers who had been nearby, including Yancy Lattimer, had heard the lieutenant's explanation. Yancy grinned broadly and said, "It's about time we got in on some action!"

Will gave his friend a brief nod to show that he agreed with that sentiment, then turned to his men and ordered them to start breaking camp. If they were going to be on the march in two hours, there was a lot of work to be done. And it would be a night march, too, because the sun would set long before they were underway.

At the end of that march, Will and all the other men might finally find out if all the training they had done over the past weeks would be enough to keep them from getting killed.

• • •

ON THE other side of the Blue Ridge, Union troops under the command of General Irvin McDowell advancing from Washington had occupied the town of Centreville, which had been abandoned by its Confederate occupants. From Centreville, McDowell hoped to forge on to Manassas, an important junction where the Manassas Gap Railroad and the Orange and Alexandria Railroad converged. Control Manassas, reasoned McDowell, and he would control all rail traffic throughout the central section of Virginia. And he hoped, as well, that a bloody

310 • *James Reasoner*

defeat would smash the spirit of the Rebels, show them the error of their ways, and force them to sue for a quick peace.

Running from southeast to northwest between Centreville and Manassas was a creek with steep, five-foot-high banks along much of its length. Those banks were thickly lined with trees, although the fields that bordered it were for the most part open. The creek was spanned by a stone bridge on the Warrenton turnpike, and there were half a dozen or so other places where it could be forded fairly easily.

The creek was known as Bull Run.

McDowell's plan was to feint at the center of the six-mile-long line of Confederate defenders arrayed along the southern banks of the creek, then swing to his left and flank the Rebels by crossing at a ford known as Union Mills. The feint was to be directed at Blackburn's Ford. The commander of the Union forces carrying out this maneuver had gotten greedy, however, and decided to push on across Bull Run when he encountered only token resistance. The resistance was slight because the Confederates were luring their enemies into a trap. The jaws of that trap snapped shut in the form of a hail of bullets, and the Federals were routed back across the creek, a badly beaten bunch.

Meanwhile, General McDowell had discovered that his opposite number, General Beauregard, had concentrated his forces south of Blackburn's Ford, so McDowell's plan to attack from that direction was ruined. With the fiasco at Blackburn's Ford, and with a much stronger opponent facing him than he had supposed he would find, McDowell had no choice but to pull back and formulate another plan. In the meantime, orders had gone out to General Robert Patterson's forces in the Shenandoah Valley to engage the Confederates under General Johnston and keep them busy, so that they would not be able to come to the aid of Beauregard. Patterson, who had been too late at Harpers Ferry, moved out toward the town of Winchester, where Johnston's troops were supposed to be headquartered.

He was too late again. The Confederates were already on the move.

• • •

WILL HAD been on a few night marches that had been conducted for practice, but this was the real thing. The Thirty-third Virginia, along with the other regiments under Johnston's command, had moved out shortly after darkness had fallen and was now marching almost due south toward Piedmont Station. The trip would take most of the night, and there was no guarantee that trains would be waiting to carry them back through Manassas Gap when they arrived. But they had to make the effort. Their fellow soldiers back east, brothers in spirit and sometimes in blood, needed them.

Dust rose from the road, kicked up by thousands of tramping feet, and clogged the nostrils of men and horses alike. Will took off his bandanna and tied it around his mouth and nose, and that helped some. He hoped the scouts up ahead kept them on the right roads. A wrong turn in the darkness could be disastrous.

Weariness set in, a tight band across Will's shoulders. He kept his horse moving, reminding himself that he had it easier than the infantrymen under his command. He could ride, while they had to march with their rifles and packs. At least a night march like this, while just as dusty, was not as hot as it would have been during daylight hours. There was that to be thankful for, too.

Finally, the sky began to turn gray in the east. Within the hour, the troops reached Piedmont Station. "Thank the Lord," proclaimed Darcy Bennett, who was a religious man when he hadn't been drinking. "I ain't overfond of trains, but right now I wouldn't mind ridin' for a while."

A whistle sounded through the fading shadows. Will grinned. "There's your train, Sergeant."

312 • *James Reasoner*

The locomotive didn't look very impressive, and neither did the old boxcars. But the men piled into them, grateful for the chance to lay down their packs for a while. Will saw that his dun was loaded into one of the cars carrying officers' mounts, then joined his company in their boxcar. Darcy looked up in surprise from the floor of the car, where he was sitting cross-legged like everyone else. The floor was littered with straw, and the car smelled as if it had previously carried livestock. Darcy asked, "What are you doin' here, Cap'n?"

"Figured I'd ride with you boys," Will replied as he found a spot and sat down so that he could lean his back against the wall of the boxcar. "If we can fight together, I reckon we can ride to the battle together."

Darcy grinned. "You ain't much like some o' them other officers, Will—I mean, Cap'n."

Will just grinned, tugged the brim of his hat down over his eyes, and said, "Wake me up when we get where we're going, Sergeant."

• • •

McDowell sat in Centreville and pondered, while Beauregard sat in Manassas and waited. The Thirty-third Virginia, under Jackson, arrived on the afternoon of July 19. Over the next twenty-four hours, several more brigades converged by rail from the Shenandoah Valley. McDowell and the other Yankee officers had no idea that Patterson had failed in his mission to keep the Confederate forces in his part of Virginia occupied.

With the reinforcements came Johnston, the senior officer of the Confederate Army. Beauregard was ready to turn over command to Johnston, but Johnston decided that he would share the responsibility with Beauregard, since the younger man had been on the scene longer and knew the ground. Beauregard, who still had his forces massed on the southern part of the defense line from Mitchell's Ford to Union Mills, had been planning to attack across Bull Run the next day, flank McDowell, and get behind the Union troops, cutting them off. Johnston agreed with that plan and left Beauregard's deployment of troops as it stood, which meant the northern sector, from Mitchell's Ford past the stone bridge to the northernmost crossing at Sudley's Ford, would be only lightly guarded. The Confederate officers went to sleep that night confident that the morning would bring them glory and triumph.

• • •

HURRY UP and wait. *That ought to be the army's motto*, Will thought as he stretched out in his bedroll and tried to sleep. He and his men had arrived at Manassas a day and a half earlier, expecting to be rushed into battle, and instead they had done nothing except sit around and wonder when something was going to happen. The Yankees were out there, no doubt about that; the glow in the sky from their campfires could be seen from the Confederate positions, even here in the rear behind General Bonham's men who were posted at Mitchell's Ford. The Yankees hadn't turned tail and run after their defeat at Blackburn's Ford a few days earlier—well, they hadn't run very far, anyway—and everybody in camp knew it was only a matter of time before they tried something else. Will knew, however, from meetings he had attended, that unless the Yankees moved soon, General Beauregard was going to beat them to the punch. Tomorrow, Sunday, July 21, the Confederate troops would storm across Bull Run and take the fight to the Northern aggressors.

An insect buzzed around Will's ear. He slapped it away, knowing it would soon be replaced by another one. He and his men hadn't bothered setting up their tents and were making do with bedrolls spread on the ground so that they could move the camp quickly if need be. Will sat up, sighing. Sleep was going to be hard to come by tonight. He wondered how things were at home. Cordelia had proven to be a faithful correspondent, writing several letters each week. Mac and Titus and Henry were generally too busy to put pen to paper, or so they claimed. Will knew from Cordelia's letters that Henry had recovered from the bullet wound and seemed to be as good as new. He knew, too, that there had been some sort of trouble between Titus and Duncan Ebersole over Polly. Will had been expecting that, but he still didn't like to hear it. At least Polly wouldn't be stirring up any more friction between Titus and her father; Ebersole had sent her to stay with relatives in Norfolk for the time being, perhaps even for the duration of the war, Cordelia hinted.

Abigail was all right, praying for victory against the Northerners. Once a week, she and Cordelia went into Culpeper to work with a group of women who sewed uniforms and flags for the Confederate troops.

The family had even had a letter from Cory, according to Cordelia. He was in Missouri, and even though he hadn't been specific about what he was doing these days, he had intimated that he was involved in some sort of lucrative business, just as he had always claimed he would be.

Will reached into his pocket and took out his watch, flipping open the case so that he could peer at the face in the starlight. If he held it just right, there was enough illumination to see the hands pointing toward two o'clock. *The wee hours of the morning*, he thought. He'd heard it said that a man was closer to death in those hours than any other.

He snapped the watch shut and lay down again, determined to get some sleep.

• • •

MAC ROLLED over in bed and sat up. He was groggy from having his slumber disturbed so abruptly, and for a moment he couldn't figure out what had done it. Then he heard the sound, a rhythmic thudding that was familiar to his ears: the hoofbeats of a horse pacing back and forth.

Mac swung his legs out of bed and went to the open window, pushing aside the curtain to look out. He stiffened as he saw the silver-gray form trotting back and forth in the yard. The stallion! He hadn't seen it in months, and now here it was, right in his own yard.

But why? The horse wasn't paying any attention to the barn, wasn't going after the mares inside there, as it had on the night Will and Mac had tried to capture it. Instead it was just dancing around skittishly, and as it looked up and saw Mac peering down from the upstairs window, it suddenly reared up on its hind legs and pawed the air. A shrill whinny rang out.

Then the stallion wheeled around sharply and broke into a gallop, disappearing out of the yard in a cloud of dust. Mac stood transfixed, knowing it would do no good to pursue the horse. The stallion would be long gone by the time he could get downstairs.

Mac's hands were shaking a little as he gripped the window-sill to steady himself. It was as if the stallion had come here tonight just to see him, he thought. To warn him? Maybe, but of what? Had the stallion even really been here, or was he losing his mind?

There were no answers. Nor was there any more sleep for Mac that night.

• • •

WILL FINALLY dozed off again, but it seemed as if he had barely closed his eyes before someone was shaking him awake with a heavy hand on his shoulder. "Cap'n!" Will recognized the urgent voice as belonging to Darcy Bennett. "Cap'n, wake up!"

Will pushed himself into a sitting position and asked, "What is it, Sergeant?" When he looked around, he realized to his surprise that the sun was already up. It was Sunday morning.

"Scouts just come in with the news that the Yankees are on the move."

That brought Will fully awake. "Are they advancing on Mitchell's Ford?" he asked as he got to his feet.

"No sir. They're heading up to the northwest, toward Sudley's Ford."

A chill went through Will's body. Sudley's Ford was at the very end of the Confederate defensive line. If the Yankees were swinging that way, it meant they were trying to flank them and get behind them. Beauregard and Johnston had been expecting such a flanking maneuver, but they had been convinced it would come from the south rather than the north.

Will pulled his suspenders up and clapped his hat on his head. "Where are the other officers?" he asked.

"General Jackson's sent for all of 'em."

Then that was where he needed to be, too, Will knew. He buckled on his pistol and saber and said to Darcy, "Have my horse saddled, Sergeant."

"Already got one of the men tendin' to it," Darcy assured him. "You goin' to see the general?"

"Damn right."

It took Will only a minute or two to locate the group of officers gathered around General Jackson, who stood on a slight rise with a field glass held to his eye as he squinted off toward the northwest. Will hurried to join them, receiving a quick nod of greeting from Yancy as he did so. Yancy looked solemn, yet excited at the same time. All of the officers were being quiet, and in the distance, a few faint popping sounds could be heard. Will knew what they were.

Gunshots.

Jackson sighed and lowered the field glass. "That'll be the skirmishers," he said, and all the officers knew he was referring to the distant shots. "If we hear any cannon fire in the next few minutes, we'll know the rumors of a Union attack are true. They may still be just feeling us out, though."

Jackson didn't sound convinced that he considered such a possibility very likely. Neither did Will. After the Yankees' failed assault of a few days' earlier, they had to be champing at the bit to get back into action.

Sure enough, within a quarter of an hour, a rumbling began to be heard coming from the northwest. It sounded a little like thunder, but the sky was clear, a dazzling, cloudless blue. The only storm today was that of war.

Jackson took a deep breath and announced, "Gentlemen, the battle is joined."

"What are your orders, sir?" asked Yancy.

Jackson tugged at his beard. "I have none, at the moment. We were posted here to reinforce the rear and to support General Longstreet when the advance on Centreville is ordered."

"And you plan to stay here while the battle is being fought over yonder?" The question was jolted out of Will before he could stop it.

Jackson's deep-set eyes glittered angrily as he turned his gaze toward Will. "What would you have us do, Captain?" demanded the general. "Should we disobey our orders?"

"That's not what I'm saying, sir," Will responded, figuring that he'd better try to show a little more military decorum. "It's just that General Beauregard positioned us here because he thought if there was an attack it would come in this direction. Seems to me a fella ought to be able to change his plans if the circumstances change."

"There's something to be said for that theory, Captain," Jackson admitted. "Resoluteness and sheer, mule-headed stubbornness are sometimes two different things. I'll take your comments under advisement."

Will nodded. That was as much as he or any other junior officer could hope for.

He and Yancy and the other captains stood on the rise with Jackson for several minutes, and as they did, the sound of cannon fire to the northwest gradually grew louder. Finally,

Jackson turned his head and ordered, "Tell your men to be ready to move out when the time comes."

"Yes sir," Will and Yancy said together, and the sentiment was echoed by the other officers.

"One more thing," said Jackson as the captains started to turn away. "I'm told that some of the Union soldiers wear blue and some wear gray, much like us. To prevent any tragic mistakes, I want you and all your men to each tie a strip of white cloth around your arm." He paused, then continued, "In addition, just to stave off any confusion, at each opportunity you should strike your left breast with your right fist and shout, 'Our homes!' Is this understood?"

Will understood, all right. He understood that such mummery might cause a fatal delay in reloading and firing. However, orders were orders, and he would pass Jackson's commands on to the men in his company.

A glance over his shoulder as he headed back to his company showed him Jackson pacing back and forth restlessly on the crest of the small hill, listening to the sounds of battle. Will figured those distant shots were like a siren's song to Jackson, calling to him with a seductive power that would not be long denied. They would be moving before the sun was another hour higher in the sky, he thought.

Will's prediction proved to be correct. Within an hour, the order came from General Jackson. Absent any orders to the contrary from Beauregard or Johnston, the Thirty-third Virginia was moving out and marching northwestward, toward the fight.

Chapter Twenty-one

WILL TOOK off his hat and sleeved sweat from his forehead. It was almost midday, and the sun was beating down with scorching intensity. The men were exhausted after marching four miles from their previous position at the rear of the forces at Mitchell's Ford. Will could see the weariness in their faces. But there was excitement and anticipation there, too, because the gunshots and cannon fire had grown increasingly louder with each step the men took toward the hill that now rose in front of them.

The call came back down the line of marching men: "Captains forward!" Will heeled the dun into a trot that carried him alongside the troops to Jackson's position in the forefront of the advance. Jackson sat there like some sort of shabby medieval knight on a charger, glaring toward the hill and the battle that was obviously raging just beyond it.

The officers gathered around him, and Jackson dismounted to bring out a map from inside his coat. He unfolded it so that all the captains could see and jabbed his finger at a spot on it.

"That's the hill yonder," said Jackson. "The house on top of it belongs to a family named Henry. Gentlemen, we are going to advance up that slope and establish a defensive position just this side of the crest."

"We're not going over?" Will asked. He added, "Sir."

Jackson shook his head. "Not yet." He smiled. "Don't worry, Captain Brannon. I'll wager that we shall all breathe our share of powder smoke before this day's work is done."

Will wasn't worried, just anxious to finally test himself and his men in battle. Jackson had ordered that they dig in defensively on the hillside, though, so that was what they would do.

He rode quickly back to his company and waved them on. The blue-clad Thirty-third, each man with a strip of white

321

cloth tied around his arm, marched up the hill with other regiments and stopped some twenty feet short of the top. The Confederate soldiers stood there, some of them shuffling their feet, seemingly at a loss as to what to do next.

General Jackson would tell them. He waved Will and Yancy forward and ordered, "Take a gander over the hill, gentlemen, and see what the situation may be."

Will liked the sound of that. He nodded and acknowledged the order enthusiastically. With Yancy alongside him, he kicked his horse into a run that carried him over the crest of the hill and down the other side.

The sight that greeted his eyes caused Will to rein up his horse. More than a dozen cannon were set on the hillside, lobbing shells toward the Union batteries in the distance. The noise was terrific, and the air was filled with powder smoke.

Will looked down the slope and saw thousands of men struggling for their lives in a sea of different shades of blue and gray. Stabbing through the cloudy countryside were the orange tongues of flame that licked from the muzzles of both sides' rifles. Adding to the scene, Will saw horsemen gallopping back and forth madly.

One of them spotted Will and Yancy and wheeled his horse toward them. "What unit are you with?" he shouted over the din.

"General Bee, sir!" Yancy exclaimed, snapping a salute. "The Thirty-third Virginia, sir!"

"Jackson's bunch?" the officer in command of the Fourth Alabama asked. "Take me to him!"

"Yes sir!" Will said. He and Yancy wheeled their horses and rode back over the hill. Something buzzed past Will's ear as he topped the rise, and it took him a second to realize that it was probably a bullet. He blew out a breath, knowing that he had just come within inches of a head wound.

Will would have to worry about such things later; there was no time now. With General Bee riding beside them, Will and Yancy headed for Jackson's headquarters.

They found Jackson still astride his horse in front of the defensive line formed by the Thirty-third Virginia. Bee rode straight toward him, and as he reined in he growled furiously, "General, they are beating us back!"

Jackson drew himself up in the saddle and proclaimed, "Then send them on, sir, and we will give them the bayonet!"

Bee nodded, and the expression on his face said that he was somewhat mollified. He sketched a salute to Jackson and turned his horse to ride back over the hill. Jackson motioned for Will and Yancy to follow him but called after them, "Bring me back a report this time, not a general!"

The two captains rode after General Bee, catching up with him on the far side of the hill as he gathered some of his men around him. They were a ragtag bunch. Will didn't see even one of them who didn't have some sort of wound. A lieutenant whose face was half-covered in blood from a gash on his forehead asked, "What do we do now, General?"

"Die if we have to," Bee shot back, "but either way, we shall conquer!" He turned and looked toward the hilltop, evidently not realizing that Will and Yancy were within earshot. "There stands Jackson, like a stone wall."

There was something in Bee's voice, but Will wasn't sure if it was disdain or approval. Was Bee thinking that Jackson should have come over the hill to help him? That could have easily resulted in the Thirty-third getting shot to ribbons, just like the Fourth Alabama had been. Jackson's defensive position atop the hill was strong, though, strong enough that he might be able to stop the Yankee advance. Now that Will had thought about it, he believed that Jackson was doing the right thing, frustrating though it had to be.

Bee waved his men back into battle. "We'll join what's left of Bartow's and Evans's regiments," declared Bee. "That's all that's left to us."

As the bloody, exhausted troops surged down the hill, Yancy turned to Will, "Let's get back to the general." They galloped over the rise, and this time no bullet came close enough to Will for him to hear the wind of its passage.

Jackson was waiting for them. Just loud enough to be heard over the noise of battle, Yancy said to Will, "I wouldn't mention anything to the general about what Bee said of stone walls."

"Don't worry," said Will. "I wasn't planning to."

As they rode up, Jackson looked at them curiously, and Yancy said, "General Bee is leading his men back into battle, sir. Colonel Bartow and Colonel Evans are still in the field as well."

Jackson nodded. "If the Yankees get past them, we'll be waiting." He turned his head and called for Colonel Newcomb. When the burly Newcomb rode up a moment later, Jackson told him, "Find General Beauregard. Tell him that we have established ourselves on Henry House Hill and that here we will stand."

Newcomb frowned. "I'd rather stay here where the fighting is, sir."

"You have your orders, Colonel," snapped Jackson. Newcomb nodded and reluctantly turned his horse.

Yancy sighed in relief and said quietly to Will, "I'm glad he didn't send us."

"I wouldn't have gone," said Will.

"You would have disobeyed a direct order?" Yancy didn't sound convinced.

Will nodded. "It's time to fight. It's past time."

"You're a real fire-eater, aren't you?" Yancy remarked with a grin.

Will had never thought of himself that way. When he was wearing the sheriff's badge, he had always considered himself just a man with a job to do. And today his job was to stop the Yankees, here and now. It was all he could do to stay put on this side of the hill, instead of giving in to his instincts and galloping over there to fight alongside General Bee.

"The Yankees will come to us," Will predicted. "I intend to be here when they do."

• • •

EARLIER IN the morning, Confederate forces under the command of Colonel Nathan Evans had rushed to the defense of Sudley's Ford when it became obvious that was where the Yankees intended to cross Bull Run. Evans and his men had been unable to stop the Union advance, but once the Yankees had crossed the creek and were turning toward the Confederate positions, Evans had led a gallant fight that delayed the advance for over an hour. That had given Bee and Bartow the opportunity to come to his aid, and although the combined Confederate forces had been pushed back by the Union troops, they had sold each foot of ground dearly for a time. Then the strength of the Yankees proved to be too much, and the shattered remnants of the Confederate regiments had fled, regrouping to mount a new defense only after they had crossed Young's Branch and reached the bottom of Henry House Hill.

A mile to the south, General Johnston was establishing a new headquarters at another house commandeered for that purpose. His job was to send any reinforcements that might arrive—and there were some—on up to the makeshift frontlines being manned by Jackson's Virginians and a motley assortment of survivors from the regiments of Bee, Bartow, and Evans. Beauregard galloped back and forth behind the lines, determining the actual positioning of the troops that awaited the next Yankee push. The Confederate line, running from north to south along the crest of the hill, consisted of the 8th Virginia; Hampton's Legion, a militia force commanded by Colonel Wade Hampton; the 5th Virginia; the 2d Virginia; the 27th Virginia; the 4th Virginia; the 33d Virginia, just below the very peak of the hill; then the remnants of the 7th Georgia and the 49th Virginia. A short distance to the south, well hidden in a grove of trees so that they could strike with surprise if need be, was Colonel J. E. B. Stuart's 1st Virginia Cavalry. All told, by midafternoon there were over six thousand men on that hill,

326 • *James Reasoner*

as well as a dozen cannon. But they were facing a much larger Union force.

The Federals had pulled back a bit right after noon. Johnston, Beauregard, and the other Confederate generals theorized that they were just catching their breath before launching another attack. That proved to be true. With no warning, the Union lines parted, and five cannon mounted on caissons emerged and were trundled forward to the base of the hill. The Union artillerymen were closely followed by infantry, and the Confederates standing watch at the top of the hill quickly passed the word back: the Yankees were coming, leading with their cannon so that a barrage could weaken the Confederate line before the infantry poured over the hill for the close work with bayonets.

The death stroke was about to be launched.

• • •

WILL AND Yancy were standing next to Jackson with several other officers when word of the Yankee guns being brought into action arrived. Jackson clenched a fist. "Let them come," he hissed. "Let them come all the way up the hill."

"General . . . ?" one of the officers asked worriedly.

"When the Yankees show their faces, the whole line will greet them with a shout, and with bayonets." Jackson's bearded face was fierce. "I am tired of fighting this battle at long range."

That was good news to Will. He turned to Darcy Bennett and passed along the orders, and Darcy shouted them to the rest of the company. Everyone along the Confederate line tensed. Will hurried over to the dun, swung into the saddle, then drew his saber. He felt strangely lightheaded, as if he could not get enough air in his body. It wasn't fear he felt, although he was afraid; no sane man could fail to be afraid for his life in these circumstances. Nor was it strictly anticipation. It was a mixture of the two, Will decided. He had experienced something like it before, in those moments when he had been forced to draw his gun when he was sheriff, but those had been fleeting sensations, born in the heat of the moment. This had been building all day. It had been building for months, actually, thought Will, ever since he had enlisted back in Culpeper.

A smattering of gunshots broke out. Confederate riflemen at the crest of the hill had been unable to wait. Disobeying Jackson's orders, they began firing on the Union artillery batteries. Several gunners and some of the horses pulling the cannon dropped under the withering fire. Apparently deciding that they had advanced far enough, the Union officers in charge of the guns ordered their artillery crews to open fire. Moments later, the cannon began to roar, and cannonballs smashed into the Henry house itself.

Will felt white-hot rage course through him at the sight of the shells striking the house. He had been told that the Henry family was still inside, waiting out the battle. Yet the Yankees were directing their fire right at the noncombatants. Will urged the dun to the top of the hill and saw the Union infantry swarming around and past the artillery batteries, beginning their charge up the hill.

"Fire!" Jackson shouted, and the command went all the way along the line.

The Confederate troops stood up and aimed their rifles down the slope. The volley they fired scythed through the Union forces, cutting them down like so many stalks of ripe wheat. As Will saw the Federals go down, he waved his saber over his head and bellowed, "Charge!"

Down the hill the company went, with Will leading the way. Behind him, the infantrymen ran forward, yelling at the tops of their lungs. In a matter of seconds, they plunged into the mass of Union troops, who were still trying to recover from the deadly volley. Will slashed right and left with the saber, coating the blade with Yankee blood. Dust rose and enveloped him, a fine coating of it sticking to the sheen of blood on the saber.

A Union soldier came out of the billowing dust and threw himself at Will. Will saw the man coming but didn't have time to avoid him. The soldier leaped high and tackled him, knocking him off his horse. Will landed hard, and the saber slipped out of his fingers and skittered away from him.

The Yankee seemed to be unarmed, but he was determined to kill Will with his bare hands. His fingers locked around Will's throat. He had one knee on Will's chest, pinning him to the ground. Will tried to throw the man off, but the Yankee's weight was too much.

Suddenly, the Yankee stiffened. He was leaning over Will so that his grimacing face was only a foot away from Will's. The man's mouth opened and blood welled out. Will saw the point of a bayonet protruding an inch or so from the center of the man's chest. He fell to the side as his eyes began to glaze over.

Darcy Bennett yanked his bayonet out of the Yankee's body and bent over Will to offer him a hand. "Come on, Cap'n," he said, raising his voice to be heard over the chaos. "Are you all right?"

Coughing a little as he dragged air through his abused throat, Will nodded. "Thanks, Darcy," he rasped. He looked around for the dun.

"Your horse run off," said Darcy. "Don't know where he got off to—"

Suddenly, a thudding sound interrupted Darcy, and the big sergeant stumbled back a step. Will looked at him in horror as Darcy slowly lifted a hand and pressed it to his chest. "Lordy," Darcy gasped in a hollow voice. "I'm hit."

Then he fell over backward, a dark bloodstain spreading under the widespread fingers of his hand.

"Darcy!" Will yelled as he dropped to his knees next to the sergeant. "Damn it, Darcy—"

"Brannon!"

Will couldn't believe his ears. He turned his head and saw a familiar figure standing ten feet away. Something had happened to Ransom Fogarty's cap during the battle, uncovering his ginger-colored hair. Smoke curled from the barrel of the rifle in his hands. His ugly freckled face split in a grin as he sneered, "I won't miss with this bayonet, Brannon!"

He lunged at Will, the rifle held low so that he could thrust with the bayonet. For a split second, Will crouched there frozen, and in that instant he cursed himself for forgetting about the Fogartys. He had never believed that they had given up their grudge against him, and now he knew he was right. Ransom was trying to kill him, and in the confusion of battle, no one would know that the Yankees weren't responsible for his death.

Will's instincts kicked in, and he threw himself to the side, avoiding Ransom's charge. He rolled over, and as he did, he saw his saber lying on the ground a few feet away. He reached for it desperately as Ransom shrieked a curse and came at him again with the bayonet.

Will had to roll again as he grabbed up the saber. As he came over onto his back he thrust up blindly at the crazed figure looming above him. The saber ripped into Ransom's groin. Ransom's own momentum sent the blade slicing through his insides. He screamed and dropped the rifle to clutch at the saber as he stumbled. He fell, wrenching the handle of the saber out of Will's hand.

Will pushed himself onto his hands and knees. A few feet away, Ransom Fogarty was twitching and moaning as blood pooled under him. His face was dead white, the freckles standing out starkly against his pallor. A ghastly rattle came from his throat as his features went slack.

Will staggered to his feet. There was still a battle going on, though he saw that his men seemed to have taken control of the Union cannon. Some of them were trying to swing the big guns around so that they could fire back down the hill toward the Yankees.

"Cap'n . . ."

Will whirled around and saw Darcy holding himself up on one elbow. The bloodstain on the front of his jacket was large, but Darcy was still alive. If Will could get him off this hill, he might recover from the bullet wound. *A bullet that had been meant for me*, Will reminded himself.

He rushed to the sergeant's side and knelt to get an arm under Darcy's shoulders. "Come on, let's get you out of here," he said as he struggled to get the burly sergeant on his feet.

"You best . . . leave me here . . . ," gasped Darcy.

"No," Will said flatly. "We'll both get down off this hill, or neither one of us will."

He half-carried Darcy up the slope, his left arm slung around Darcy's waist. As they topped the rise, someone behind them shouted, "Turn around, Brannon!"

Will stopped, thinking *not again*, and turned enough to see George Fogarty pointing a rifle at him. Even in the midst of a battle, the Fogartys were so consumed with their hatred for him that they could forget all about the thousands of Yankees trying to kill them.

That was George's mistake, because before he could pull the trigger of his own rifle, a Minié ball slammed into the back of his neck and burst out his throat. Will saw the spray of blood, saw George drop the rifle and fall forward in the unmistakable loose-limbed sprawl of death, and he muttered under his breath, "Go to hell, Fogarty."

He resumed trying to get his friend down the far side of the hill, away from the battle, and they disappeared somewhere on the slope in the clouds of dust and smoke, the roar of the cannon, and the cries of dying men.

Chapter Twenty-two

THE UNION batteries were taken and retaken several times by each side during that long, bloody afternoon. Each time the Confederates stormed over the hill, they inflicted major damage on the Federal forces before the Yankees were able to regroup and drive them back again. Beauregard and Johnston continued pouring reinforcements into the battle from the rear, but the Yankees under McDowell did not have that option. Most of their men were already in the field. However, McDowell committed a strategic error by not taking advantage of his superior numbers and staging a full-scale assault on the Confederate position. The piecemeal attacks that he ordered failed to dislodge the Southerners from their hilltop stronghold and at the same time fatally depleted the strength of the Union forces. One by one, the Yankee units began to fall back, whether they had been ordered to do so or not. Seeing this, Beauregard immediately ordered a counterattack.

The rout was on.

By this time, Darcy Bennett was in a hastily erected Confederate field hospital at the Lewis house, where Johnston had set up his headquarters earlier. The surgeons had promised an anxious Will Brannon that they would do everything they could for him. Will had found a horse and galloped back to the frontlines, hating to leave Darcy but knowing that he had a duty to the rest of his men as well.

He returned to a celebration. Hearing someone hailing him as he rode up to the Henry house, he turned and saw Yancy Lattimer striding toward him. Yancy was grinning, despite the bloody bandage that was tied around his left arm.

Will nodded toward the bandage and wryly said, "Jackson told us to use white cloth, not red."

"Well, it started out white," Yancy responded with a shrug. "Are you all right, Will?"

"I'm fine," Will said as he dismounted. "What happened to the Yankees?"

"I imagine most of them are still running toward Washington, those who haven't already gotten there. I think we chased them halfway to the Potomac. And what a sight it was, too! You know, hundreds of people came out from Washington to watch the battle."

Will frowned. "Civilians?"

"That's right. They drove out in their fancy carriages, and some of them even packed a lunch." Yancy shook his head. "I reckon they got more excitement than they bargained for. I saw some Yankee soldiers commandeering carriages and using them to run for their lives." Yancy took a slightly crooked cigar from the breast pocket of his uniform jacket and lit it with a sulphur match. "By the way, that dun horse of yours is over yonder in a rope corral. I found it earlier and brought it back. Gave me a scare, too, because I figured you were dead."

"Nope, just tending to some business." Will didn't explain what that business had been. He wasn't alone in helping wounded friends back to the field hospital. All he knew was that he couldn't allow Darcy Bennett to die without doing everything he could to save him. All the way back to that field hospital, Will had been thinking about Luther Strawn.

A group of officers rode past, among them General Jackson. Yancy grinned again and nodded toward the general. "There goes old Stonewall," he said dryly.

"What?"

"Stonewall Jackson. That's what they're calling him, because he stood like a stone wall against the Yankees."

"Well, I suppose General Bee probably meant that, too. At least I'd like to think so."

Yancy was shaking his head. "No point in disputing a legend, Will. Especially not one like this."

Yancy was right, Will decided. Jackson had made the correct military decision by following orders and digging in on the hilltop. If folks wanted to look at that from a little different angle than how it had really been, they weren't going to get any help from Will.

"At least it's over," Yancy went on after a moment. "We showed that we can whip the Yankees. The North will have to listen to reason now."

Will grunted in surprise. "After what happened here today? I'm glad we won, too, but all today's fighting will just make things worse."

"What in blazes are you talking about? We beat them!"

Will looked around the battlefield pocked with shell holes, littered with broken and discarded equipment, and highlighted with dark stains still drying on patches of bare ground. He thought about the Fogartys and about a blood debt that had driven them to come after him and his whole family, even leading them to enlist so they could kill him with impunity during the heat of battle.

A lot more blood had been spilled here today, on both sides. And with it came debts that neither North nor South would soon forgive, debts that each side would feel could be washed away only with more blood.

But that wasn't what a dashing young officer like Yancy Lattimer wanted to hear, thought Will, so he just smiled tiredly, clapped a hand on Yancy's shoulder, and said, "Maybe you're right. I hope so."

Then he went to reclaim his horse. Sooner or later, there would be more fighting to do, and Will would be ready.

• • •

SUNDAY WAS Abigail Brannon's favorite day of the week. She and her children had been to church services that morning, of course, and then they had spent a peaceful Sabbath at home.

Now the house was dark and quiet. Mac, Titus, Henry, and Cordelia were all asleep, and Abigail should have been, too. But she was restless, unable to sleep, so she did what she always did in times of trouble.

She turned to the Lord.

With her bones creaking a lot more than they used to, she knelt beside her bed and clasped her hands together and closed her eyes, even though the room was dark. She felt God's presence in the room as she began to pray, and almost immediately, peace washed over her. She asked blessings on her children, one by one, beginning with Mac and going on through Titus, Cory, and Henry before ending with Cordelia.

Then she paused. The silence stretched out almost painfully before Abigail said, "I know You've been watching over Will for me, too, Lord. Keep him safe. Maybe . . . maybe someday, he can come home, when this war is over."

And she whispered "Amen" into the darkness.